The Empire State Series

A WEEK in NEW YORK

AUTUMN in LONDON

NEW YEAR in MANHATTAN

D1052872

LOUISE BAY

ISBN - 978-1-910747-02-5

The Empire State Series: Part One

A WEEK in NEW YORK

LOUISE BAY

CHAPTER
One

Anna

"Has he tried to contact you?"

I could barely hear Leah through the booming of the bass. We were perched on stools at the oh-so-cool bar in TriBeCa and we had to lean in to each other to be heard. I'm not sure if hearing her would have helped me make sense of what she was saying—we were three cocktails in. But I got that she was talking about Ben—she hadn't really talked about much else.

Leah was my best friend in the whole world. We had met at law school, and until recently, we'd shared a flat. She was supremely protective of me, and I of her. Talking about men and drinking cocktails is what we did, and we did it so well. The subject of our conversation tonight was Ben—my most recent ex.

"He wouldn't dare. Probably knows I'd rip his balls off." I shrugged and sipped on my Manhattan. I had to drink Manhattans while I was in Manhattan, didn't I?

"I just can't believe it," Leah said for the 57th time that evening.

I shrugged again and looked over Leah's shoulder and saw a face in the shadows looking at me. He raised his glass and nodded in my direction. Did I know him? He looked familiar. My eyes darted back to Leah.

"And you didn't have any hints?" she asked.

"I mean, he was different from other guys I had dated. But no, he never dropped it into the conversation that he was mixed up in crazy shit and owed money to the wrong kind of people."

Ben the biker had turned into the boyfriend from hell—or Ben the Bastard as Leah now referred to him. He had always been so sweet to me. I thought he was going to be different. I thought I'd finally made a good choice after having precisely no luck with men for years. But I'd been delivered a reality check—Ben the Bastard was a bastard. The crazies he'd owed money broke into our flat and scrawled a crazy-assed threat across the bathroom mirror in Leah's room. They hadn't taken anything, which confused us. About a week later, Ben confessed and I went to the police.

The police had called earlier today and confirmed that Ben had confessed to them, as well. It had been a threat to scare him into paying back what he owed.

"So you're going to sell your apartment?"

"Well, I still call it a flat, but yes, I'm going to sell it," I smirked. Leah started calling her mobile a cell as soon as we landed at JFK. I couldn't pass up an opportunity to tease her sudden Americanization.

I'd decided on the plane that I was definitely going

to sell my flat. I'd not felt right about the place since the break in. Daniel, Leah's boyfriend and all around perfect man, had arranged for an alarm to be installed. But Leah had moved in with him, and I hated being on my own. Even though I knew the police were handling it, I still didn't want to be in the flat. I didn't tell Leah that because she would have moved me in with her and Daniel, and as much as I loved them, I didn't want to be living with them and interrupting their sexy time. Especially when I wasn't having any of my own.

Leah, as she couldn't stop telling me, couldn't believe it. But I stopped hearing from him around the time of the break-in, and so I had a niggling at the back of my brain. I'd never had much luck with the men in my life. They started off really great, but then around the three-month mark something always went wrong. I went off them, or they became clingy, or they had crazies breaking into my flat. Same old, same old.

When Leah invited me to keep her company on a week's trip she and Daniel were making to New York, I jumped at the chance. It was an opportunity to get away from London and my flat and any complications of the male variety. Daniel would be working a lot, apparently, so we'd have plenty of girl time. And girl time was just what I needed. After Leah's last break up, we'd flown to Mexico for a holiday. Flying west seemed to get her over her heartbreak. Let's hope it did the same for me.

The bartender slid some more drinks in front of us—a Manhattan in front of me and a replica of the disgustingly sweet concoction that Leah had ordered earlier. I looked at Leah and she shrugged and picked up her drink. I gently pushed her wrist, persuading her to put it back on the bar.

"We didn't order these," I said to the bartender.

He pointed at the man I half-recognized. "They're courtesy of the gentleman at the end of the bar."

Sirens blared in my head. Oh no. This wasn't happening. I didn't want male attention. I didn't want any complications. The familiar stranger caught my eye and raised his drink again. Ungratefully, I rolled my eyes and sat back in my chair. Leah looked at me pleadingly.

"Fuck it," I said and grabbed the fresh cocktail. I might as well drink it. It didn't mean I had to talk to him.

"So, Daniel has this friend," Leah said.

"Not interested."

"He's a really nice guy."

I shook my head.

"But you always told me the way to get over a man is to get under another."

"I would never say something like that."

"You did and you know it."

I grinned. I so would. "I'm not dating."

"What? Ever?"

"Look, I just found out that my last boyfriend was

mixed up in a whole lot of crazy. I'm not on the market. I need to give myself a timeout. I have shockingly bad taste in men."

"You totally do not."

"What about the guy that picked up the waitress while I popped to the loo."

"Well, he was a douche. But you still need a bit of fun in your life."

"She's right," a voice said from behind me. I turned to find the familiar stranger looking down at me

Leah popped off her stool, grinning. "I have to go to the restroom."

"Restroom? Not loo?" I teased, and rolled my eyes. She was about as subtle as a brick.

The stranger lowered himself into Leah's seat. I could feel him looking at me while I stared into my drink.

"I have rules," I blurted.

He didn't respond so I looked up to see if he was paying attention. He was looking straight at me with bright blue eyes. I stared back at my drink, unnerved. Ok, objectively he was handsome, the tall and dark variety, but no doubt a total shit because he was here talking to me and I was a shit magnet.

"Rules about fun?"

I nodded. "Rules if you want to get laid tonight."

"I'm listening," he said, without missing a beat.

Did I have rules? Well, now I had to think of some.

"I don't want to know your real name. Make something up."

He shook his head. "No. No, that's not going to work for me. You're not going to be screaming another man's name tonight. My name is Ethan."

Our eyes locked and my breath caught in my throat.

"Look, I'm sick of being lied to. If I don't expect anything from you I can't possibly be disappointed."

"I promise you won't be disappointed."

I took a beat and said, "I don't want to know anything about you. And I won't tell you my real name."

"You British girls seem to have a certain charm about you."

"If you don't like it, feel free to leave me alone." I really wasn't in the mood to mess about.

"I'm not going anywhere. I'd like to see how this plays out." He grinned at me and I felt the corners of my mouth twitch. I wanted to hate him. "So you know I'm Ethan. And I work in construction?" He asked instead of told me.

It was very clear from his Cayman Islands tan and the Rolex on his left wrist that he didn't work in construction, but he'd lied at my request, so I had no room to complain. I felt a shiver down my spine. This might be fun.

"I'm Florence."

He shook his head. "No. You're not Florence."

"I know, but I'm not going to tell you my real name. I told you, there are rules."

"That's fine, but your made-up name isn't going to be Florence. It's about as sexy as an old shoe and you're a sexy girl. You need a sexy name."

I raised my eyebrows at him. "Ok," I said cautiously. "Kate?"

He shook his head again.

"Whatever. Choose something."

I could see him thinking. I was interested to see what he'd come up with. How did he see me? "Anna," he said finally.

What?? Did he know me? No. We lived 3,000 miles from each other. Did I look like an Anna? It must be just some kind of weird coincidence. What did it matter if he used my real name, anyway? I'd never see him again after tonight.

Leah came back from the restroom at that moment, interrupting any debate I might have with Ethan over his invented name for me.

Ethan reached out to shake Leah's hand. "I'm Ethan. We were just leaving, but we'll see you home."

I giggled. He was pretty sure of himself, that was for certain. "I did not—"

"My boyfriend's driver is outside. I can see myself home." She grinned like an idiot.

"Ok, then we'll walk you out," Ethan said, as if we were a couple or something.

13

Daniel's driver was chatting to a man who turned out to be Ethan's driver when we got outside. I said goodbye to Leah, promising to call her in an hour to let her know where I was and that I was ok. Ethan opened the door to his car and gestured for me to get inside.

"Do you know Daniel?" I asked.

"Daniel who?"

"Daniel Armitage."

"I know of him, but I've never met him. Why do you ask?"

"Your driver seems to know his driver."

"Leah's boyfriend is Daniel Armitage?"

I nodded and he nodded in response.

"Where are we going?" I asked, slightly panicked. Why hadn't I asked before? I'd just got into a car with a stranger without asking any questions. What was I doing? I pulled out my phone to text Leah.

"Columbus Circle. Mandarin Oriental," he said to the driver.

I told her where we were going and that I'd text her later to let her know I was ok. I swallowed and leaned forward to unwind the window to let the warm air of the New York summer spill in. OK, well if we were going to a hotel. He meant business. And when I say *business*, I mean *sex*. I'd never been into one-night stands. I didn't like the idea of a stranger seeing me naked. But this stranger was particularly attractive and I was here in

New York City to blow off some steam and have some fun, right? It was the city that didn't sleep, and when in Rome ...

My right leg started bouncing. A nervous habit. I only noticed as I caught Ethan noticing. He dragged his eyes from my leg up to my eyes and smiled.

"There's no need to be nervous. We won't do anything you don't beg me to do to you," he whispered in my ear.

Wow. My stomach tilted and I shifted in my seat, and went back to staring out the window.

CHAPTER Two

Ethan already seemed to have the key to a ... our ... the room. We made our way up in the elevator without speaking. Without touching. I was more nervous than I wanted to be. I could do sex with no strings attached. What was the big deal?

When we reached the door, it swung open to reveal a huge living room overlooking Central Park. It was the most romantic thing I'd ever seen. The ceiling was decorated in what looked like gold leaf. The floors were dark and gleamed against the lights of the city. It looked like a place where a Roman god would live.

"Fuck," I said, failing to keep what was in my head in my head.

"It's a great view, isn't it?"

I nodded and walked toward the window, placing my hands on the glass as I stared out. I wanted to know who this guy was. He certainly wasn't in construction. Maybe he was a gangster. I reminded myself that it didn't matter. I wasn't here for romance or to get to know him. I was here for fun. Distraction without complications.

"Can I get you a drink to go with that view?"

"Whiskey, please," I replied without turning around.

I heard him clink about behind me as I tried to make out various landmarks. "I think I can see the Dakota Building," I said, as if I were sightseeing, forgetting I was talking to a stranger I was about to have sex with.

"It's unusual for women to drink whiskey," Ethan said.

"I guess you'd know." Again, I didn't mean for the comment to slip out of my head. Or maybe I did. Maybe I wanted to see what response it would solicit. But there was no response.

"Show me what you're looking at," he said, standing behind me, close. I could feel his body heat rolling off him. He handed me my whiskey and dropped his arm around my waist to pull me against him. I stiffened slightly and then relaxed. This was nice. The drink, the view, the Roman god. He smelled of something. Something intoxicating. I couldn't think what it was. Money. Sex. Power.

My finger stabbed the glass. "There. Is that the Dakota Building?" I pointed at the green-roofed building on the west of the park.

"I don't think so. I think the Dakota is on the East side."

"Oh." I tipped my head back slightly and it fell on his chest. He was tall. Very tall.

He pushed his cheek against mine and lowered his mouth to my neck, his breath tickling my skin. I wanted him. I really wanted him.

"I have more rules."

He kissed my neck. "Tell me."

"You have to wear a condom."

"Right this moment?" he teased.

"No, later when ... if."

"What else?" He kissed my neck again.

"We're not exchanging numbers or email or saying we're going to see each other again."

He moved to the other side of my neck and kissed me again. I could feel myself soften slightly with each touch of his lips.

"Ok," he replied. "Is that it?"

"For now," I said. My brain was fuzzy and I couldn't think of anything else.

"Good." He pulled away from me and I turned to see him sit down on the sofa opposite the window. "Undress for me."

I paused, just for a second or two, but there was no saying no to him—and I didn't want to say no. I fumbled with the top button of my shirt and then steadied my hand and undid the rest of the buttons. I peeled off the tight-fitting blue silk shirt and let it fall to the ground. I looked at him and he was looking me directly in the eyes as he took a sip of his drink. I felt my underwear dampen.

He was just gorgeous, the kind of man you'd find on

a billboard in Times Square, but not on a sofa opposite me, waiting for me to get naked. I found the zipper of my skirt and I turned around so my back was facing him as I pulled it down. Bending at my waist, pushing my butt toward him, I stepped out of it. I gave him a quick look over my shoulder. His eyes had darkened and he licked his lips. He actually licked his lips, like he was getting ready to devour me. I turned to face him in my underwear and heels.

"I'll take care of the rest. Come here," he growled. I felt heat rush to my sex. I walked across to him and stood between his knees. "Where do I start with you? You're so beautiful. Like a perfectly wrapped present that gets more exciting as the layers come off."

I had to stop myself from enjoying his words. I wasn't here to be romanced. I was here to have fun.

He sat forward suddenly and delved into my underwear, his thumb finding my nub instantly. "You're already wet for me," he said as his fingers slid along my folds, coating his fingers with me as his thumb circled my clitoris. My legs softened and my hands fell on his shoulders to steady myself.

He looked up at me. "You like that?"

I gasped and nodded, unable to speak.

"I knew you would. I knew when I saw you across the bar, rolling your eyes at me. I knew this is what you wanted, what you needed." His fingers quickened and I twisted my hips in some kind of futile resistance. "Stay still while I make you come."

I tipped my head back as his fingers and thumb continued their work. My whole body felt hot, on fire. The heat was emanating from between my legs and spreading throughout my body. I could feel my nipples straining at the lace of my bra, begging for attention. My shoulders rounded forward.

"Take it off," he said. "Your bra. Now. Take it off."

I felt myself shudder at his words. Unsteady and half-crazed, I unsnapped the clasp of my bra and stripped it off.

"Oh, yes. You are perfect. Perfect tits. Perfect pussy."

"Oh god," I said. "Oh god. Oh god." I was gasping for breath.

He reached behind me and pushed me harder on to his hand and he plunged his fingers into me. "I'm your god tonight, beautiful. Now come for me."

And I couldn't help myself: My eyes closed and a blinding white light filled my head as my climax crashed over me.

I felt myself weaken, and then Ethan's arms around me. Had I fallen? I felt softness all around me. Ethan was leaning over me—we were in bed.

"Hey," he said.

"Hey," I said, barely conscious. What the hell just happened? I'd always associated good sex with intimacy and maybe love, but this man did mind-blowing things to my body and I'd just met him.

"You look spectacular when you come." He bent his head and took a nipple between his teeth. I was writhing off the mattress as he alternated grazing and sucking one breast and then the other. My hands pushed into his hair and he pulled me up so I was facing him. For a second he looked at me before inching forward and taking my bottom lip between his teeth. I wanted him again, desperately. I wanted to see him above me, pushing into me, filling me. I grabbed at his back and pulled his shirt from his trousers and scratched down his back. He groaned and plunged his tongue into my mouth, urgent, hungry. I reached down for his fly, impatient for more of him. He kneeled up, bringing my mouth with him as his stripped his shirt off. I pushed him away and turned over and onto all fours.

"Hurry. I want you inside me," I said.

"Fuck, beautiful."

I heard him rustling behind me, first with his clothes and then a condom wrapper. I turned and looked over my shoulder and he was staring at my ass.

He kneeled behind me and I felt his hands on my hips. My skin fizzed at his touch and I pushed back, wanting to feel more him.

"Back into position," he growled. "I'm going to fuck you so hard you're not going to remember your own name." And he pushed into me so forcefully that my elbows gave way and I had to steady myself. I was full of him—so full it bordered on uncomfortable. I wasn't sure if it was because he was big or was because he was deep. Really deep. He withdrew slowly—I was aware of every part of him. His hand found my shoulder, giving me support and him resistance, and he plunged in again, hard and deep.

"Jesus," I cried out as I felt him at the end of me.

"Yes, baby. That's it. We're going to be doing this all night."

He found his rhythm and I could do nothing but comply. Right then, I would do whatever the hell he asked me to do. And he was the sort of man who would ask for everything.

"All night. We're going to fuck until you're sore and still begging me for more. Do you hear me?"

"More. Harder," I choked.

He grunted and increased his rhythm, pushing farther and farther into me. The rumbling of my orgasm started somewhere far off.

"I can feel you. You feel so good. And you're close. Aren't you?" he asked.

"Yes, so close."

And then he pulled out and I felt his fingers fall from my body. Panicked, I looked over my shoulder.

"I have to see your face. On your back."

I scrambled to my back, desperate to feel him again, and he pulled me down the bed closer to him and pushed into me again. *Oh yes, that was it ... right there.*

He didn't take his eyes off of me as my orgasm built again. He put one of my legs over his shoulder and the change in position sent me hurtling toward that light again. I arched off the bed as my orgasm gripped me. Ethan's rhythm didn't alter, not for a second, and each stroke pulled out another level of pleasure until I was sure that I would pass out. When it finally subsided enough for me to open my eyes, he was above me still, pushing into me, looking at me.

A second after our eyes met, I felt him tense and watched his eyes cloud as his climax washed over him.

He rolled off me, disposed of his condom, and his hands felt for my body and pulled at me, bringing me closer to him. I got up and went to the bathroom. I was here to have fun, not to cuddle.

I sat on the edge of the bath, still weak from my orgasm, still not quite understanding how sex could be that amazing with a man I just met. I groaned and pushed my hands through my hair. I had to get out of there, before things got awkward. I grabbed a robe from the back of the bathroom door and drew it around me.

As I peeked out the door, Ethan lay sprawled on the bed looking at the ceiling, as if defeated. I smiled and headed to the living room.

"Anna?" I heard him call from the bedroom. I ignored him as I picked up my clothes from the various points around the room at which they were discarded.

"What are you doing?" he asked, his voice closer now. I looked up and found him looking at me from the doorway.

"Umm. I'm finding my clothes. I need to get going—"

Ethan strode across the room, grabbed me by the bottom, lifted me over his shoulder, marched back to the bedroom, and threw me on the bed.

"You're not going anywhere. I told you we're going to fuck all night, and I'm not nearly halfway finished."

CHAPTER
Three

Ethan

It was hot. Even this early, it was too fucking hot. I was sweating already and I hadn't even reached the Turtle Pond. I had been close to waking her up and burying myself in her again this morning, she looked so fucking sexy as she slept. But I didn't do morning sex. So I left her there, looking sexy as hell, and now I was running off my hard-on.

Wrong choice, bud, my dick whispered to me. No morning sex was a rule of mine. I liked that she had rules, too. I grinned as I remembered her trying to think them up on the spot. Mine were set in stone and no morning sex was at the top of the list—Number One. Number Two was no sleepovers. Everything looked different in the morning. More real. And I didn't do real. Not with women. It was only ever sex. Great sex. Lots of sex. Lots of women. But nothing more. More than that was too complicated, and rule Number Three was I didn't do complicated.

I wasn't sure who fell asleep first but I hadn't gotten around to leaving the hotel. I'd booked the suite earlier in the day. I didn't bring women back to my place—rule

Number Four—and I was tired of schlepping over to bridge-and-tunnel land. Did no one live in Manhattan anymore? The Mandarin Oriental always impressed, and besides I loved the view from the Oriental Suite.

My cell rang and I took it, pleased to have a distraction. "Scott," I answered.

"Hey. How'd you do last night?" It was Andrew. We'd known each other since college and we had a healthy competition between us in everything we did.

"Good. I'm out on my run."

"Man, I'm sorry you didn't score." He was baiting me and I wasn't biting. "Maybe you're just too old for the young, hot girls these days. You should think about settling down before the quality of women who will fuck you dives too low."

"You have me bent over double from laughing, you prick."

He knew she was hot. He knew I would have fucked her, just as I told him I would when I first caught sight of her across the bar last night. When I went over to her, Andrew had left to go home to Amanda. His wife. Of five years, although they'd been together since college. Ten years fucking the same woman. Or not fucking her, as Andrew so often complained. Jesus. I knew I couldn't do it. I didn't even pretend it was a possibility. I had rules and I didn't keep them to myself. I was clear with the women I fucked. I didn't pretend it was anything other than sex. There were no broken promises, no ambiguity. They never wondered if I would call—I never took their number.

There were a few women that had my number and I saw semi-regularly. And when I say *saw*, I mean *fucked*. Joan, who called me whenever she was between boyfriends. I was happy to help her out. Phoebe who lived in Boston but came to New York once a month and was a fantastic lay. And Fiona, who hadn't called in a while, maybe she got married or something. But I never called them. Not ever. That was rule Number Five.

"Mandy wants to know if you're still coming up to the Hamptons this weekend. I think she has a friend she wants to introduce you to."

"Fuck, Andrew. I'm not fucking one of Mandy's friends again." Mandy had introduced me to Susie last December. I'd been clear—very clear—with her that I didn't date. She seemed to be cool with that and she had great legs, so I'd taken her back to her hotel. The sex had been very average and then she tried to give me her number, which I politely refused, and she had gone bunny boiler crazy. Mandy was pissy with me. Andrew had tried to talk me into going to dinner with her. It was a fucking disaster.

"If I come to the Hamptons this weekend, I won't be fucking any of Mandy's friends under any circumstances. Can you tell her that? Can you make it clear that it's not a case of not having found the right woman? It's that there are too many right women for me to limit myself to one. Tell her, bud, or it's going to get ugly."

"You're a dick."

I grinned. "Likewise."

"Later."

I hung up.

"Anna" had been anything but average last night. She had been exceptional. Feisty, demanding, hungry, responsive. My dick twitched at the images invading my head. I picked up the pace to try to shake it off. When women understood that it was only ever going to be one night, it was better. They let go. Unusually, last night, it had been Anna who had made it clear that there was going to be no follow-up. That had never happened to me before. I found myself grinning. Her accent was cute. Her ass was better. Perfect—round, smooth, firm. I felt stirrings again. She was on vacation, right? Only stateside for one week. Enforced no strings. I'd already broken the no sleepover rule. I might as well use it to my advantage. I stopped dead. She would be naked right now. It was still early. I looked at my watch. I'd only been out fifteen minutes. I'd been planning on running for an hour, giving her time to get out before I got back. If I ran back now, she'd still be there and I could wake her with my tongue between her legs.

Fuck.

Morning sex didn't count as real if you knew they'd be 3,000 miles away within a week. I started the run back to the hotel.

Anna

I awoke sore. I could feel the half-formed bruises on my neck, on my thighs, on my breasts. I smiled at the cause and then froze. Shit, I hadn't meant to fall asleep. I had been about to get dressed and head back to Daniel's place when Ethan had carried me back to bed, and true to his word, he had fucked me all night. Oh god. I'd never had so much sex in one night, never had such amazing sex, and never begged for it, as he told me I would, over and over. I squirmed, feeling myself dampen at the memory. Was he still here? I couldn't bring myself to look. I couldn't hear him breathing, but the bed was as big as a small country, so that was no wonder. Did he live here? In a hotel? I had so many unanswered questions. But, I told myself, I came here for fun, not answers.

I rolled to my side and swung my legs off the bed. The bed was empty. I held my breath, trying not to make a sound, so I could hear if there was any noise on the other side of the door.

Nothing.

I grabbed the robe that had been discarded beside the bed and pulled it around me, wincing as the movement brought my attention to my sore back. I headed to the bathroom and lowered the robe, angling my back at the mirror, to see if I could see the cause of the pain. My back was grazed. Oh yes, that was from the part of last night where I was up against the wall, my legs wrapped around Ethan's waist as he pounded into me, pushing me farther and farther up the wall. Friction burns. I blushed and tried to suppress a grin.

Tentatively, I opened the door to the bedroom into the living room. Not a sound. He was gone, but his suit was still strewn across the living room. I felt disappointed, and then embarrassed at my disappointment. It was just sex. I gathered my clothes, took them back to the bedroom, and dressed quickly. Should I leave a note? What was one-night stand etiquette? No, it was just sex—no note required.

I called Leah and she answered on the first ring. "Don't even speak to me. I know I'm a slut." I said before she'd even said hello.

She screeched. "Don't you dare say that. You're just having yourself some fun. I want to hear all about it but we've got to have some culture with our booze. Get yourself back here to change. I want to go to that place you said was around the corner."

"You want to go to The Frick?"

"Yes, that's the one."

"We're going to talk about fucking in The Frick? That doesn't seem very appropriate." We laughed.

"You can tell me all about it and then you can tell me again over lunch and cocktails. Let's go somewhere fancy. Get the concierge to book something on the way out."

I slipped out the suite, down the elevators, and without a single shred of embarrassment, despite my evening attire, spoke to the concierge who booked lunch for two at what I supposed was a very expensive restaurant. I headed out into the humidity of a New York morning in July. It was only just 7 a.m. but it was already stiflingly hot. Once I orientated myself, I realized I was about ten blocks from Daniel's apartment, but I couldn't walk, not in these heels. Ten blocks was a long walk of shame. Except I wasn't ashamed. I felt great, like I'd scrubbed a layer of something unpleasant from me, and I was now fresh and ready for my next chapter.

"So, I bet he was amazing. He looked like he would be amazing," Leah rambled as we strolled through Central Park, coffees in hand, taking in the morning parkgoers, killing time while we waited for the Frick to open.

I grinned. He was amazing. The sex. The sex had been amazing.

"I have no complaints."

"So, you see, you should take your own advice—it

works!" she bumped my shoulder with hers. "Are you going to see him again?"

"I told you, Leah, it was just sex. No kissing on the mouth."

"Eww, you didn't kiss him on the mouth but you let his penis inside you?"

"No, I mean figuratively." He'd been an excellent kisser. An excellent everything. "You know, no emotional involvement."

"Oh, like from *Pretty Woman*," she said. I nodded. "What is it with you and that film?"

I shrugged.

"So, what if he calls and asks you out again?"

"We've not been out to go out *again,* and anyway, he doesn't have my number." Should I have left him my number or a note or something? No, it was just sex.

Leah raised her eyebrows at me. I didn't know if it was disbelief of disapproval. Both, probably.

"It should be open now. Let's go." I wanted the subject changed. I was in New York! I wanted to enjoy it. I picked up the pace as we headed to The Frick. The streets seemed relatively peaceful. The commuters were all behind their desks, leaving the streets to people who had to endure the July heat—tourists like Leah and me, couriers, students, nannies pushing strollers, schoolchildren on trips away from home.

"So you're going to marry Daniel?" I asked. She'd

accepted his proposal weeks ago but I'd heard no mention of it since.

Leah didn't respond straight away. "Yes, but there's no rush."

"I thought when you know, you know. You know?"

We laughed. "I know," Leah answered. "I can't imagine being with anybody else. He makes me happy and I want to make him happy, forever. It doesn't matter if we're married or not."

"That's nice," I said. I meant it.

"It will happen for you."

I smiled at her and shrugged my shoulders. "It's all about fun for me now. I've tried to find 'it' or 'the one' and it hasn't happened, so I officially give up. I want fun. Nothing complicated."

The air conditioning in the museum was a godsend. "Shall we just stay here all day? We can be cool and cultured at the same time."

"No doubt our very expensive restaurant will have A/C and we can get a cab. It's too hot to walk." Leah always looked perfectly beautiful, but even her glossy straight hair had the start of a frizz around it. I'd long since given up with mine. The humidity took the hint of a natural curl and turned me into Diana Ross.

"Ok, as long as I can day drink, I'll let you take me to lunch."

"I'm honored."

"You should be."

CHAPTER
Four

Ethan

I scanned the restaurant but I couldn't see her. Maybe my intel was wrong.

I'd felt cheated when I got back to the hotel. I was hoping to put my hard-on to good use and clear my head. But she'd cleared out. No number. No goodbye. You'd think she would have hung around to see if I was coming back. We'd had fucking phenomenal sex. I'd made her come five or six times.

I didn't like it when things didn't go my way, so I'd made a few discrete enquiries with the lobby staff, who I had hoped might have put her in a cab, but better than that, the concierge had booked lunch for her for later today. Anna was meant to be in this restaurant this lunchtime.

"So what's the big news?" Andrew asked.

"What?"

"Why have you dragged me out to lunch?"

"Dragged you? You're my bud."

"I saw you last night, dude. I'm sick of you."

"Fuck you."

"Did you get laid?"

I raised my eyebrows.

"Dude. Come on. Did you?"

I grinned at him.

"Fuck you," he said.

"That's what I thought."

I heard her laugh and looked up from my menu. Yes, it was her at the door. She was with her friend from the night before, the one that was seeing Armitage. She didn't see me as she made her way behind the waitress to a table across the room from us. She looked different from last night. Somehow better than I remembered. Even though it had just been a few hours since I last saw her, the sight of her warmed something in me. I quickly looked back at my menu before I could see where she was seated. What the fuck was I doing? I was fucking stalking this girl. Suddenly I realized what a pathetic prick I was. "Let's order," I huffed and immediately caught the eye of a waitress who scurried over.

"So, you still haven't told me what we're doing here," Andrew said.

"Shut up and order," I barked. "I'll have the rib eye, rare, with spinach. And a beer." The waitress gave me the look. The look that said she'd go down on me right there if I asked her to. It calmed me. I grinned at her and she blushed. Not my type.

I slung my arm on the back of the booth and relaxed. On a quick scan of the restaurant I couldn't see her.

Maybe we could have lunch and I could get out without running into her. What was I thinking coming here?

"I spoke to Mandy about setting you up. I guess this is why we're here."

"Was she ok about it?" I liked Mandy; we'd been friends a long time. I didn't want to piss her off, but I really didn't want to be fucking her friends again.

"She told me your penis would shrivel up and fall off, but you're off the hook. No more set-ups. For now, anyway. But you're coming to dinner on Friday right? Come over in the afternoon and we can play tennis."

Andrew and Mandy's place in East Hampton had a tennis court. I was using my sister's place. She had moved to London with her husband last summer and didn't make it back very often since they had their daughter Izzy, so I took full advantage. It had a good-sized pool and some great running routes nearby. I was looking forward to emptying my mind of the day to day this weekend. Work was a bitch at the moment and I needed to clear my head.

"Dude, is that that girl from last night?" Andrew indicated behind me.

I really hadn't thought this through. Was I going to go over and speak to her? Ask her out? Fuck.

I shrugged but didn't look.

"Seriously, I think it is. Take a look," he pushed.

I glanced over my shoulder and my eyes locked with

hers. I couldn't help but grin. She looked shocked and blushed but didn't look away. I knew how far that blush dipped beneath her shirt.

"Excuse me a minute," I said.

"Careful. You might have to marry her if you speak to her after you've fucked her."

There was something in her eyes that hadn't been there the night before. She looked ... relaxed.

"Nice to see you again, girls," I said as I arrived at the table. Except I was looking only at Anna, who was smiling at me. That was a good sign.

"Wow, this is a small town," Leah said. "Some things are just meant to happen, I guess."

I pulled my eyes away from Anna and looked at Leah, who was looking very happy. That was another good sign. Anna couldn't be pissed that I hadn't been there when she woke up, given Leah's welcome.

"Nice to see you again. Are you two enjoying your day?" My eyes went back to Anna. She looked great. None of the makeup from last night, and it suited her.

"Join us," Leah said. I caught Anna shoot her a warning look.

"I'm sure Ethan has better things to do than join us for lunch," Anna clipped.

"I don't, actually." I gestured at Andrew to come over. "We're joining this table," I said to a passing waiter. I moved to Anna's side of the booth and she scurried along the bench. I rested a hand on her thigh and she stopped moving away from me. She might not want me here. She might have wanted me to disappear after last night, but now I was here and I could change her mind.

Andrew came over, clearly a little confused. I hope he played along and didn't say anything that made me want to punch him. Unlikely.

"So, do you two work together?" Leah asked.

Anna's leg began bobbing up and down. She was nervous. Cute.

I moved my hand, stroking her and pushing her skirt slightly farther up her thighs. She tensed and I grinned as she gave me an imploring look.

Andrew was chatting away to Leah, telling her about his job.

"You'd left when I came back from my run," I said so only she could hear. "I was hoping to give you a morning workout."

She blushed again but didn't reply.

"I'd like to see you again." The words came out before I realized what I was saying. Why else was I here? I wanted a bit more of her. Just another night and I'd quench this thirst I had for her.

"Ethan."

"Dinner tonight?" I asked, ignoring the warning in her voice.

"That wasn't the deal."

"I don't remember making a deal," I said as my fingers dipped under the hem of her skirt.

"I have *rules*," she whispered.

"Give me your phone."

Her hand covered the phone on the table and my hand moved up her thigh.

"Ethan," she whispered.

I grazed the seam of her underwear. "Give me your phone and I'll stop."

She looked me directly in the eye and dropped the phone into her purse.

Fuck. She wanted this. I slid my fingers under her underwear and found her beautifully wet for me. My heart raced as I dragged my fingers along her sex. She moved forward and put her elbows on the table, joining the conversation between Andrew and Leah. My fingers found her clit and I started circling. She agreed with Leah on something she was saying about their morning. I couldn't hear. I wasn't listening. She was a great actress. It was like she wasn't fazed by the fact I had my fingers all over her. I found myself watching the three of them as if I weren't there. All I could concentrate on was the sweet pussy coating my fingers, like honey dripping from her. I could feel myself hardening. Could I maneuver us to the restrooms? I wanted to be inside her.

The waiters appeared with our food. Without looking at me, Anna reached into her bag and handed me her phone. I wasn't sure if I was pleased or disappointed. I withdrew my hand from her underwear and wiped my fingers on my napkin.

I typed my number into her phone and then pressed Call. I felt the familiar vibration against my chest. I saved my number on her phone and tried to think about something—anything—that would stand my dick down. Andrew was talking about proposing to Mandy. That would do it. *Thanks, dude.*

"So you're living the fairytale?" Leah asked.

"No," Anna said. "You're living the fairytale. Daniel was the last handsome Prince out there. The rest of them..." she shook her head as she trailed off. Someone had clearly done a number on her. Idiot.

"So what are you up to this afternoon?" I asked. I didn't like to see that sadness in her.

"Well, Anna needs to rest. She didn't get much sleep last night." Leah winked at me and Anna rolled her eyes. I laughed. She'd rolled her eyes at me last night. I didn't often have that effect on women.

"We're just going to go back to the apartment and lay like broccoli, be still like vegetables, and watch movies," Anna said.

"Well, I have a lot of construction to do so we better make a move."

"Construction?" Andrew asked.

"Come on. Let's leave these ladies to their afternoon

of *Pretty Woman*. Nice to see you again, Leah." I turned to Anna. "And you." I cupped her jaw. "I'll call you about dinner." And I kissed her square on the lips, for just a second longer than was appropriate.

"Dude," Andrew said to me as we walked out the restaurant.

"Don't say a fucking word," I warned.

Anna

"He likes you, Anna," Leah said. "Anna?"

"I heard you. I don't want to talk about it. There's nothing to say."

"But don't you think it's amazing how you bumped into each other, like, just hours after you left him? It's like fate bringing you together or something."

It *was* weird how we bumped into each other. And there was none of that post-casual sex awkwardness. I supposed he had had lots of practice.

"Leah, I'm going to have to kill you or throw up on you unless you stop talking."

Ethan and Andrew had just left.

"Excuse me." I gestured to the waitress. "Please can we have the check?"

"The check has been paid, ma'am. Mr. Scott said you can order anything you like. Can I bring you something else?"

Mr. Scott. Mr. Scott.

"Ma'am?"

"Oh. Nothing. Thanks."

Leah was grinning at me like the cat that got the cream.

"Right, let's go and get in bed and watch movies," I said, ignoring her grin.

"*And* he knew you were quoting *Pretty Woman* when you were on about the broccoli thing."

"Shut up, Leah." I'd caught that, too. It was cute.

"He's, like, your perfect match."

"Shut up, Leah."

"He's very sexy."

He was. I pushed my lips together to stop myself from smiling. "If I hear another word out of you about it I'm going to change my flights and go home." I shifted out the booth and then we were in the oppressive heat.

"Let's get a cab back to Daniel's," I said, holding out my arm.

"Ok, just one more thing, and then I'll shut up." I didn't say anything. "I saw you give him your phone. Did he give you his number?"

I shrugged as I moved toward the cab that had pulled in.

"Is that a yes?"

"I've not looked. I guess he did."

"And did he ask you out again?"

Had he? I couldn't remember. He'd said something.

His touch had been distracting. I could still feel him between my legs.

I shrugged again. "I can't remember."

"You can't remember if someone who looks like that asked you out?" Leah scoffed. "He's almost as handsome as Daniel."

"He's way hotter." I grinned.

"I knew you liked him!"

"I didn't say I didn't know he was hot. Jesus. I slept with him. I'm clearly attracted to him. I'm just not interested in having more than one night. With anyone."

"Who said anything about a relationship?" Leah asked. "Just enjoy a fling and see where it goes."

"It's not going anywhere. It's not like I'm going to bump into him again."

"He's going to call you."

"Whatever."

This was what vacations were all about. Wrapped up in the world's softest duvet, in PJs, eating chocolate and watching movies. Leah and I were arguing over which movie to play next. Obviously, we'd started with *Pretty Woman*. Although Leah protested about watching it for the millionth time with me, I knew she secretly loved it.

"There's no way I'm watching *The Vow*. It's a bullshit film," I said.

"You know it's not bullshit. It's one of your favorite films ever. But we don't have to watch it if it's going to make your mood plummet farther downhill. What about *Sweet Home Alabama*?"

"If it hasn't got Ryan Gosling in it, I'm not interested."

"You don't think Josh Lucas is hot?"

"I'm not saying he's not hot. I just think Ryan is hotter."

"Ryan has a funny eye."

"How can you say that? He does not!"

I heard my phone ring from somewhere in the bed and I dived below the duvet to retrieve it. Fuck, where was it? The name "Sex God" flashed up on the screen and I grinned. I should ignore it. But as I didn't actually know who it was, although of course I did, I pressed Accept.

"Are you stalking me?" I answered.

"No, I'm calling you. Calling someone after a night of incredible sex is not normally considered stalking, as far as I'm aware. But I like the way you see the words 'Sex God' and you assume it's me calling."

He thought the sex was incredible, too? I'd supposed it was par for course for Roman gods like him. I squeezed my thighs together.

"Oh." It was all I could think to say.

"So, I'll pick you up at 7 p.m."

Leah was grinning at me so I sidled into the

bathroom, shut the door, and perched on the bath, chewing my finger.

"Anna?"

"Uh huh."

"7 p.m."

"I ..."

"Tell me your address so I can pick you up."

"I can't leave Leah. I'm staying with Leah and Daniel. It's rude."

Leah popped her head around the door. "You can totally leave me and Daniel."

"Leah, get out. And stop listening at the door! Unbelievable."

Ethan was laughing. "So, 7 p.m.?"

"You're persistent."

"Apparently I am when it comes to you."

God, he knew just the right thing to say. "820 Fifth Avenue. The Penthouse," I said.

"I'll see you at 7 p.m."

And he hung up.

CHAPTER Five

It was fifteen minutes to 7 p.m. and I was pacing up and down. I shouldn't be doing this. Last night was meant to be a one-off.

"I shouldn't be doing this," I said to Leah, who was fiddling about in the kitchen, trying to make us cocktails.

"Got it. It tastes almost like a proper one."

She came out the kitchen and handed me what I think was meant to be a mojito.

"Drink it," she ordered.

I took the drink and sniffed it.

"It's not going to poison you."

I needed a bit of liquid courage, so I took a sip. My eyebrows shot up. "It's good," I said.

Leah nodded. "I told you. Listen: Just have a good time tonight. I don't know why you are so nervous. He's hot, but so are you."

"And that, Leah Thompson, is why I love you."

She beamed. "Right back at you."

I didn't know why I was nervous. It wasn't because I was about to have dinner with a Roman god. Well, that wasn't the whole reason. I guess I was just so sick of trying to find the right guy and going through this process of getting dressed up, flirting, touching, kissing. Sharing things and then being hit with the inevitable realization that he wasn't the right guy. It had just been another waste of time. It was exhausting. I was sick of it.

Ethan definitely wasn't the right guy. Way too smooth. Way too charming. Way too 3,000 miles away. Way too ...

The intercom buzzed and Leah answered.

"You look beautiful," he said when I opened the door. He kissed me on the cheek. What else could I do but let him? He was way too hot.

I'd dressed conservatively on purpose. I didn't want him to think I was a sure thing. Even though I was totally a sure thing, I didn't have to dress like it. I'd worn palazzo pants and a long-sleeved, silk, cream shirt. The concession to sexiness was that shirt buttoned low so I couldn't wear a bra with it.

"Thanks. Let's go."

"Do you want to come in for a cocktail?" Leah shouted from behind me.

I shook my head. "No," I shouted back.

"I wasn't asking you," she replied.

"Let's go," I said to Ethan, and he backed out the door as I grabbed my clutch from the console table and I pulled the door behind us.

"Cocktail making isn't a core skill for Leah," I explained.

Ethan nodded.

I felt his hand on my back as we waited for the elevator.

"You look beautiful. Did you enjoy your afternoon?" he asked.

I nodded.

"*Pretty Woman*?"

I nodded again.

"You? Did you have a good afternoon... constructing?"

Ethan laughed throatily. "I was a little distracted after seeing you at lunchtime, but yes, it wasn't bad."

Way. Too. Smooth.

"Thanks for lunch," I said quickly realizing I'd not thanked him sooner.

"It was my pleasure."

"Thanks for dinner."

He laughed again. "Don't thank me yet. You might hate it."

Ethan's driver met us on the curb, and like the night before, I slipped in and rolled down the window.

"You don't like the air conditioning?"

"I like the cool. The breeze. Do you mind?" I asked.

He shook his head and looked at me as if he wanted to say something else. I had to look away. His eyes, I'd forgotten how blue they were.

After a few moments he spoke, "It seems that you're a little distracted. Was I wrong to be so insistent about dinner?"

I shook my head. "No, sorry." I turned to look at him again. "You know. It's just." I shrugged.

He drew his eyebrows together. "No, I don't know. Tell me."

"It's just that there are rules, and yet here we are. And I want to be here, but I don't want to be *here*. Do you know what I mean?"

"Not really."

"I'm just sick of this cycle of disappointment I seem to be in. Hence the rules."

He turned my hand so my palm faced up, and then linked his fingers through mine.

Ethan

It's not that I'd never held a woman's hand before, it was just that I'd never felt the *urge* to hold a woman's hand before. I wanted to touch her, to soothe her, to take away the cloud that seemed to surround her. I just didn't know how.

"What cycle of disappointment? I've never had a problem getting it up, if that's what you're worried about."

Her head snapped around and she looked at me and laughed—a genuine, full, unaffected laugh. "I believe that. Maybe you're the fun I need," she said almost to herself.

"Maybe I am."

"I'm sorry. I'll be better company when we get to the restaurant, I promise."

"I don't want you to be anything but yourself. You don't have to put on any act with me."

She stroked her thumb across my skin and I squeezed her hand.

We arrived at the restaurant sooner than I would have liked. I enjoyed having her next to me in the car with no one around us. I was close to suggesting we just go back to the hotel right now. But that would sound like I wanted to get into her underwear, which of course I did, but it wasn't just that. I didn't want to share her.

I knew instantly I'd chosen the wrong restaurant. We walked in and heads turned toward us, straining to see who had just arrived. It didn't suit her. She wasn't going to be impressed with seeing some powerful hedge fund guy or some Hollywood actor. I'd gotten this totally wrong. Fuck.

We were showed to our table toward the back of the restaurant. I was jumpy. I was very close to fucking this whole evening up.

"You ok?" she asked as we sat.

"Yeah, I guess."

"Sorry for going all Sylvia Plath in the car."

I laughed. "You don't have to apologize. I just want you to be yourself. I'm just a bit concerned this restaurant isn't the right place for you."

"Really?" she looked around. "It seems nice. You don't like it?"

"It's fine. I just don't think it's the type of place that I should have brought you. I should have picked a better restaurant."

"It looks plenty fancy enough."

"That's the point. It's too much I think. You suit something ..."

"You don't think I'm worth taking somewhere fancy?" She was smiling but it concealed an edge to her question.

"I think you're worth taking to the fanciest place in New York City. But I'm not sure you'd like it as much as you'd like something a bit more relaxed. Less pretentious."

She raised her eyebrows at me. "I can do fancy," she said simply.

A very nervous waiter came over and went through the menu with us. I watched her as she smiled and nodded at him, trying to put him at ease. It was a kind thing to do, and when he left he looked like he was a little bit in love with her.

"What are you going to order?" I asked.

She was looking over my shoulder, not at the menu. She shrugged. "I'll have whatever you have."

"You will?"

She nodded. "I hate menus. I hate the deciding, so I prefer not to look."

"So now I have to order something I think you'll like. Like a test."

"God no, that's awful—what kind of women do you normally date? Just order what you want. It'll be fine."

"But if you don't like it?"

"Then I won't eat it, but I'm sure it'll be fine. It's not a test, honestly."

I ordered. Sea bass. I wouldn't normally order fish, but women liked fish, didn't they?

"I don't date," I said when the smitten waiter had taken our order. Or my order for both of us.

"What?"

"You asked me a question about the kind of women I normally date."

"Oh, yes. You don't date?"

I shook my head.

"Oh, right. I can see there's something of a monk about you."

I laughed. "I didn't say I was a monk. I said I didn't date."

"I'm not following you. You don't like to call it dating?"

"Call what dating?"

"Dinner, drinks, back to your hotel. Do you live there?"

"No, I don't live there. I just ... book that suite sometimes."

"Somewhere to stay with your non-dates?"

"I don't stay there." Why was I telling her this stuff?

"You're talking in riddles."

I took a deep breath. "I don't do the dinner, drinks, dating thing usually ... or ever. I book the suite, I fuck in the suite, but I don't stay over."

She looked at me but didn't say anything.

I waited and she still didn't say anything. Fucking hell. I knew I was going to fuck this up. This restaurant. Telling her about my relationships, or lack of them. What was I thinking? I should never have run into her at lunch. This was a disaster.

"You haven't said anything," I reminded her.

"I don't know what to say." She gulped down half her glass of wine. "You don't need to woo me. I fucked you last night. I'll fuck you again tonight. You didn't need to bring me to dinner. You don't need to tell me that I'm different—that you don't normally sleep over, but you made an exception for me; that you don't normally take women to dinner, but you made an exception for me. I told you last night. I don't want the bullshit. I can take it if it's only sex. That's all I want. I just want the truth."

She took her napkin off her lap and pushed it onto the table and stood up.

"Let's go," she said. "Let's get to the bit where we're fucking. That's what we're here for. The rest of this is just bullshit."

I reached across to her and circled my hand just above the wrist. "Sit down. Please." She looked beautiful. Unguarded.

It hadn't occurred to me that she'd think it was a line. But I guess she didn't know that I didn't do that. I didn't need to do that. She didn't know that I had a no-bullshit policy. Why would she? She'd been fucked over by a series of douchebags full of lines like that. Why would I be any different?

She hesitated, but she sat down, her eyes fixed on the wine glass in front of her. I grabbed the bottle from the bucket beside the table and shooed away the waiter who came to assist. I topped up her glass.

"Thank you," she said.

"I'm going to promise you something."

She shifted in her seat, uncomfortable.

"I know you don't want me to, but I'm going to do it, anyway. I'm going to promise you that I'm not going to bullshit you. You can choose to believe me or not. I'm not going to tell you that I'm going to tell you everything, but everything I do say to you will be true. I like you. You're funny and sexy and amazing in bed. You're here for a week. Then you're gone. You've said you need a little fun in your life and I'm happy to oblige. Why don't we just hang out for the week? We can have some fun and then say goodbye. No bullshit. No promises. Just great sex and a few laughs."

She looked at me for the first time since she sat down. I could tell she was trying to think of a funny response. I grinned at her and she took a sip of wine rather than grin back, although I could see the twitch at the corner of her mouth. Wow, she was stubborn.

"Is that such a bad offer?"

"No bullshit," she repeated.

"I promise. But that doesn't mean I'm not going to pay you a compliment."

"You can only do that if it's not bullshit. Not because you think it's what I want to hear, or what you think you need to say to get me into bed."

"Agreed." I nodded. "You look beautiful tonight."

"Fuck off," she grinned.

"You do. Suck it up, buttercup."

CHAPTER Six

Anna

Once we'd established our no-bullshit rule, I allowed myself to relax. We'd laid it out there. I was here for a week. And I wanted some fun and some good sex. No complications, no promises, no bullshit. He was easy company. And easy on the eye, that was for sure. Was it possible to be as handsome as he was without being a total douche? Well, he put on a good act, because he seemed funny and charming and nice to the obviously very nervous waiter, despite the fact he wouldn't let him pour our wine. I was determined to just let myself enjoy the here and now.

Dating back in London was never about the here and now. I was always skipping ahead, fast forwarding the relationship in my head. Would my friends like him? Would my parents like him? Could I live with his quirks? Would he be a good father? It didn't have to be like that with Ethan. It was only ever going to be for a week, so I was forced to live in the moment.

"Shall we go and find a cocktail bar and an after dinner drink?" he asked.

I shook my head.

"No?"

I shook my head again. "I want to see you naked again."

"Well that's a coincidence. Because I want to see you naked again, too."

He grinned and asked for the check.

Unlike the night before, our car journey this evening was full of chatter. He seemed to know every building in New York City and pointed his favorites out as we drove along. A couple times he pulled me toward him so I could see better.

It seemed we were headed back to Daniel's apartment. "Where are we going?"

"The hotel. Is that ok?"

I nodded. Had I hoped we would go back to his place? Maybe a little. But it didn't matter where we were going, because wherever it was I was going to have the best—or the second best, after last night—sex of my life. He stroked my cheek with his thumb and leaned in and kissed me softly on the lips. It seemed, romantic almost. He pulled away and put his hand around my shoulders and pulled me closer.

When we got out the car, he held his hand for me and I took it and we crossed the lobby as if we were a couple. As we got in the elevator, despite being surrounded by other guests, my skin started to fizz. I knew what was going to happen when we got up to his suite. The delay of only minutes felt too much. I looked up at him, to try and see what he was thinking. He looked back at me with darkened eyes and shook his head and looked away.

"Don't," he said quietly and the fizz of my skin grew. His hand on my hand was not enough. I needed to feel him.

As the last guests got off the elevator, the door hadn't quite shut when Ethan released my hand. For a brief moment I was confused, until he pushed me against the wall of the elevator and kissed me hard. His tongue pushed straight into my mouth, and his hands thrust into my hair, as if he couldn't stop himself. I reached around his neck, drawing him closer. He smelled so good. It had been less than 24 hours since my body had been taken by him, but I felt like it had been months. I felt a longing from somewhere, like it was never going to be enough with him.

He pulled at my clothes, releasing my shirt from my pants, and his hands spread up and across my naked back.

He reached for my leg, drawing it around his waist and he pushed me harder against the wall. I curled the other one around so he was holding me up. I felt his erection against me, but there were too many layers between us.

His mouth was still on mine, his tongue desperate and thrusting, when he released me from the wall and carried me from the elevator. Then I felt another wall behind me, and he pressed his hardness against me, making sure I knew he was ready for me.

I needed his shirt off. I clawed at his collar, fumbling for the buttons, his mouth having found my neck, nipping and sucking. Not gentle, but desperate like he had to taste me.

I started to make my way down his shirt, undoing the buttons, when he pulled away.

"We need to get in the room," he whispered. "Or I'm going to fuck you right here."

I realized we were in the hallway, just outside the elevators. I'd assumed we'd made it into the suite. I giggled and buried my head in his neck as he pulled me off the wall and moved toward the door. I should have got down from him. He should have released me, but I needed his body against mine. I pulled him tighter to me as he opened the door. He strode down the hallway of the suite and I pulled back slightly to look at him as he walked. He looked purposeful and determined and I let out the tiniest sigh. He was so handsome.

"Fuck," he said. "When you look at me like that, it does something to me. It flicks a switch in me."

I felt my back against the mattress as he leaned over me and I relaxed my hold on him.

"Seriously. Naked. Right now," he said as he went for the zipper to my trousers, tugging at it. I pushed his fingers away and took over and he reached for the buttons on my blouse. "Look at your gorgeous tits," he said as he spread my blouse open. "I need you right now," he said as he fumbled for his own zipper.

"So take me. I'm yours to have. You have my body for a week."

I shrugged off my blouse and kicked off my pants as he finished undressing and found a condom. He crawled up my body, pressing his flesh against mine.

"You're mine to have," he repeated to me as he thrust into me. My legs parted farther and my knees drew up either side of him at the feel of him, as if trying to make more room for him. He watched me and my reaction. For a second, I couldn't make a sound; I was so caught up in the sheer feel of him inside me. And then from the back of my throat I heard myself groan.

"Oh, that's it baby. Take it all," he said as he thrust into me again. Long, hard, pounding strokes.

"Ethan. Ethan. Ethan," I screamed.

I felt myself clench around him and I dug my fingernails into shoulders. Oh god, he needed to slow down. I wasn't ready for this. I wasn't ready to feel this so quickly. My hands grabbed at his arms and then started to push at his chest.

"Ethan. Slow down. I can't." But he kept me there, pushing into me, deeper and deeper and deeper. "I'm going to..." I couldn't get my words out before I felt myself falling, and there I was floating, feeling nothing and everything as my orgasm washed over me.

I opened my eyes. Ethan had stilled and was watching me. "You look so incredible when you come. You *feel* so incredible when you come."

"For you."

"For me," he repeated and started his rhythm again, and I saw the moment his orgasm started and spread through his body. God, he was sexy. He was my Sex God.

He rolled off me and went into the bathroom, and I climbed under the sheets and lay back on the bed.

"I thought it might have been a fluke," he said when he came back into the bedroom.

I sat up on my elbows and looked at him.

"Last night. Me coming like a teenager. I thought it must have been fluke. But it's you, Miss Anna." He crawled over me and kissed me on the nose and lay down on the other side of me. "Come here," he said, inviting me to scoot into the crook of his arm.

Ethan

Her skin was amazing. It glided over mine like warm silk. I liked stroking it and I liked it touching me. Her leg was hooked over mine and her hand rested on my chest. I'd just come like a teenager. Jesus, what was with that? It was the look on her face that pushed me over the edge a few minutes ago. It was the way she tried to resist her climax for a few seconds before giving into it and opening herself up entirely to me. It was like I could see everything about her when she came. All there, laid bare. Fuck, I could feel myself hardening again. I reached across to cup her ass.

"What are you thinking about?" she asked.

"You."

"You liar."

"I told you, no bullshit." My hand dipped and her leg inched up. I sat up and pushed her gently onto her back, leaned over to her and took one of her nipples. It pebbled in my mouth and she moaned. So reactive. I felt her hands in my hair, urging me on. I wanted to taste her. All of her. I moved lower, trailing kisses down to her stomach, across to her hipbone, and she shuddered. She was ready again. She wanted it as much as I wanted it, and that realization was the biggest fucking turn on. I delved my tongue into her folds and I held her knees out, giving me the best fucking view. She looked so incredible lying there, disheveled, only just recovered from having my dick bring her to her first orgasm, but still ready for my tongue to take her to her next. She wanted it. She wanted me. I heard myself groan and she arched off the bed. I thrust two fingers into her and circled.

"Hold still, Miss Anna. I'm going to make you come so hard, you're going to forget yourself."

She answered with a moan. It was the only answer I

needed. My tongue found her nub and pressed flat and hard before circling. She thrust her hips off the mattress, pushing herself into my mouth. I pushed her back down and my tongue replaced my fingers and I tasted deep inside her. She tasted just like honey. I couldn't get enough.

I could tell she was close when she twisted to try and escape me. I reached up and found her hands, then took her wrists and held them under her ass. That was the perfect angle for me—it held her still. I kept sucking and tasting and licking until I felt her tiny shudders. I could tell she was almost there.

"Ethan," she cried. I wasn't sure if it was a cry of pleasure or pain. Either way, I was in control of it. I could bring her over the edge or leave her right there. Fuck, my dick was throbbing. The power I felt. I increased the pressure of my tongue and there it was. She was over. She held her breath as she came, for so long, as if she forgot everything else. I released her hands and they went straight to my hair as I sucked the last remaining waves of her orgasm from her. Jesus, my cock ached for her.

I lay beside her, propped up on one elbow, and watched her as she came around. Her eyes eventually opened and she looked at me.

She absentmindedly stroked my chest. "You have magic in your touch." She said it in a way that let me believe I was the only one who could do that to her. That only I could make her body respond that way. Fuck, I wanted her again, badly. Before I had the chance to grab her and push my cock into her, she rolled out of bed and went into the bathroom.

I lay flat on my back, staring at the ceiling. If I died now, after tasting her and fucking her, I'd feel like I'd achieved something in my life. Fuck my job—making her come like that was the biggest fucking thrill.

As she came from the bathroom, she looked at me and then down to my hard-on, which I quickly covered with a sheet. I was constantly ready to go around her; it was verging on embarrassing.

I moved up the bed, rested against the headboard, and held my arm out for her to lie next to me. But instead, she took my hand in hers to steady herself as she climbed astride me, her eyes never leaving mine. She leaned forward, pushing her pussy back along the length of my cock, and pulled my bottom lip between her teeth.

I sat up, grabbed her face in my hands, and kissed her hard on the lips, pushing my tongue through to meet hers. She responded, her mouth open and ready—just like her. She trailed her fingers up my sides so lightly, with such a contrast to the heat and passion I felt from her, the way she moved above me, that it was as if those fingers told me something more, something deeper about her.

Jesus. How did she do that, open herself up to me like that? Without even realizing. But I knew. And I knew then that I had to be careful with her. She was feisty and passionate, but also gentle, sweet, and breakable.

I moved my hands to her magnificent tits. They were just fucking perfect. Natural, firm, not too big, and it felt like they were made for me. I felt harder than ever. I looked across to the bedside table. She followed my eyes and reached over for a condom, which she handed to me. After fumbling around like a 15-year-old, I placed my hands back on her hips and pulled her onto me. I loved having her above me like that, pushing down at her own pace. Her eyes left mine and to watch me move in and out of her. I tilted her chin so she looked at me again.

"You like to watch that?" I asked.

She nodded.

"Tell me," I said.

She hesitated. For a moment I thought I'd pushed her too far.

"I like to see your dick fucking me."

"Jesus," I groaned. My cock was throbbing and I was aware of every inch of her clamped around me. My hands dug into her hips as I tried to get deeper, quicker. She responded and moved with me to speed up her rhythm and pressed her nails into my shoulders as her head fell back. God, she was so sexy. I was going to make her come again. I wasn't sure if it was the feeling of fucking her or watching her getting fucked, but I wasn't going to last long. Not breaking our perfect movements, I reached down and my thumb found her clitoris. Instinctively, she backed away and I tried to hold her in place.

"No," she gasped.

"Yes, baby. Let me make you come."

"I can't, not again."

"You can and you will." And I flipped her to her back and drove into her.

"Ethan. Please. Harder."

That was it. I was done for. I pushed my thumb back to her clitoris and roughly rounded the bag of nerves as I kept up my rhythm. Her hips tilted up to meet my hand and my dick, driving me harder into her, just as she wanted. I felt my orgasm begin to rumble at the base of my spine. I kept my eyes open, wanting to see it on her face as well. Just a split second later, there it was, her eyes shut lazily, I felt her breathing stop, and I relaxed and allowed my climax to take me over.

I collapsed on top of her, totally spent and totally needing more from her.

I could fuck her forever. *What?*

I pulled out and went into the bathroom to dispose of the condom. I needed to clear my head. Shake it off. I splashed some water on my face and looked in the mirror.

I don't do complicated, I reminded myself.

When I opened the door to the bedroom, she was sat on the edge of the bed and was pulling her shirt on.

"Are you leaving?" I asked. How long had I been in the bathroom?

"I was cold, but yeah, maybe I should go." I was a dick. She wasn't leaving, and now it looked as if I was thinking she should. She hadn't said it as a question, but her eyes were asking. I didn't answer. I wasn't sure what my answer would be.

She looked away and stood up, her eyes going to the floor, looking for her things. I walked up to her and drew her to my chest. Her hands hung limply by her side. She was upset—upset with me—and I hated myself for it.

"Stay," I said into her neck.

"I should go."

"I want to wake up with you tomorrow." No bullshit. It was what I wanted.

"Just a week," she said. I wasn't sure if she was talking to me or herself as she unbuttoned her blouse and shrugged it off her shoulders.

I didn't push her to explain. "Let's get you into bed if you're cold." I walked her backward into the bed and guided her under the covers. "You need body heat to warm you, beautiful," I said as I pulled her back to my front and fit her perfectly into my body. "Sleep."

CHAPTER Seven

Anna

There was a distinct giddiness about my mood as I let myself back into Daniel's flat the following morning. I had woken up to Ethan trailing kisses along my body. He told me he was hungry and that he wanted to taste my honey. Who was I to argue? I loved the way he was so keen to make me come.

There was something about him that was almost addictive. I couldn't get enough of his body, his touch. If someone said that I could trade any hope of a normal existence and spend the rest of my life in that bed with him, I think I'd sign on the dotted line. Even now, twenty minutes since I last saw him, I wanted him again. And who was he? He was a stranger to me, and I to him. But I think part of him knew me better than anyone else. The way he looked at me, through me, and right into the center of me. Somehow, that ability to see me in a way others didn't meant he could do things with my body that no one could. No one had.

Leah was right. It was impossible to think about anything else, and Ben in particular, while I was with Ethan. Maybe I could fly to New York every time I got heartbroken. Ethan was almost worth getting heartbroken for.

"Are you mad?" I asked Leah as we sat down at a table at a coffee shop on Prince Street.

"What about?"

"Me spending time with Ethan."

"Yes, I'm super-mad that you are happy and having fun and being distracted from Ben the Bastard while I get to have super-hot and very loud sex with my super-hot and very loud boyfriend."

"Well, when you put it like that."

"Are you seeing him again tonight?"

"Err." How had we left it? He had dropped me at Daniel's on his way to work, but he'd left some of his stuff in the suite; he was in a fresh suit this morning, not wearing the same clothes from last night like I was. But he'd just kissed me and told me he'd see me later. "We didn't make any plans," I said, trying to sound breezy but I felt a pit in my stomach. I hoped that wasn't it. I hoped I would see him again. I reached into my bag and to find my phone. Nothing.

"Daniel has this reception thing at the hotel tonight and I said I would go with him. You should come."

"Sounds fun." I was trying to seem enthusiastic.

"But if Ethan calls, then go do your thing."

I smiled tightly. I shouldn't want to see him this badly. "You are the most awesome friend in the world."

"Uh uh." Leah shook her head. "No, that title belongs to you."

My phone rattled against the table.

SG: What are you wearing?

A warm spread across my chest at his text and I laughed.

"Ethan?" Leah asked and I nodded as I typed a response.

Me: My oldest jeans, and a T-shirt with a hole under the arm. Super sexy.

SG: You'd make a garbage bag look super sexy.

Me: Shut up.

SG: No bullshit.

SG: I can leave work by 6 p.m. tonight. Meet me at the hotel?

I laughed. He was all for getting down to business. No dinner and drinks tonight. Well, it was fun, not romance that I signed up for.

Me: Only if you promise to be naked when I arrive.

SG: You drive a hard bargain. See you then.

I looked up to find Leah looking at me and my wide grin. She wiggled her eyebrows. "We need to go underwear shopping."

"We do?"

"We need to get something to seduce our sexy men with."

"Well, A, he's not my man, and B, I think he's a sure thing. But ok, let's go."

Leah took me to an amazing lingerie boutique. She'd been there before when shopping alone in New York, thinking of ways to distract Daniel. She warned me it could be expensive, but assured me it was worth every penny. When we walked in and were handed a glass of champagne, I knew there was some serious money going to be spent.

Going through the racks I realized I hated shops like this. There was not a single item in the boutique that I didn't want to try on. As I started to select items, an assistant took them to a changing room. Dangerous. I couldn't remember how many I'd selected.

"Hey," Leah loud-whispered at me. "Come look." She held up a bra that I could sue the owner of the boutique for misrepresentation over. It was no more than a few strips of material, none of which would cover an actual breast.

"Kinky," I said.

"I have this one. It always goes down well ... or ensures Daniel does."

"Leah Thompson. I'm shocked. I thought you were going to be a virgin until your wedding night."

We both giggled.

My eyes darted to the rack next to her. This was clearly the kinky section. I picked up even more things to try on and finally made it to the changing rooms.

I could imagine Ethan ripping off everything I tried on. That was a good thing, but an expensive thing. The beautifully soft lighting that made me feel like Heidi Klum didn't help. I tried a very simple black bra and panties, which were entirely sheer. I loved them and decided I had to have them. I was sure Ethan would love them, too. I grabbed my bag to find my phone so I could text him and tell him what I was doing, and then the champagne suggested that showing him might be even more fun. I arranged myself so I was leaning on my side in front of the mirror, one hand reaching up against the wall. I then snapped a photo. Was I really going to do this? I typed out a message.

Me: I'm doing a little retail therapy. What are you up to?

I hadn't even changed into the next set when my phone buzzed.

SG: Charge it to my card and don't take it off. Wear them tonight. I'm in an all-day meeting and now I'm hard and want to be inside you.

Shivers rippled across my body and my nipples tightened under the sheer fabric. I wanted him inside me, too.

I chose three sets. One had a bra and bustier, so

maybe that might count as four. Oh, and then there was the corselette and the teddy. Shit. I wasn't going to let him pay and I wasn't sure my credit card could handle it, but it would be worth it to see his face when I wore them. *Would I get to wear them all by the end of the week?*

Ethan

The meeting I was in was a total waste of time. Clients moaned about lawyers' fees but loved wasting our time. I considered announcing that I would double our rates if this meeting went for more than another 30 minutes. I wanted to get out of here. It was coming up to 5 p.m. and I had much better things to be doing with my time than listening to this old guy complain that he was going to make $5 million less than he was expecting on the deal we were all killing ourselves to make happen. I headed to the counter with the coffee and poured myself a cup. I glanced around to make sure nobody was nearby and found Anna's text. She looked incredible. Her eyes were naughty, but her pose a little coy. She managed to do sexy and sweet at the same time. How was that even possible? I couldn't wait to see her in that underwear and then peel it off her.

Finally our meeting wrapped up and I headed back to my office.

"I have 19 messages from Mr. Dillon and then about 200 from BoNY," Susie said as I walked past her into my office.

"Fuck, what does Dillon want?"

"Something about an article in the FT. I had a look but couldn't find anything."

"Shit. I'll call him from the car."

"Where are you going?"

"I'm leaving for the day. Unless there's a fucking apocalypse, I'm not answering my phone."

"Is everything ok?" Susie asked. She looked concerned, like I was unwell or something.

"Fine. I'm just taking the night off."

"Is your sister ok?"

Susie had worked for me for nearly ten years. And over the course of that decade, the only time I dropped things at work was for my sister. And then there was tonight, with Anna.

"Yeah, she's fine. I just have a friend in town who I really want to catch up with. I'll see you tomorrow."

I headed out the door and down the elevators to flag a cab. No need for my driver tonight. We weren't going out. I could feel the blood in my veins and I could hear my heartbeat. Just the thought of her on her way to meet me had my body reacting. I checked my watch. I wanted to make sure I arrived before she did. I had a promise to keep.

I'd left a key at reception for her so she didn't have to knock.

I still had my watch on and it was telling me it was 6:10. Where was she? I heard a rustling in the lock and grinned and shifted on my seat. Was she going to think I was a total dick? I was sitting at the dining room table, naked apart from my tie, my legs on the chair beside me, one knee bent.

She saw me as soon as she walked into the room and just stood still. The sight of her almost made me forget my line.

"How was your day, dear?" I asked, looking at her and adjusting my tie.

She looked beautiful in some kind of long t-shirt that was too short for other men to see her in. She didn't take her eyes off me. Shit, was she going to respond? Her face broke out into a wide grin.

"I like your tie." She walked toward me, dropping her bag on the floor.

"I wore it for you," I said as she sat on my lap.

"You are my favorite person in the whole world right now. For this week."

I swallowed. Fuck. I felt winded and full of … something—light, warmth. I wasn't sure. I grabbed her ass and brought her closer to me and she buried her face in my neck.

"You're my favorite person in the whole world right now too."

"How do you know *Pretty Woman* so well?" she asked, pulling away from my neck so she could look at me.

"I have an older sister. I know every fucking line from that movie."

"Sounds like I'd like your sister." She blushed and put her head back in my neck. I stroked her back.

"Yes, I think you would. She'd like you, too. She lives in London, actually."

"She does? Have you visited?"

"Yes, last year when their daughter was born."

"Oh," she said quietly. I wanted to see inside her head, see the question she didn't ask me. She could ask me anything. I wanted her to ask me everything.

"I have a present for you." Her mood shifted from quiet to excited and I found myself grinning at her as she leapt off my lap. She turned so her back was facing me and reached for the hem of her t-shirt and stripped it off in one swift movement.

Fuck me. I was faced with her perfect ass wrapped in a black silk bow. I was speechless. Maybe it was my lack of reaction that caused her to spin around to see if I was watching. I watched the bow disappear as she revealed what looked like a normal pair of panties. My eyes met another black silk bow wrapping up her perfect tits.

Fuck.

Best. Gift. Ever.

"Your gift to me is your body?"

She nodded and blushed again as I stood in front of her.

"And I can do what I like with it?"

She nodded.

"You are the sexiest thing I've ever seen. All my Christmases just came at once."

"Ethan," she scolded.

"No fucking bullshit." I bent down and threw her over my shoulder and carried her into the bedroom. "Let's get you unwrapped."

I put her down on the bed and watched her watching me. Something shifted. I wanted her, but it wasn't just lust I felt. I reached to her chest and pulled the ends of the bow to reveal my gift, keeping my eyes on her. As I felt the material loosen, my eyes went to her chest just as her beautiful skin was revealed. Her nipples were puckered and waiting, as if they were being offered up to me. I couldn't resist.

"Jesus, beautiful. You look amazing." I dipped my head and grazed her nipple between my teeth. "You taste amazing." She arched her back and I slipped what was left of her bra off her shoulders, running my hands down her back. "You feel amazing."

CHAPTER Eight

Anna

I lay half-exhausted on my stomach. Ethan was in the bathroom, disposing of the second condom of the evening. Jesus. I'd never wanted a man physically in the way I wanted him. Of course I'd desired men before, but not like this. I wanted to give him everything.

"You are wearing a very sexy look, Miss Anna," he said as he came from the bathroom. I opened my eyes.

"I'm sure I look thoroughly disheveled."

"You do. You wear it well. I like that I caused it."

I grinned.

"Let's get you some dinner."

"I'm not hungry."

"You have to eat. Do you want to stay in and order room service?"

"You want to go out?" I turned and sat up on my elbows.

"*You* wanna go out?" he asked.

"I asked you first."

He sighed.

"I don't mind. You choose," I said.

"I don't want to share you with anyone tonight."

My stomach flipped over once, then twice, and I grinned. "Well, my body is yours, so I guess we're staying in."

After finally negotiating with Ethan that I was allowed to wear a robe while we ate, room service knocked at the door and I quickly went to the bathroom to try and stem the tide of mascara that was trying to escape from my eyelashes down my face. He was right, I did look disheveled. I took a hairbrush from my bag and tried to improve the situation.

"Anna," he called.

I splashed some water on my face and then wandered into the living space. Wow. He'd turned the lights down and there were just a few candles flickering on the dining table. The lights of the city illuminated our feast. There was music playing. I bet he'd wooed a few women in this suite like this. I sighed, but couldn't help but grin at him as I took my place kitty corner to him so we were both facing the view of the park.

Ethan had ordered for us both, so it was a surprise when he unveiled risotto and poured some crisp cool white wine into our glasses. He sat back and looked at me and patted my legs, and then lifted them up so they were resting on his lap, being soothed by his hands.

"A girl could get used to this." Shit, I hadn't meant to say that aloud.

He grinned at me.

"Sorry. I just meant that I feel very spoiled, and it's lovely. Thank you."

He nodded. "You deserve it. You did bring me a great gift this evening."

"You seemed to have fun with it," I replied, trying to be nonchalant.

"I did. You as well, I hope."

"Always. You ..." I shook my head.

"What?" he asked.

"It's just you seem to know exactly what my body needs and wants. No one has, ever... Not like you." I wished I could have sewn up my mouth right then. *Shut up, Anna.*

He smiled at me and then focused on his plate, stroking my legs in his lap as he ate his risotto. I stirred mine.

"I'm supposed to go to the Hamptons this weekend with Andrew and Mandy."

And there it was: his excuse to get out of Dodge. I'd said too much. *Fuck, Anna. No complications, remember?*

"Cool." I continued to stare at my food.

"Will you come with me?" he asked, and my stomach twisted and spun.

I looked at him sideways to see if maybe I'd heard him wrong.

"We could get out of the city and spend the weekend together before you go back to London."

I wanted to say yes. I *really* wanted to say yes, but I could feel myself opening up to him. I could feel my guard coming down, and he was peering across the threshold, about to step inside. In normal circumstances between two normal people, that might have been a good thing, but we were supposed to be just having fun. I was getting over someone else. He wasn't meant to be the guy that got to know me, that took me away for weekends, that gave me more orgasms in the past three days than I'd ever had in my life. He was meant to be uncomplicated fun. This felt like it was verging on complicated.

"Jesus, I can see the cogs in your brain working at a million miles an hour. What are you thinking? No bullshit."

"I'm thinking I don't know you."

"I'll tell you anything you want to know, but you'll have to tell me some stuff first."

I pursed my lips at him. "Go on," I said.

"First, you tell me your name."

I nodded. "And?"

"And then second, you come to the Hamptons this weekend."

"Anything else?"

"You tell me about what or who you're escaping."

"What do you mean?"

"The guy. The guy before New York."

I started to remove my legs from his lap, but he

dropped his fork to his plate and held them where they were.

"I'm not sure I want to know you that badly," I said under my breath.

"The construction thing is bullshit, I have an older sister, I work too hard, I've slept with too many women and mushrooms are my favorite food."

"So now, you have to tell me," he said.

"My name?" I asked staring at my plate. I took a deep breath. "Anna. No bullshit."

"But I chose your name." He sounded confused. I stayed silent, playing with my risotto. "I chose your *real* name?" I could tell he was looking at me, but I couldn't bring myself to look up.

"Like you knew me before you met me," I said so quietly I almost couldn't hear myself.

"I think I did," he said.

Ethan

I was thrown off balance by Anna's revelation. It felt like it meant something—something big—and that made me feel fucking uncomfortable. It was new territory for me. I didn't do meaning or anything big. I stared at my plate. Fuck.

"Tell me about the guy." I wanted to know, and I needed the distraction from my own thoughts.

"Tell you what?"

"What happened that made you need to get away. To have these rules."

"You know what we need?" She jumped up from the table and dived into her bag. She retrieved an iPod.

She wasn't going to be pushed.

"An '80s dance-off."

I couldn't help but grin at her. "I would say that that's exactly what we *don't* need."

She bent over the iPod station until music blared. She spun around, her eyes bright in expectation. "Come on, dance with me." Her hands flew up in the air and she started to jump up and down. "I love this one."

It was Duran Duran, I was pretty sure. I did *not* love it, but I enjoyed watching her love it, even though she was dancing like a complete lunatic.

I stood and folded my arms as I watched her, determined that I wouldn't join in. She came over and grabbed at my robe. I laughed at her as she dragged me a few feet toward the music. "I'm not dancing to this shit."

"Dancing is the best distraction there is," she said as she spun around and continued to jump and move in front of me. After a few minutes the music faded and the beginning of another song, a better song, drifted between us. It was Chaka Khan's classic, *Ain't Nobody*. Her laughter faded and she turned and started to walk toward the music. "What about some Blondie?"

My arms unfolded and stopped her and I turned her around and pulled her toward me.

"Dance with me," I said pulling her arms up around my neck, then sliding mine around her waist and moving to the music. The beat was sensual and yearning. I'd forgotten how much I liked this song and I liked dancing to it with her. I'd not danced with a woman since high school. I didn't often listen to music anymore, but listening to this I wondered why. The music matched my mood completely and the voice was telling me everything I wished Anna would say to me. Jesus. I was fucked.

Her head rested on my chest and I pressed my lips to her hair. We stayed like that until the song drifted out and something I didn't recognize replaced it.

"Ethan," she whispered against my chest and I squeezed her tighter to me. "Take me to bed."

"So this weekend, we'll leave Friday lunchtime," I said as I emerged from the bathroom after disposing of another condom.

"I haven't said I'll come with you."

"But you said your body was mine."

"I lied."

"You did not." I dived back into bed and dragged her back toward me, wrapping my arms around her waist.

"I tell you I'm a liar and you don't believe me?"

"Nope."

"You're crazy."

"I'm not. I just know you." She couldn't hide anything from me. I knew that now. "Do you want to pick you up from Armitage's apartment?"

"I have to speak to Leah. I came to New York to spend time with her, and anyway, I'm not so sure that it's a good idea if I come with you."

I didn't say anything. I wanted her to want to come with me. I didn't want to have to convince her. She wriggled around in my arms to face me.

"Do you know what I mean?" she asked.

I laughed. "No. Why don't you just cut the bullshit and say what you mean."

She kicked me and I wrapped my legs around hers so she couldn't do it again.

"I just mean that, you know, this ... the hot sex we're having ... Our week of fun, I'm not sure how it translates to a weekend away in the Hamptons and meeting your friends and not having hot sex because we're down the hall from these people I've never met."

I pushed her back around so her back was against me again. "Oh, now we're getting to it. I'm not worth the effort if you're not going to get your rocks off," I said. She giggled and I maneuvered my hardening dick against the crease in her perfect ass.

"Like you could handle it. You're ready to go again, Sex God."

"I'm always ready around you. And anyway, it's

not a problem because we're staying at my sister's, and Andrew and Mandy will be at their place. We can still fuck like rabbits."

She pushed back on my dick, increasing the friction. I reached down to her pussy. Her breathing quickened as my fingers found her clit.

"And don't you think it sounds a bit— Oh god, yes."

"Sounds a bit *what*, beautiful?" I stilled my hand and she quickly placed her hand over mine and started moving my fingers.

"Don't stop," she breathed. Fuck, this woman was insatiable. "Sounds a bit ... oh God ... against the rules."

"Game's changed, baby." I hooked her leg up and back over mine and grabbed a condom, tearing it open with my fingers and mouth, trying not to waste another second, and I sank into her. It felt like home. It felt like the first time. I was going to come in about ten seconds if I didn't concentrate. I slowed my pace and nibbled along her shoulder, my fingers circling and pushing. The sounds she made told me she was close. I realized I knew this about her and it made me want her more.

"Look at me. I want to see your face," I said.

She turned her shoulders and her eyes met mine. They were full of lust and confusion and questions.

"Feel this?" I asked as I drove into her. She nodded. "No one else can make you feel like this, can they, Anna?" Her hand came to my shoulder and she shook her head. "Tell me."

"No one makes me feel like you do." And as she said it she clenched around me and her breath held. She was there and I couldn't hold back for a second longer. I increased my pace, pushing myself closer to her, closer to my climax, and then exploded into her.

CHAPTER Nine

Anna

"What are your plans for the day?" Ethan asked me as he came out of the bathroom after his shower.

"Sleep." I was exhausted. The frequent interruptions to my sleep were welcome, but I could quite happily spend the day in bed snoozing.

"You're not staying in bed if I'm not there with you."

"Are you always this cheerful in the mornings? It's annoying," I huffed and turned over away from him.

"You're cute when you're sleepy and grumpy."

"Go to work."

I felt the mattress dip on my side of the bed and his hand stroked my ass. "I might have to work late tonight." My stomach twisted. "Did you hear me?"

I sat up and nodded, pulling my knees to my chest. He looked at me. "Do you have plans? Tonight? I mean later?"

I shrugged. I'd kinda assumed that I'd see him tonight. He'd become a habit in just a few days.

"You could stay here tonight, and then we could go up to the Hamptons first thing Friday."

"You don't have to work Friday?"

"I can do some calls from the car on the way up there. I should be able to manage a day off."

"Ok," I said. I was half-delighted, half-terrified. I wanted to spend the day with him Friday. I wanted to spend as much time with him as possible before I left, and I was terrified about that. I didn't want to want that. I'd promised myself I wouldn't want a man again. 3,000 miles apart after Monday should do it. I took a deep breath. "I'm in."

"I knew I'd wear you down," he said grinning at me.

"I just feel sorry for you, that's all."

He pulled my legs away from my chest and climbed over me, pinning my arms above my head. "What did you say?"

"I feel sorry for you." He dipped his head to my neck and started to suck as I started to giggle. "I know you must have been having a drought before I came along. How long had it been? Five, six years?"

"Since a woman took pity on me and let me fuck her?" he asked and I laughed and tried to break my wrists free of his hands as his mouth tracked lower and started to suck again. "Since a woman let me give her three, four, five orgasms a night?"

"Since a woman came back for seconds."

He let go of my wrists and moved off me.

"Hey, are you going to finish what you started?" I asked, propping myself up on my elbows.

"I have to get to work. Stop distracting me," he said as pulled a tie on. He smiled, but I could detect that his mood had shifted.

"Sorry," I said, trying to meet his eyes.

He nodded. I was joking. He must know I was joking.

I crawled out of bed and put on a robe as Ethan gathered his wallet and keys. I followed him to the door of the suite.

"Go do something cultural," he said as he opened the door. Then he turned, kissed me on the forehead, and left.

Fear unfurled in my stomach. I wasn't quite sure of the cause. Fear of not seeing him again, fear that I'd hurt his feelings, fear of going with him to the Hamptons, fear of complications, fear of going back to London.

I stood under the shower trying to decide whether to text him when my phone started to ring. I leapt out of the shower. It must be Ethan letting me know about plans tonight. I hoped it would Ethan letting me know about plans tonight.

It was Leah. I pressed Accept and hooked the phone under my chin while I grabbed a towel to wrap around me.

"Hey, I have a fun-packed day planned. I got those tickets for Book of Mormon and I thought we could go do the Empire State this morning. How long are you going to be?"

"Oh, great. You got those tickets. That's awesome."

"Don't worry. It's the matinee. It won't interrupt your holiday romance."

"There's no romance, Leah. And anyway, it wouldn't interrupt anything. I don't think we're seeing each other tonight." I wasn't sure if we were seeing each other tonight. How did we leave it? Fuck. This wasn't supposed to be complicated.

"Oh. Are you ok?"

"Of course. We're not attached at the hip. It was just a fling. Nothing complicated."

"Was?"

"I don't know. I'll be ready in 15 minutes. Shall I meet you somewhere?"

We agreed to meet in line at the Empire State Building. I pulled on my jeans and a t-shirt and combed my wet hair. There was no point in blow drying it in this humidity. I'd leave it to frizz. I'd brought a few more things with me last night, thinking I may be staying tonight as well but I was careful to collect everything. I didn't know if I'd be back. Before I left I took out my phone and snapped a couple of photos of the view. God it was amazing. Worth every penny this ginormous suite must have cost. When I grew up and won the lottery, I was going to live here.

Leah waved at me from the entrance to the ticket hall.

"There isn't much of a queue."

"Who'd have thought it? It's 8-frigging-15 a.m. on a random Thursday in July. Of course there isn't much of a queue." I hadn't realized how early it was until I was in the cab on the way to meet Leah.

"Alright, grumpy knickers. I'm just trying to make sure we squeeze everything in. I want to make sure it's not just the New York men you get to experience."

I rolled my eyes at Leah and then leaned in and kissed her on the cheek. "Sorry."

Without the queues we got to the top quickly and without the pushing and shoving that the crowds would inevitably bring later. The view of the park was almost surreal. Unlike from the hotel, where the view was lower, you could see the whole thing—as if a slice of somewhere else had been picked up and planted in amongst the buildings and bustle of the city.

"So you're not seeing him tonight?" Leah interrupted my thoughts that for just the twenty seconds before hadn't been full of Ethan.

"I'm not sure. We were and he invited me to the Hamptons, and then it got weird, and now I'm not sure."

"Wait, he invited you to the Hamptons?"

"Oh, yes. Sorry. I was going to speak to you to see if you would mind if I went. I guess it doesn't matter now."

"Of course I don't mind. You should go. I'm sure it's fine. He didn't uninvite you, did he?"

I shook my head. No, not yet. That would come later ... I was sure of it.

Ethan

I'd officially grown a vagina.

Make that two vaginas. I was becoming a vagina farmer. What the fuck was the matter with me? It stung when she said that women didn't want to sleep with me more than once. I mean, I knew it wasn't true, but the fact that she might think that. A vagina farmer. Fuck.

She was the greatest lay I'd ever had and I had to wear her down to spend the weekend with me. That stung, too. That was it. I needed to kick some ass and take some names. I wanted to get this work done so I could fuck her out of my system. Just after I had another look at that sexy-as-hell text she'd sent me of her in her underwear.

I worked like a maniac all day. I was sure that my associate was on the verge of quitting two or three times. I could see the panic in his eyes as I piled more and more work onto him, but I was too busy to think about it. He said that he wanted more responsibility, so he shouldn't fucking whine when I gave it to him. I was going to have to look over various documents over the weekend, but I was going to be able to get out of the office. My biggest client was on vacation, which couldn't have come at a better time. I looked at my watch. Jesus. How was it 6 p.m. already? Would she be at the hotel by now or was she spending the evening with Armitage's girlfriend? Had she said? I checked my cell for messages but there was nothing.

Me: Hey sexy. What are you wearing?

Nothing. For thirty minutes.

Anna: Hey.

Hey?

Me: Are you at the hotel?

Anna: No.

Me: When will you be there? Make sure you bring your case so we can get straight off in the morning.

Anna: Later. Okay.

Me: Let me know when you're at the hotel. I should be back by midnight.

Three hours later and I'd just come off the least useful conference call in my career. At least it hadn't generated more work. The ball was in the court of the Chinese. We had the weekend off.

Back at my desk, I checked my phone.

Anna: At the hotel bar.

The text was sent over an hour ago. The hotel bar, for Christ's sake? It was close to 9:30. No doubt a million sleazy guys had hit on her.

Me: On your own?

Anna: You haven't died then.

Me: On your own?

Anna: I'm making new friends.

New friends? New friends with dicks? My fists clenched. Jesus. I was going to end up in prison by the end of the weekend if I wasn't careful. I put some papers together quickly and left the office earlier than I should have.

I saw her as soon as I entered the bar. She was sitting at the bar, her head tipped back, and she was laughing at something the bartender had said to her. He looked like he'd just hit a home run. I knew how that felt—it lit me up when I made her laugh. I didn't like that he got to feel that, too. I'd never felt jealousy over a woman before now.

I came up behind her and rubbed her back. She was mid-laugh and she jumped when I touched her. I hated that.

"Hey!" she said a little too loudly and both her hands flew into the air. "He's here," she said to the bartender.

The bartender nodded at Anna and turned to me. "Can I get you a drink, sir?"

Anna interrupted my response "You're here! I'd thought you were gone and now you're here! My New York lover."

"I think she's had enough for both of us," I said.

"No! Have a drink. I have lots of new friends to show you. Which one do I like best?" She looked imploringly at the bartender.

"You like them all, ma'am."

"I do. I like all these cocktails. They are my friends. My New York friends." She pointed at a list of at least twenty drinks.

"Tell me you've not served her all these?"

He shook his head. "Just the first five or so. She was working her way down the list."

"Come on, beautiful. Let's get you to bed."

I signed the tab and helped her off the stool.

"My case, my case, my case," she said as she spun around and went to grab a small silver suitcase, which I took for her. I put my free arm around her waist and guided her back to the elevator bank.

"Why didn't you leave it in the room?" I asked.

"No key, no key, no key." She was pretty unsteady on her feet, but her mouth was working just fine, if a little slurry.

"Did you lose your key?" I asked.

"No, of course I didn't lose it. I left it in the room because of your weirdness this morning." She prodded her finger into my cheek. "And then I wouldn't have to bring it back and run into you when you dumped me, which would definitely happen because I have the *worst* luck with men, and that would be weirder and awkward so I left it, and then you texted me and then it was weird and now I'm here. I'm so tired." She slumped against the elevator door.

That was a lot of information to process in one go. "We're going to get you to bed, beautiful," I said and pulled her against me. I kissed the top of her head. "I'm sorry for being weird this morning."

"That's ok." She looked up at me and grinned. "I think you're awesome so I'll forgive you."

Something inside me warmed and I could feel myself harden. Jesus, how was some drunk crazy girl getting me hard?

I stroked her face. "I think you're awesome, too." She grinned, closed her eyes, and put her head on my chest.

CHAPTER Ten

She had barely said two words to me this morning. Rory was driving us to the Hamptons, which meant I could work, but I couldn't concentrate with her next to me. Not to mention the hard-on that I'd had for 12 hours.

"How are you feeling?" I asked her again.

She grunted and curled her legs under her. She was wearing her sunglasses so I couldn't see her expression.

"A little delicate?" I suggested.

She nodded. "With a good dose of humiliation thrown in."

"There's nothing for you to feel humiliated about. You're a cute drunk. I've seen a lot worse."

"Oh god. Don't, Ethan. God knows what I said to you last night. I'm so embarrassed." She turned to face the window. I unbuckled her seatbelt and pulled her over onto my lap. Her body was limp and unresponsive.

"Listen to me," I said as she put her head in her hands. I wasn't sure if she was crying. "Listen to me," I repeated, pulling her hands away. "You have nothing to be embarrassed about. You didn't say anything. You introduced me to the cocktail list in the bar, and then when I got you upstairs you passed out in your clothes. It was a pretty uneventful evening."

"We didn't have sex?"

"I'm not going to have sex with you passed out. I might have a permanent hard-on with you around, but Jesus, I can control myself."

"God. We're meant to be having a sex-filled fling. I'm not holding up my end of the bargain very well." Her hands went back to her face. I pulled them away.

"Beautiful, we're having plenty of sex, and we're *going* to have plenty of sex this weekend, believe me."

"And I didn't say anything to embarrass myself?" she asked.

"Like what?" What was she so worried about?

She shrugged.

"No. You told me you thought I was awesome."

She groaned.

"Why's that embarrassing? I am awesome," I said and I grinned at her.

She laughed, which made me smile.

"I told you I thought you were awesome, too," I said.

"You did?"

I nodded.

"Ok. I'm starting to feel a little more human."

"Can you lose the shades? I miss your eyes."

She shook her head. "I need carbs and three gallons of water before the shades come off."

Anna

After stopping for a breakfast burrito, we arrived at Ethan's sister's house around 11 a.m. The house was spectacular. With a pool and view of the ocean and a million rooms.

"No one has pools in the UK, really," I mused staring into the water.

"Well, let's make the most of it, then," Ethan said as he slapped my ass. "I want to see you in your skimpiest bikini."

"I don't do skimpy. Have you seen my ass?"

"Yes, and it's perfect. Totally nude is fine, too. Let's change."

The pool was a fantastic antidote to the humidity. I swam lazily in no particular direction, wondering what was keeping Ethan. He'd changed into his trunks, so I expected him to be in the pool already.

After a few minutes he emerged from the patio doors looking spectacular. I'd seen him plenty naked, but in the sun, wearing his shades, the sheen of his skin gave his body's contours even more definition. As if they needed it. He was my Sex God, for one week only.

"Get in this pool, you handsome fellow," I bellowed at him just as I noticed he hung up his phone.

He paced toward me and then stopped suddenly and looked at his phone, held it to his ear and started heading toward me again. I headed to the edge of the pool to meet him.

"What time?" I heard him say as he approached the pool. "Yeah, that's fine. I think. Hang on." Then he dropped the phone to his waist, sat on the edge of the pool and said, "Is 7 p.m. ok? It's only ten minutes from here."

I nodded. Did he mean we were going over to his friends' house? I guess. My stomach churned slightly and I felt uneasy.

"Yes, 7 is fine. Yes, she's here. In the pool, and she's much better-looking than you, so fuck off. I'll see you tonight."

He hung up and threw his phone on to one of the loungers and slid into the pool. It was as if the water heated ten degrees. He lifted his sunglasses onto his head and reached over to take mine from my eyes. "I haven't seen your eyes all day," he said.

"You don't want to see them; they're red and small and tired."

He wrapped his hands around my waist and pulled me toward him. I wrapped my legs around his waist. "You'd better kiss me, then, so I'll be too distracted to notice."

I took his bottom lip between my teeth. I felt him harden beneath me, and I sighed contentedly, knowing how things were going to play out. My nipples puckered and I tightened my legs around him. The water sloshed between us and made his skin silky to the touch as I brought my hands up his chest and his tongue delved between my lips. I moaned and he pulled my hips closer to him. My body had been starved of him for too long.

"Ethan," I said. "I need to feel you."

He growled, turned us around in the water, and then lifted me to onto the edge of the pool, leaping out beside me. He held out my hand and helped me up. "Come on. We're going inside to finish this. I don't want the neighbors to hear you scream."

"Can I use another guest room to get showered and changed?" I asked. It was nearly 6 and we were still lying in bed, my back to his front, after spending the afternoon having amazingly hot sex. I barely had the energy to speak. How I was going to make it through an evening of polite chat with strangers, I had no idea.

"I guess. Why don't you want to use this bathroom? I've seen you naked before, you know."

"Yes, and that's the problem. I'd like to make myself presentable. And if I stay within five yards of you, I'll be introduced to your friends looking like I've just been fucked and smelling of sex."

"Sounds perfect. I love it when you smell like me. When I know your skin has my sweat and come all over it." He ground his hips into my ass and I felt the stirring of his cock. Holy hell. Again?

"Yeah, that's kinda the point."

"So you don't trust me to control myself around you?"

"Nope."

"Makes sense," he said as I felt his teeth on my neck.

The entire day could have been measured by how far away either of us was from our last or next orgasm. Activity other than sex had been attempted—lunch, swimming, reading—we'd tried all three with varying amounts of success. But at some point Ethan would look at me or touch me in a certain way, and something would switch in us both and he would be inside me in seconds—his fingers, his tongue, his cock. It was like an unquenchable thirst that we shared.

I slapped at his hands around my waist and tried to break free.

"I need to get in the shower."

"Sounds good. I haven't fucked you in the shower yet."

"Yet again, you've just very elegantly proven my point, Mr. Scott. I need to have a shower, alone. You can control yourself for a few hours."

"How many hours exactly?" he asked, propping his head on his hand as I slid out of bed.

"Until we get back from your friends' house."

"Really? I think we should cancel." I could hear the grin in his voice.

I flicked my head around to look at him. "Don't be ridiculous. We're not animals. We can keep our hands off each other for a few hours."

"I'm not so sure."

My leg started jumping as the car pulled out. Ethan slid his hand to my knee. "Hey, don't be nervous."

"I'm not," I lied. And I stilled my leg.

He took my hand in his and squeezed.

"I should be the one who's nervous," he said.

"Do you think I'm going to embarrass you?"

"Well, obviously that's a concern." He grinned at me. "Andrew's going to have fun with this. He won't be able to resist."

"With what? Us?"

He nodded. Fear washed over me. What did he mean? Before I got a chance to ask we'd arrived.

Ethan took my hand as we walked up to the house. Just as he reached for the knocker, the door flew open.

"Hey, guys," Andrew welcomed us. Mandy stood beside him. She had red curly hair and a big smile. Her hands were clasped together as if she was about to applaud and her eyes sparkled with what looked like excitement.

"I'm so happy you're here." She grabbed me and hugged me. "And you're so pretty. I just knew you would be," she said as she ushered me down their hallway. I turned to try and catch Ethan's eye, but he wasn't looking at me. "What do you want to drink? Tell me you drink and you're not one of those health nuts? Andrew, can you get us some drinks? Cocktails?" Ethan was looking back at me and he grinned.

"Maybe not cocktails. Anna had a little cocktail incident last night," Ethan said.

"Oh, how sweet. He's protecting you. You drink, thank god. Wine?"

I'd barely had an opportunity to say anything, so I just nodded.

"And you're from England? You know that Ethan's sister is in England. I've always wanted to go. Andrew keeps saying he'll take me but, hey, sometime never."

"Jesus, woman, take a breath already," Andrew interrupted.

Mandy laughed. "Sorry, I'm over-excited. I usually have to put up with these two talking about sports and business when Ethan comes over, so it's so nice to have a girl to play with!"

"She's not for you to play with, Mandy," Ethan said and put his arm around my shoulders. "That's my job." And he kissed me on my head.

"Oh, my god. You're so cute together! I wondered if this would ever happen and now it has and I'm so excited."

"Excuse my wife, Anna," said Andrew. "She's not used to company." Mandy slapped Andrew on the arm and tutted. It was cute.

"I'm just not used to Ethan introducing me to a girl," she said to him as if I wasn't there.

"Woman," Ethan said.

Mandy squealed. *What the hell was going on?*

"Let's get you a drink so you're forced not to speak while you sip," Andrew said.

When the drinks were poured, we made our way onto the patio, where the table was set for dinner.

"This is a beautiful house, Mandy," I said. Ethan and Andrew were chatting about some game, leaving Mandy and I to talk. I wasn't sure which sport; I switched off as soon as I heard the words *league* and *ball*.

"Thank you. It was my parent's house. I inherited it. I've always loved it. I love the city but this feels like home." Mandy had calmed down. Maybe it was the wine. "Do you live in the city?" she asked.

I nodded. "Yes, and I love it."

"You'd never want to come to New York to live?"

"Oh," I was shocked by her question. "I've never thought about it."

"Would you consider it?" She nodded sideways to Ethan.

"I'm just here for a week. We're just having some fun. It's nothing serious."

She pursed her lips. "I've never met one of his women." I felt a churning in my stomach. "I know he has his share. But he doesn't spend time with them. He just sleeps with them. Like a sport or something. You seem to be something different for him."

I shook my head. "I'm here for a week, and then he knows I'm 3,000 miles away. And I just broke up with someone. It's just circumstances that are different."

"I'm not so sure," she said.

Ethan reached behind him to grab my hand, but continued his conversation with Andrew. I met Mandy's eyes as they lifted from our joint hands and she raised her eyebrows.

CHAPTER Eleven

Ethan

Back at the house, we moved around each other in the bathroom, getting ready for bed. It felt domestic, like we were a couple. Anna had been quiet in the car, and I was lost in my own head. But it was an easy silence that descended between us. I realized I really enjoyed the evening. I enjoyed sleeping with Anna, but I enjoyed hanging out with her, too. She was funny and confident and busted my balls.

I got into bed and watched her as she brushed her hair and found my eyes before joining me in bed. I pulled her perfect ass toward me and wrapped my arms around her waist.

"Hi," she said as she tipped her head back to my chest.

"Hi," I replied. "How was your evening?"

"Good. I like your friends. How about you?"

"Good. I like my friends, too. And I like that they like you."

"Yeah, that was a bit weird at the beginning with Mandy."

"It was? Which bit?" Was tonight too complicated for her?

"Just her making such a fuss over meeting me."

"Oh, I didn't catch that. But I told you they'd have some fun with it. I thought I would get more of a hard time from Andrew, to be honest."

"A hard time for bringing me? Because we're so casual?"

I sucked in some air. Was I going to say this? I didn't do bullshit. "Because I've never introduced them to a woman before."

"Never?"

"No."

"Because you normally keep your girlfriends chained up in your basement?" She was funny.

"I live in an apartment." She kicked me. "Because I don't have girlfriends. There are women I have sex with, but I don't hang out with them. I told you, I don't date." God, she was going to run screaming for the fucking hills, and I wouldn't blame her. I'd never questioned my relationships with women before, but I didn't want her thinking I was a complete dick.

"Oh," she replied. I needed to distract her.

"Are you sleepy?" I asked.

"Not so sleepy that I don't want you."

That was the right fucking answer.

Anna

The next day we barely made it out of bed. Ethan kept suggesting we go down to the beach, which was only at the end of the gardens, just beyond the pool, and on several occasions I'd agreed, but we never made it. We were in our own private world in the house and somehow it kept pulling us back, like if we stepped outside it something would be lost.

We were sitting on one of the loungers, me between his legs, leaning back against him. We were talking about his sister when his phone rattled against the side table. He picked it up and checked his message.

"Urgh." I felt his discomfort vibrate in his chest.

"What's up?"

"It's from Mandy. She wants us to go to a party tonight."

"That's nice of her to invite us. You don't want to go?"

"I think she just wants to hang out with you again. I hate parties in the Hamptons."

"So we won't go. But I think we should go out somewhere. To dinner or something. We've been in this house all day."

His phone buzzed again and he handed it to me. My heart skipped. It seemed a strangely intimate thing to do.

"What?"

"Read it."

I clicked on the phone so the message came into view.

Andrew: Dude. Get your ass to this party or Mandy's going to have my balls.

I giggled. "Those guys are really cute together."

Ethan's arms tightened around me. "They really are, but don't tell them I said so. They'll think I'm going soft."

"Mr. Scott, in my humble opinion, being soft is not something you need to worry about."

"Never around you, baby." He buried his head in my neck.

"We should go, though," I said. "I'd hate for Andrew to lose his balls. And I like Mandy and Andrew. It'll be nice."

"Really? Fuck. You won't like those parties."

I felt myself stiffen. What did he mean by that?

"You don't think the British fit into Hamptons society?"

"You'll see."

"I'm not going to be able to concentrate with you in that dress. All I can think about is that I could have it off in about two seconds."

I was wearing a red jersey sleeveless dress. Ethan's eyes had barely left me since we'd got into the car. It was a good thing Rory was driving or we would have been in an accident already. "Well, then, you're not going to like it when I tell you that I'm not wearing underwear underneath, are you?"

His eyes flashed with lust and then anger and he shook his head. "One hour is all we're spending at this god-awful party."

"Ethan. How do you know that it's going to be awful? We're not even there yet."

"I've been to this party a thousand times."

"You're so dramatic. If you've been to parties like this a lot, then you must like them."

He just growled at me and I reached across and stroked his chin. He caught my wrist in his hand and brought my hand to his lips. "An hour, beautiful."

Rory had strict instructions to be waiting for us in an hour when he dropped us. As soon as I climbed out of the car, Ethan was beside me, his arm around my waist, guiding me toward the sound of music and chatter beyond the line of trees right in front of us.

"Whose house is this?" I asked.

"Some dick banker that Andrew is friends with."

"Why are all bankers dicks?" I asked. "Do you think banking turns them into dicks or that they only employ dicks to begin with?"

"An interesting philosophical question, Miss Anna. Why don't we go back to the house and debate it. In bed. Naked. Me between your legs?"

I looked up at him and grinned. "Later. We have plenty of time."

But we didn't have plenty of time. We had exactly two nights before I flew back to London. My skin prickled at the thought. It wasn't enough time. I wanted another week with him. Or maybe just a few more days.

Before panic could overwhelm me, we were confronted by a mass of people. It felt like they were all looking at us. Ethan squeezed me closer to him as we made our way through the crowd toward the bar that had been set up at the other end of the pool. Ethan briefly shook hands with a couple of over-tanned, middle-aged men, but kept us moving.

Ethan

Jesus, I really didn't want to be here. I wasn't sure why I hadn't insisted that we stay at home. Having her in that skimpy red dress, pressed up against me, knowing she wasn't wearing underwear—it was almost painful. Even though I'd spent more time inside her today than not, I still wanted her. I wanted her to myself, without all these people getting in our way.

She didn't fit in in this environment. She didn't have to try so hard. I was so sick of this scene. I didn't understand why Andrew and Mandy were still doing it. Andrew was almost as well connected as I was, so it couldn't be for business, and Mandy certainly didn't fit in with these women—her face still looked normal and not like a frozen Pillsbury Doughboy.

Andrew and Mandy were heading toward us.

"Hey guys, you made it," Mandy said, hugging first Anna and then me.

"Yeah, we did it for a good cause—Andrew's balls," I said. Anna elbowed me in the ribs.

"Fuck you, dude," Andrew said.

"I was excited to come. Thanks for inviting us," Anna said.

Mandy clasped her hands together like an over-excited seal. "I'm so pleased you're an 'us' and you're here!"

I rolled my eyes at her excitement. I hoped she wasn't making Anna uncomfortable. She didn't want pressure to be an 'us,' I knew that for sure.

"To be honest, I'm not sure why we come to these parties. Although I like to see the women's faces. It's so bizarre," Mandy said.

"I'll go and get us some drinks," I offered. "Andrew?"

"Yeah, a beer, thanks."

"No, you dick, you're coming with me."

"Fuck you."

"Stop being children and go and get your ladies some drinks," Mandy instructed.

"She's great, man," Andrew said as we headed toward the bar.

I grinned and nodded.

"You like her."

I nodded. "Yeah, of course."

"So when does she go back to London?" I didn't want to think about it. I'd promised her uncomplicated, and I didn't go back on my promises.

"Monday." I felt my jaw tense. "Can we get a beer, a whiskey, a Manhattan, and a glass of champagne?" I said to the bartender.

"She is your perfect woman if she drinks whiskey."

I grinned and raised my eyebrows.

I felt a hand on my shoulder. When I turned, I was faced with Julie ... or Julia, or something.

"Hey, handsome," she drawled. I cringed—I didn't remember fucking her, but I knew we'd fucked. And I cringed that she had her hand on my shoulder when the only person I wanted touching me was Anna. I moved to the right to encourage her to remove her arm, but she just moved with me. Fuck. I hoped Anna wasn't watching this. Would she care? I wasn't sure, but I cared.

"Hey. This is my friend Andrew," I said. I couldn't introduce them properly when I couldn't remember her fucking name.

"Hey, Andrew," she said dismissively and turned back to me. "So, you should give me a call sometime. We could hang out again."

Fucking hell. I put every effort into never having to have these conversations. I was always clear that they would have no call from me. Ever.

"I don't think so. I'm with someone." I wasn't sure if

I said it to soften what I was saying or because I wanted it to be true.

"I won't tell if you don't."

Jesus, that made my stomach churn. As if I'd ever fuck her again.

"I'm not interested," I said. It was rude, but I didn't care. And it got the result I wanted: She removed her hand from my shoulder, called me an asshole, and walked away. Thank fuck for that. I turned to see if Anna had caught any of that, but she was talking to Mandy and that bitch Clarissa. Fuck, why had I agreed to come to this shitty party?

"I hate these parties, man."

"Me, too," he said. "I think it's going to be fun until I actually get here."

"Is this bartender on a go-slow?" I wanted to save Anna from Clarissa.

Just as we picked up the drinks, we were ambushed by the Zetter twins and some girl I'd never seen before. I worked with their father, so couldn't brush them off as easily as I had Julie. Julia. Whatever her name was. But eventually we broke free and headed back to Anna and Mandy.

CHAPTER
Twelve

Anna

"Do you have parties like this in London?" Mandy asked.

I shrugged. I didn't know what that meant. "We have parties. But indoors, mainly." She laughed. I looked over to the bar. A tall, very tanned woman wearing a very short skirt had her arm draped over Ethan's shoulder. Had he slept with her? Was she his type?

"Hey, Clarissa," Mandy said, as an equally tanned woman came to join us.

"Hi." She smiled. It wasn't a warm smile. There was something off about it. She kissed Mandy on the cheek and then held out her hand to me and actually looked me up and down. Wow.

"Clarissa, this is Ethan's girlfriend, Anna." I took her hand and shook it.

"Ethan's *girlfriend*?" she asked.

I should have set her straight. I should say that we were just friends, or lovers, or ... how would I describe us? 'Oh, I'm just having hot sex with him for a week to get over my ex'? I was pretty sure that wouldn't be appropriate. And besides, I liked to see Clarissa squirm, which was apparently what she was doing.

"Nice to meet you," I said.

"Yes, we had dinner together last night. They are so cute together," Mandy said.

"Well, nice to meet you, too," Clarissa said. It felt like she had to force the words out. "I was just on my way to the ladies room, so excuse me." And she turned and walked away.

"She is such a grade-A bitch," Mandy confided. "She's been trying to land Ethan for years. She's pissed as hell to meet you."

"But I'm not his girlfriend, Mandy. You got that, right?"

She shrugged. "Well, you're both putting on a pretty good act, and it's as close as he's ever come."

There was no point in arguing with her. I glanced over at the bar and Ethan was draped in a different woman now, and there were two others that were also hovering around him. I felt a pang of jealousy. Would one of them be next in line, after me?

"He's attracting his fair share of admirers over there." I nudged Mandy as I looked over at him. He caught my eye and I quickly looked back at Mandy.

"He always does. Look at the man, for Christ's sake. He's hot and rich and charming, and most importantly, unattainable. He's not short of women who want him. I'm sure every woman he fucks just wants to be the one who tamed him."

"Don't you think it's a bit cruel of him to have a series of one-night stands with women who want something more?"

"I've had this discussion with him a million times. He says to me—and I believe him—that he makes it clear from the outset that he's only in it for one night. He has these rules to keep things from getting 'complicated,' as he puts it."

"Rules?" I prompted. I thought I was the one with the rules.

"Yeah, like, he never stays the night with them. He never takes them back to his apartment, never takes their number. A couple he sees more than once, but only if he thinks they can handle his rules, and even then, never more than once a month. So the waters don't get muddied, or so he says. There are others. I can't remember them all."

"So he's like an ethical man-whore?"

Mandy laughed. "I suppose. I keep thinking he'll grow out of it. He's been like this since I met him in college. But he never has, until you."

"Mandy, the rules may have been flexed a bit, but only because I live 3,000 miles away. There's not going to be a happy ending here."

She shrugged. "Maybe."

Before I could convince her, Ethan and Andrew came back with our drinks.

"You've been making new friends," I said softly to him.

He shook his head and bent his head to kiss my neck. "You're the only new friend I want to make this evening," he whispered into my ear.

My skin tightened with goose bumps and my hands snaked around his neck.

"Get a room, guys," Andrew admonished, and grinning, we turned back to them as Ethan slid his hand over my pantyless ass. Why had I suggested we come to this party? I was an idiot.

Eventually, I started to enjoy myself. Mandy was sweet, kind, and funny, and I loved seeing how she interacted with Andrew. I found out they'd met at college and had been together ever since. Ethan seemed to be the third wheel in their relationship, which I thought was super cute. How this god of a man could be a third wheel, I had no idea.

I was coming back from the ladies room and heading back to Ethan when I checked my watch. We'd been here for an hour and a half, and I was done. Ethan was right: I didn't fit in here. It felt weird. I liked Mandy and Andrew, but I wanted it to be just the two of us again.

As I approached our group, I noticed Clarissa was at Ethan's side. Jesus, I hated that woman and I'd spent all of five minutes in her company.

I slid the other side of Ethan to Clarissa and I warmed as his arm came around my shoulders.

"You ok?" he asked, just so I could hear.

"Our time's up. I want you take me home and get me naked," I said.

"You don't have to ask me twice," he said as he threw back the rest of his whiskey and found a passing waiter to give his glass to.

"Excuse me, guys. My girl wants to take me home and ravage me, so we're leaving." And apparently that was his goodbye. He took my hand and started to pull me to the entrance. I grinned at Mandy and Andrew and waved goodbye.

The next morning I woke to an empty bed. *This is how it will be when I get back to London.* Tonight would be my last night in New York. My heart was heavy as I dragged myself up. I turned the shower on and steam bellowed from the stall.

I stood under the water for what seemed like hours, wondering if Ethan would appear and jolt me out of this cloud I was in. It was so hot it almost burned, but it felt good. Eventually, I got out, pulled on my jeans and a t-shirt, and started to pack my stuff while my hair dried in the air.

"Hey." Ethan appeared at the doorway in shorts and a bare chest, sweaty and god-like, as usual.

"Hey," I said.

"You were sound asleep and I didn't want to wake you. I went for a run."

"I never mind you waking me." I meant it to sound flirtatious, but it came out sounding melancholy.

"Are you packing?"

"No, I'm churning butter," I snapped. I was in a horrible mood.

He ignored my bitchiness. "What do you want to do today?" he asked, passing beside me and into the bathroom. "Anna?"

"I don't know. I guess we have to head back to the city. You have to work tomorrow and I need to pack properly."

I didn't know if he heard me, but he didn't respond. I heard him step into the shower. I finished my packing and took my case downstairs and placed it by the door.

Only a few minutes later, he came into the kitchen looking so handsome I thought my heart would stop. His hair was wet and his white shirt made his skin shimmer slightly. I sighed.

"So, first things first," he said, wrapping his arms around me as I sat at the breakfast bar, and then placing my arms around his waist when I didn't respond. He took my face in his hands and brushed his lips against mine. Then he placed small, feather-light kisses at the corner of my mouth before running his tongue along the seam of my lips. I heard myself sigh and he took it as a sign to continue and pushed through my lips, his tongue meeting mine. I squirmed in my seat. My reaction was to want to be closer to him. My knees parted and he took half a step forward, opening them still wider. His tongue grew more insistent and passionate. His hands dropped to my back, pressing me against him. I reached around for the button to his jeans, but he pulled away and our kiss finished, two hours too early.

I was left a little shaken. That wasn't his normal reaction to me

Ethan

"So has that kiss knocked you out of your bad mood?" I asked. The two words she'd spoken to me this morning had been a little bitchy. It was a side to her I hadn't seen. It was funny, but I guessed she wouldn't want me to tell her that.

"Maybe," she said, but her smile told me that it had.

"So, we could head back to the city after lunch if you like." I moved around the counter to pour myself some coffee.

"Ok. Could we go to the beach this morning? It's just we've not seen it since we've been here, and it'd be nice. You know. Before we go."

"Sure. Anything you want, beautiful."

"I should probably call Leah and tell her I'll be back this afternoon."

"But you won't be back with Leah this afternoon," I said. Tonight would be her last night. Was she thinking she wouldn't spend it with me? There was no fucking way I was letting that happen.

"Huh?"

"Tonight, when we get back to the city. You'll spend it with me."

"Ethan, I've spent every night with you. Leah will think I'm the worst friend in the world."

"So another one won't matter. Give me your phone."

"Why?"

"I'm going to call Leah and tell her you're staying with me tonight."

She grinned at me. "I'll tell her. You're such a bully."

"You eat it up," I winked at her. "And go and change into a bikini while you're at it." The sight of her in a bikini gave my hard-on a hard-on. How could wearing clothes actually be more of a turn on than not wearing clothes?

I was finishing my oatmeal and coffee when she came back into the kitchen wearing some cut off shorts and a vest top. Fucking perfect.

"Come on, we're off to frighten the wildlife on the beach," I said, pulling her from the door.

We set our towels on the sand and I watched as she stripped off her T-shirt and shorts. Why did she want to go to the beach again? We could have so much more fun back at the house.

"Stop staring, you perv."

"I'm just trying to capture mental images for my spank bank."

"God, you're a pig today."

I grabbed her and pulled her down into my lap. "I told you, I'm your god." My hand delved beneath her bikini bottoms and I hardened as I felt how wet she was.

"You are always so wet, beautiful."

"Ethan, we're on the beach."

"And I'm going to make you come on the beach," I said. I felt her relent and relax against my fingers. She knew there was no point in fighting me. I held her orgasm in my hands and the power I felt over her body made me harder than a baseball bat. My fingers slid deep inside her and my thumb circled that bundle of nerves that I'd come to know so well. Her breath quickened and her hand pushed against her chest, but my free arm was encircling her. She wasn't going anywhere.

"Don't fight it, baby. You know what I do to you. Give in to me."

Her head tipped back and she whimpered my name, over and over. Jesus, that was hot. How could she ever think that I could ever have her call me another name? And then her breathing stopped and I watched as her orgasm crashed over her.

I stroked her gently and pulled my hand away and cradled her tighter against me.

"God, Ethan. You know me so well. I mean, you know my body so well."

"Don't forget it, baby." I said it before I realized what I'd said. But it was true: I didn't want her to forget what I could do to her. I wanted every man that came after me to fall short by a hundred miles. So short that she'd give up trying to find anyone and she'd come back to me. Andrew was right. I really liked this girl. If she lived in New York, I could imagine dating this girl. Like, spending all my time with her, just like this week had been, but every day. The thought was shocking, but in the best of ways. And then reality broke through. She didn't live in New York. She lived 3,000 fucking miles away on another continent. I squeezed her again in my arms.

"You're so good. Like, the best ever," she said sleepily.

"I bet you say that to all your lovers."

"Anything to keep all my men happy." She opened her eyes and grinned at me.

"Right, that's it." And I picked her up in my arms and strode in the sea to the tops of my thighs and dumped her into the cold water.

She emerged her hair draped over her face. "Fuck! That's arctic, you pig."

I laughed at her and she splashed me and then leapt on me, wrapping her legs around my waist and her arms around my neck. I walked deeper into the ocean so the water was at waist height and I pushed her hair from her face.

"I meant it. You gave me more orgasms during our first night together than any man has ever given me."

I felt like someone's fist had tightened around my heart. "You don't need to try to make me feel better."

"I mean it. You know my body better than anyone." And she hugged me tight and I squeezed her back.

We spent the rest of the morning walking along the shore, collecting shells that she said that she wanted to take back to London. There wasn't a soul on the beach. Or maybe there was and we just didn't see them.

CHAPTER
Thirteen

Anna

"Have you forgotten anything?" Ethan bellowed from upstairs. He'd asked me about three times already. I didn't forget things. That was not the type of thing I did. I was perched on my suitcase at the front door waiting for him.

"I'm all set, as you say in this country."

"You don't say that in England?"

I shook my head. "Nope."

"Who knew?"

"Everyone in England?"

"You're hilarious. Have you thought about taking your act on tour?"

He made me laugh aloud. Only a very few people could make me laugh like that. "You've guessed my secret. I'm a closet stand-up comedian."

"Come on, crazy. Let's get you back to the city."

I opened the front door and went to grab my suitcase, but Ethan beat me to it. He took his bag and my case out to the car.

As Rory pulled out and I clicked on my seatbelt, I turned to him. "Thank you for a lovely weekend."

He looked at me, as if he was trying to uncover more meaning behind what I was saying. "Thank you. You're great to hang out with." He pulled my legs to his lap and stroked up and down as he watched me, watching him.

"Are we going to go out tonight?" I asked him.

He shook his head. I grinned. I guessed he'd want to make the most of the time we had left by keeping me naked.

"Are you going to be busy this week at work?" I asked. We never talked about his work. I liked that about him. So many of the people I hung out with in London spent their free time talking about their jobs. I didn't really ever notice it until I spent time with Ethan. We had everything else to talk about.

"I'll make sure I'm busy. I'll need a distraction with you gone."

I knew how he felt. I was pleased that I was leaving the city, where reminders of him would be all around me. It would make it easier.

I squeezed his hand.

"Hey, sleepyhead." I felt Ethan brushing my cheek and my eyes opened. How long had I slept? I had my head on his lap. I didn't remember dozing off.

"Hey, are we back?"

"Almost," he said. I looked out the window but didn't recognize where we were. We turned and went into an underground parking lot. Rory pulled up and I heard the trunk pop. "We're home. Come on."

I clamored out of the car, still a bit dazed from my nap. Why hadn't he dropped us at the entrance? I said goodbye to Rory and caught up with Ethan, who was holding the door open for me. Through the door was a small elevator lobby.

"I'm sleepy," I said.

"You can sleep when we get upstairs, beautiful."

"No, I need to wake up. I want to enjoy our last night together."

We stepped into the elevator when it arrived. It didn't feel as if we'd gone many floors up when the doors opened and Ethan gestured for me to step out. This didn't feel like the hotel.

"Where are we?"

"Home," he said setting our bags down in the entrance lobby.

"Home?"

He nodded. "Come on, I'll show you around."

"*Your* home?"

"Come on." He took my hand in his as he opened the door into a huge white living space with dark wood floors. Two walls were just complete glass and you could hardly tell what belonged inside and what belonged outside.

"This is where you live?" I asked. Mandy had told me that he didn't bring women back to his place. Maybe he'd rented it.

"Yes, crazyhead. I don't live in the hotel."

"Oh," I said.

"Are you disappointed? The view isn't as good."

"No, I just..." I wandered over to the window. How could he think I would be disappointed? "I didn't know, you know. And are you kidding me? It looks like we're floating on the water. Is that the Hudson?"

I looked back to him and he was grinning. "Yeah, it's great isn't it?"

"You're just trying to impress me, hoping I will give up my virtue. It's very manipulative, Mr. Scott."

As I stood looking out he came to stand behind me and wrapped his arms around my waist. I rested my arms on his. "I would never make you do anything you didn't want to do. I told you that the first night we met," he said softly.

I leaned my head back to rest on his chest. "You did, and you've kept your word. I've had an incredible week with you, Mr. Scott. I'll remember it forever."

He squeezed me tighter. "Follow me. I want to see you come in my bed."

Immediately I felt heat between my legs at his words and I grabbed his hand as he led me through a door at the far end of the room. We went down a long, windowless corridor and then into a dark room. It was a complete contrast to the airiness of the living space. He switched the lights on low and closed the door behind me. I watched him as I shifted from one foot to the other, his blue eyes burning with desire just as they always did before he had me. He stepped forward as I stepped back. And then my ass hit the wall and he kept coming toward me. He placed his hands either side of my head and then bent toward my lips.

"Kiss me," he said.

I trailed my fingers up his chest. And then up his neck, I brushed my thumbs across his lips. His eyes closed and I knew I had to remember his face just like that. My hands reached around his neck and I pulled him toward me. I took his bottom lip between his teeth, like I knew he liked, and then sucked and bit. I pushed my tongue against his and he reached around me and cupped my ass. I loved his obsession with it and I grinned against his lips. Kissing him was not like kissing anyone I'd kissed before. I realized that, from now on, there would be a Before Ethan and an After Ethan divide in my life. Before Ethan, kissing was always a prelude to the real stuff, but I could kiss Ethan forever. I was sure that he could make me come just by kissing me, with no other part of his body touching me. I sighed. And he pulled me away from the wall and walked me over to the bed. I held my hands up above my head and, breaking our kiss for just a second, he stripped my shirt from me in one quick movement.

"Give me your phone," I said to Ethan. He had ordered Chinese and we were sitting on his sofa picking at the 187 dishes he'd had delivered. I was wearing a Columbia University T-shirt I'd found on a chair. He was in his boxers. It might have been the best evening this week, and that was saying something.

Ethan got up, walked to the console table on the other side of the room where his phone was, and came back and handed it to me.

I tapped and scrolled, trying to find my name in his contacts. "I can't find me," I said, looking up at him. He took the phone from my hands pressed some buttons and then handed it back. I was under Beautiful Anna. Oh, sweet mother of god, why couldn't I find a man like this in London?

I brought up the menu and hit delete and then tried to find our text messages.

"What are you doing?" he asked me gently.

"Deleting me from your phone," I replied, while scrolling through his messages. He didn't respond.

"This is going to be harder than it should be for me, and I need to make sure there's no ambiguity left behind.

No promises to break, no room for disappointment." I knew that if I left him a way to contact me, I would spend my days back in London wishing and hoping. When I wasn't looking, Ethan had gone from Uncomplicated Fun to something else. I didn't want to think what. I deleted our message thread. Done. We were done after tonight. My stomach churned and I felt something in the back of my throat.

He reached for me and dragged me on to his lap, my phone still in my hands as he pushed my hair off my shoulder and kissed my neck. He wasn't making this easier.

"Sometimes I forget that I didn't know you my whole life," I said.

"Anna," he replied and kissed my neck again. "My beautiful Anna, I'd never break a promise to you."

I turned and held his face in my hands. "I know you think you wouldn't, but it's inevitable. And I can't do it again," I said, dropping my hands to my lap. "I can't hope or wish for anything but a perfect evening this evening, which is what this is. Thank you, Ethan. You put my heart back together and made me believe there could be something better out there."

He didn't say anything. Part of me was relieved— but there was something, a voice right at the back of my head, that was urging him to ask me to stay, to tell me we could be together, we could make it work between us, that it wasn't just a fling for him, that he felt something. Something more, something different. I wanted him to tell me that he felt for me what I felt for him. But I got silence.

No promises, no ambiguity, no bullshit.

Ethan

I didn't know what to say. She sounded so sad. I wanted her. I wanted her to live in the city and for us to hang out and date and all that stuff. But she was right. She lived 3,000 miles away and we'd known each other a week. She'd seen parts of me I'd never shown anyone, but we'd still known each other for a week. And I'd never had a relationship with a woman that lasted more than four hours. A week was a lifetime in my world, but in reality it was still a week. Fuck. It was an impossible situation and she was making the right decision. The sensible decision.

If we stayed in touch, how would that play out? My job wouldn't allow me to fly out to London regularly, and even if it did we'd probably only see each other once a month or something. I'd seen plenty of relationships poisoned by distance. I didn't want to poison what we had. I didn't want her to end up hating me. This week we'd escaped reality. There'd been no expectation, no everyday shit to muddy the waters. But still, there was something between us. Did she feel it?

She picked up her phone and started prodding at it. Presumably deleting me. Maybe it was *because* she felt something that I'd just been deleted.

I needed to let her walk away.

No promises, no ambiguity, no bullshit.

My hands tightened in hers as I pushed into her. I watched her below me. Her mouth opened a fraction wider as I pushed right up to the hilt. Jesus, she felt amazing. Her eyes never left mine as I began my rhythm above her. God, I would miss this. I would miss watching her reaction to me. I captured her nipple in between my teeth. She arched into me. I bit down and she screamed.

"You're so fucking perfect," I whispered as I switched to her other breast. "So fucking incredible." I felt her pussy tighten and I groaned. Jesus, I was going to come in about twenty seconds if she kept that up.

"Ethan," she moaned.

"Tell me, baby." I loved it when she told me what she wanted, what she liked.

"Don't ever stop."

I knew I could fuck this woman, and only this woman, for the rest of my life. My thrusts came harder and deeper. I could tell she was close.

"You don't want me to ever stop fucking you?"

"No, not ever. I need you inside me all the time," she whimpered.

God, she could be my undoing. I watched her as her breath hitched and she fought against my hands that pinned her to my bed. Beautiful. And mine, for tonight.

I saw her orgasm pass over her as her face tensed and then relaxed.

"Oh god. Oh god. Oh god," she cried out.

She made me feel like a god. She squeezed her thighs against me, and before I had a chance to stop it I was emptying myself in her. Her pleasure had become my trigger.

I slumped forward, putting all my weight on her, stretching our arms out, my body touching as much of her body as possible.

"You are the sexiest man I've ever met," she said, her voice returning to normal after her breathless panting of mid-orgasm words. I wasn't sure which I preferred.

"Right back at you, beautiful."

I pushed myself up on my elbows so I could look at her. She looked at her best like this. Post orgasm. Like she belonged to me.

"God, you're so beautiful," I said and I moved out of her and disposed of the condom.

I pulled her perfect ass toward me and wrapped my arms around her waist. I loved how she fit so exactly.

"I need you to do something for me tomorrow," she said.

"Anything."

"Even if you think it's weird?"

"Even if I think it's weird," I reassured her.

"When we say goodbye tomorrow, I need you to act like we're going to see each other again that evening. Like it's just like the last seven mornings."

I felt like someone punched me in the gut. And a piece of me broke.

Anna

Daniel was staying in New York, so it was just Leah and me flying back together. We were flying first class, thanks to Daniel. All that meant to me was unlimited booze—and I needed to get smashed. I needed to erase Ethan Scott from every corner of my mind.

"Can I get you something from the bar, miss?" the flight attendant asked.

"Sure. Can I get a whiskey, please?" Oh god, whiskey reminded me of him. "Actually, make that champagne, please." She nodded. "Actually, can you make that two?" I got a tight smile but at least she didn't dare say anything.

"Are you ok?" Leah asked.

"Of course I'm ok," I snapped. "Sorry. I just need a drink. I'm a nervous flyer."

"Yeah, right. It's ok to be upset."

"No, Leah, it's not. It's not ok at all. I knew the guy for a week. I'm being ridiculous and I just need a drink."

"When it works it works. I knew with Daniel on the first date. I tried to fight it. I was engaged to another man, for crying out loud, but I knew."

"Even if I did know, it doesn't even matter. We live on different continents. And anyway, it's done. We haven't got each other's numbers."

"What do you mean? You texted each other, of course you have each other's numbers."

"I deleted them. On both our phones. It was a fling, Leah. I can't have myself think it was anything else. It's better this way."

She squeezed my knee. "Well, at least you know there are good guys out there. We can find you someone else when you get back. Daniel has a cute friend, Adam, who's available."

Leah was just trying to be nice, but there was nothing I would like less than to think about dating someone else. I was going to let myself wallow for a little bit. I'd drink a bit too much, eat a bit too much, and work long hours. Then when I felt at an all-time low, I'd pick myself up and start again.

No promises, no ambiguity, no bullshit.

The Empire State Series: Part Two

AUTUMN
in
LONDON

LOUISE BAY

CHAPTER
One

Anna

"Just a drink? What have you got to lose?" Leah was trying to convince me to go on a date with one of her boyfriend Daniel's old college friends.

"Leah, please. I've said no about a hundred times. Can you drop it?" I replied.

"I just hate to see you so sad Anna."

"I'm not sad. I don't know what you mean."

Leah sighed. "You know exactly what I mean. You've been like this for months, since we came back from New York."

"I've just had a lot going on since we came back. The flat—work has been busy. You know people are saying that we all might be out of jobs if the rumors are true about the firm being in trouble, and I've had so much work since Mindy left. There's just a lot been going on and I've been distracted." But although that was all true, Leah was right, I'd been under a black cloud since being back in London. Everything had just seemed a bit muted, and I couldn't bring myself to feel enthusiastic about anything.

"You're not going to lose your job. And even if you did, you could walk into another tomorrow."

I'd managed to change the subject from New York. I wanted to scrub it from my memory and I wanted to relive it constantly at the same time. I'd had a perfect week with Ethan. I didn't know if it was because we were both clear on our expectations—that the week would be uncomplicated and about enjoying ourselves and, most importantly, limited to only one week—but I'd never felt so comfortable in a man's company before. There had been no pressure, no expectations, no bullshit. We'd just concentrated on enjoying ourselves and each other. He made me laugh—out loud—not many men could do that. I liked him and I liked the person *I* was around him. By the end, it had felt like there was something more between us. The fact that he'd brought me back to his place the last evening we had together had made me feel like I was special.

"You could call him," she said.

"Who?" I pretended I didn't know who "him" was.

"You know who. Ethan."

"I don't want to call him. It was just a holiday fling. And if I did want to, I couldn't because I don't have his number any more than I did the ten thousand times you've mentioned this before."

"You could Google him."

I'd not told Leah, but I'd already briefly tried to internet stalk him with no success. There were plenty of Ethan Scotts but nothing that I could see was relating to my Ethan. I was grateful in a way. No ambiguity. No promises. No bullshit.

"Drop it, Leah."

"Okay. Let's change the subject. When does the flat go through?"

My flat had been on the market since I came back from New York and I'd just accepted an offer. I was so relieved to be moving after the break in. I hated being in that place alone. Even though they'd not taken anything, the fact that uninvited strangers had been in my home was still terrifying.

"Hopefully within a month. The buyers want to move quickly."

"But you've not found somewhere else? What are you going to do? I've told you, you can stay with Daniel and me if you've not found somewhere."

I shrugged. "Thanks." For once in my life, I didn't have a plan and I didn't want one.

"You could move to New York," Leah said.

"Jesus Christ, Leah. I have to get back to work." I stood from our table at our regular lunchtime place.

"Sorry," she mumbled. "I just want you to be happy," she said.

"I don't need a man to make me happy," I replied.

Leah ignored me. "Are you coming out on Saturday?" she asked as we climbed the stairs, making our way out of the basement into the rain of an autumn afternoon in

London. It was a great time of year. It matched my mood perfectly: dark and dreary.

I shrugged. "It depends on work."

"It's Saturday night, Anna."

"I'll see."

We kissed each other goodbye and headed off in opposite directions.

I should make the effort to go on Saturday. It was our friend from law school, Alice's, birthday. Work was busy but not busy enough to be working weekends. I was a little worried about my job. Leah was right, I probably could find something else but I'd been happy where I was and I liked the people I worked with. But if the firm was in trouble, we could all lose our jobs no matter how hard I worked.

The bustle of the office disguised my mood. No one noticed that I wasn't participating, that my mind and my heart were elsewhere. It felt like they were all moving at a million miles an hour and that I was stuck in treacle, unable to keep up. I shouldn't take breaks at lunchtime. It broke my concentration and allowed 'him' to seep through the cracks. If I kept busy, it kept him at bay. That's why I'd been spending so much time at work recently. It was when I wasn't in the office that I imagined bumping into him. The way I had the lunchtime after our first night together. Leah had told me it was fate and I'd scoffed. As far as I was concerned scoffing was mandatory when someone said something was fate. But part of me, a part I kept buried deep, away from sunlight and reality, wondered if she might have been right. And it was thoughts like that, that were driving me a little closer to insanity.

He could be in London right? He could be visiting his sister. London isn't so big. Thirteen million people isn't so many, right?

Wrong Anna. You're an idiot, Anna.

I shot an email to Leah and told her I would go along on Saturday. I wasn't going to get away with not going without a lot of grief, so I might as well give in now and not waste the energy. On balance, it was the easier option. I'd been working such long hours that I was almost up to date with everything. I needed a project. A distraction. Maybe finding a new flat would be a good place to start. I closed my office door and started trawling through the property websites. I called about a couple of places and set up appointments after work and on Saturday. I thought about seeing if Leah wanted to come with me but decided against it. I didn't want her constantly reminding me of Ethan. I didn't need reminding.

I'd never told Leah, or anyone, that I'd developed . . . feelings . . . I suppose would be the best way to describe it, for Ethan. She knew the sex was amazing. She knew I'd spent every night with him and she'd seen my black mood After Ethan. Before Ethan, I'd never really spent more than three months in a relationship with a guy and although, most of the time, it was their bad behavior that ended things, it never took me long to recover. Ben the Bastard, and what he had gotten me mixed up with, had been awful. It meant I didn't feel comfortable in my own home, but I wasn't day dreaming about Ben and fantasizing that things could be different, that we could still be together. I'd never done that before. I'd been pissed off. I'd been hurt, but I'd just moved on. Ethan, on the other hand, was following me around like a ghost and I didn't know how to shake him off.

Ethan

Usually, I didn't like flying, especially long haul. Today it didn't bother me. I had too much to do to distract me from the fact we were thirty thousand feet up in a metal tube and the pilot was probably asleep, drunk or fucking the cabin crew. I had too much to think about. Tomorrow was a big day. I had to prepare. I'd not read the communications pack that had been couriered to my apartment yesterday and we were having interviews with press and meetings with clients all day tomorrow, and before that a meeting with the staff at 10 a.m. to announce the merger.

And then there was Anna to think about. I should never have brought her back to my apartment on that last night. Since then, I'd seen her in every room. She looked so fucking amazing coming in my bed. It was all I could see when I tried to sleep in there. I'd started spending my nights in the guest room because those images of her refused to leave me.

I liked that I could make her laugh out loud and that when she did, it was unaffected, with her whole body. We'd laughed a lot. I didn't normally have fun with women—it had always been about the sex before Anna. And she'd seemed to understand about the demands of my job, which had surprised me. She hadn't been sulky or demanding when I had to work—she got it. What I liked most of all was that she didn't seem to give a shit about all the New York pretenses—the parties and the important people. She was real and she had gotten under my skin in a way no woman ever had.

When the tin tube in which I was so precariously sitting hit the tarmac at London Heathrow in six hours, we would be in the same city. Breathing the same air. I wasn't sure how I felt about it. Part of me was excited that I might see her again and part of me thought that that spelled complicated and I didn't do complicated.

If I wanted to find her, there were ways. But I hadn't decided if that *was* what I wanted. I knew I wanted to fuck her again but I knew that my dick didn't always have my best interests at heart. My brain knew I didn't need the distraction—work was going to be demanding.

And she might be distracted with someone else. It had been months and she had an appetite as voracious as my own. The thought churned my stomach. I hoped it was her vibrator keeping her hunger at bay rather than some prick who didn't know how to make her come.

"Would you like another whiskey, sir?" The blonde flight attendant leaned over, giving me a view of her less-than-perfect tits.

She wasn't my type. I wasn't sure what was my type anymore. I was going through a dry spell. I was busy at work and well, every woman I met I compared to Anna and they just didn't seem to make me laugh like her, or get me hard like her or do that cute thing waving their hands in the air when they talked like her.

"No. Thank you," I replied.

She lowered her voice. "Well, if there's anything you want, anything, you just let me know."

There was nothing subtle about her. Not her overly made up face, not her fake tits and not her come-on.

"No, thank you," I replied again. I didn't want her hovering around me for the rest of the flight. She should go and find someone who would be more appreciative of her lack of subtlety.

I'd been sent over to London by the New York office. Apparently, according to our communications manager, I wasn't allowed to say "head office". Fucking politics. New York *would* be head office. This wasn't a merger, it was a takeover. I would be overseeing the "merger" of the New York law firm, where I was partner, with the London law firm Allen & Smith. Our firms had been in talks for months about a transatlantic merger but when Allen & Smith posted less than stellar profits three months ago, we knew the time was right. They were vulnerable, and we were ready. Without us, Allen & Smith would have probably gone into liquidation. I had been assigned to London for three months to head up integration. I wasn't sure if integration was strictly the correct word. I was here to make sure London was doing what New York told them to do.

When I got the first few days over with, I'd decide what to do about finding Anna. I didn't need to think about it until then. I needed to work. To focus. I opened up my laptop and started preparing for Monday.

My sister had become mildly hysterical when I'd announced I was coming to London. As soon as I'd told her, she'd started making plans on the spot. She had me mentally moved into their guest room in Hammersmith, wherever that was, and firmly palmed off with one the single mothers she knew. Eventually she gave in to me living on my own on the promise that I would have dinner with her and James and baby Izzy at least once a week. Izzy was a woman I could cope with. Jessica, not so much. I don't know how James put up with her.

She still insisted on meeting me at the airport as if I were a child. I would have preferred to wait to see her when Monday was over but it was one less argument to have with her. Jesus, she was hard work at times. But I couldn't help but grin when I saw her and James waiting for me with a placard with my childhood nickname, Bond, written on it when I came out of baggage. I was obsessed with James Bond as a kid. The fast cars, the booze, the women. What wasn't to like?

I scooped Jessica up in a hug as soon as I saw her. "Stop nagging me," I said.

"I've not said a word," she said, pushing me away.

"Yes but you were about to," I replied, ruffling her hair.

"Don't touch my hair." She slapped my arm. "I don't nag. I wouldn't know how." I looked at James who rolled his eyes as we shook hands. I chuckled.

"So where's my favorite girl?" I peered into the stroller to see Izzy fast asleep.

"Don't wake her. She's being a terror at the moment," Jessica said.

"Like mother, like daughter," I teased.

"Better that she's like me than you." Jessica sneered at me.

Why did we revert to being thirteen around each

other? I needed not to take the bait. "Come on—I need to prep for tomorrow so I need to get checked in to my hotel."

"Why won't you stay with us?" Jessica whined. She did nothing but give me a hard time but she wanted me living with her? She was full of contradictions.

"Because you're a terror and I'm going to be working a lot. We discussed this. Come on."

We drove into the city and they dropped me at my hotel. I was going to stay here and see apartments the following week. I was here for three months so I didn't want to be living in a hotel the whole time. As I checked in at the desk, I scanned the lobby. *She could be here.* What was she doing? Had she woken up with someone this morning? My gut clenched. I needed to focus. Tomorrow was a big day. It was an important time for the firm. There wasn't room for distractions or complications.

CHAPTER TWO

Anna

My hangover hit me hard. It was 4 p.m. and I was still lying in the dark on my sofa watching *Sweet Home Alabama*. The day had been a complete write off. I should have learned by now that I couldn't drink white wine without a huge hangover. The problem was I couldn't drink whiskey any more, not since New York.

Despite myself, Alice's birthday had been fun. Leah was right, my mood had been off since New York. I'd pulled back a bit from things, from life, and I didn't want to carry on like that. I'd plastered on a smile at Alice's party and found that by the end of the night the smile had been genuine. Two guys had asked for my number and instead of rolling my eyes and dismissing them, which had been my reaction to anything male since I'd come back from New York I had agreed to take theirs. And who knows, I might use one of them. I missed Ethan but I'd only known him a week, he didn't want anything more from me than what had happened between us and he was a continent away. I wanted to find an Ethan in London. Despite my hangover, I felt as if I'd pressed the reset button and by tomorrow everything should have reloaded, ready to start again.

The next morning my new, positive attitude had decided to stick around so I dressed to kill and got into the office early. Except when I arrived, it didn't seem that early. Passing through reception, there were people taking up seats, mobiles clamped to their ears. I checked my watch. Eight. It was weird, reception never had anyone in at that time.

I wandered over to Julia, the head receptionist, who looked frazzled. "What's going on?" I whispered.

She shrugged. "Who the hell knows? But I've got Americans coming out of my arse."

I winced "Sounds painful. I'll let you get on with it."

As I made my way to my desk I noticed the partners in our department huddled in one of our meeting rooms. Something was up. Maybe we were going into liquidation. Jesus. I was prepared for a new start but I didn't want to kick things off by losing my job.

Twenty minutes later, a few more associates were milling about and there was unmistakable tension in the air and not the good, sexual kind. I grabbed the phone and dialed Leah.

"Something is going down," I said in my best spy-like voice.

"Well as long as he's hot, I'd say open wide."

"Leah, what the hell is the matter with you? Your mouth's dirtier than mine these days," I said, genuinely shocked.

She giggled. "I know, it's Daniel. He's a bad influence."

"I don't want to know. Anyway. There's definitely something up. I'll rephrase that before you twist my words. Something is going on. Everyone's jittery, there's a bunch of activity in reception, and the partners look like they've been throwing up all night. It's freaking me out."

"I'll see if anyone here knows anything and I'll text you."

Leah worked at another law firm and gossip among firms spread like wildfire. She was as likely to know something about my firm as I was.

"Okay, good. Shall we meet for a drink tonight?" I suggested.

"Yeah. That would be great." Leah sounded shocked, I'd not been out much recently.

The partners filed out of their huddle and a murmur passed across the office. People were exchanging glances. What had happened? My secretary caught my blank expression and whispered for me to check my email.

All the associates were summoned to a firm meeting at 10 a.m. It was official. We were going under.

I tried to concentrate on work but found myself surfing job websites. Was Leah right? Would I find something easily? Well, I wasn't going to find anything between now and 10 a.m.

Ethan

Since landing in London, the pull toward Anna had become stronger. She was becoming bigger in my thoughts and she wasn't going away. I was going to have to track her down. I knew that now. The obvious way was through her friend's boyfriend—Daniel Armitage. I could call him or maybe one of the other partners knew him – they probably ran in the same circles. Yes, Armitage would be the way in.

I picked up an unknown number calling my cell.

"Scott," I answered.

"Hey, Ethan. It's Phoebe."

Phoebe was one of the few women I'd fucked more than once. She lived in Boston and came to New York for work regularly. I didn't have her number. She called me if she was in town and wanted to get laid. Until now I'd been happy to help her out.

"So I'm in town and wondered if you were free tonight, say around ten?"

"Actually," I said closing the door to my temporary office, "I'm in London, for work, and . . ."

"Okay, so I'll call you next time."

"Er, Phoebe . . ."

"Yes?"

"You know that I've never bullshitted you about our . . . relationship." This was harder than I expected.

"Yes, Ethan, I'm not in love with you, don't worry that handsome face of yours."

I laughed, trying to sound casual. "Yeah, I know you would never be that crazy. It's just . . . well, I don't think we should catch up anymore when you're in town."

"Oh. Okay. Did you go gay?" She laughed again, in a little less assured way this time.

"Sorry, I just, well I met someone."

"Oh wow. First George Clooney, and now you? Well, I'm happy for you, I really am. Look, I've gotta go. Take care now." The phone went dead.

Relief pooled in my stomach and I collapsed back in my chair. It was only a half-lie. I had met someone and even though we weren't together, our week together made my arrangement with Phoebe seem kinda sleazy.

Now I needed to focus. To concentrate. We were about to head into the conference room to make the announcement to the staff. Later today, I'd put a call into Armitage and see if I could find Anna.

"Ethan, just to recap, I'll speak for about ten minutes and then introduce you," Frank, the outgoing senior partner addressed me. I nodded, half listening. There was no need to fucking recap. We weren't conducting brain surgery, this was a staff announcement about a merger.

Would Armitage tell me where she was? Would she be back with her ex? *Get your head in the fucking game.*

We filed into the conference room. You could feel the tension in the air, it was heavy. Lawyers didn't like surprises and here was a room full of them scared out of their wits. As I scanned the room, eyes tried to catch mine, trying to see what was going to be announced seconds before the person next to them. My attention swept left and right and I tried to force a smile. I wasn't here to announce bad news, after all. This was good for everyone. Their firm wasn't going under and it would have if it hadn't been for us.

My eyes were pulled to a group of lawyers at the side of the room, and something I couldn't quite make out caught my attention. The faces gradually came into focus and there, standing behind the throng of chairs, she stood. Anna. *My Anna.* Looking straight at me, her mouth open, as if she'd seen a ghost.

Fuck.

I looked away quickly, and looked at the floor, trying to get my head together. My brain was fuzzy and I couldn't organize my thoughts properly. She was here? She was a lawyer? The floor disappeared from beneath me as I tried to make sense of what I'd seen. I was meant to be saying a few reassuring words. She looked amazing. Different. Had Frank stopped speaking?

Fuck.

Get your fucking shit together, Ethan. I brought my fist to my mouth and cleared my throat.

I looked up, stared straight ahead and tuned into what Frank was saying. He sounded beaten, exhausted.

As he introduced me, I clapped him on the back. "Thanks Frank. I'm delighted to be here today with a number of my colleagues from New York to announce what will be the start of a new dawn for both our firms. Allen & Smith has a fantastic reputation for quality and client service and we're all looking forward to working more closely together in these coming weeks, months and years. The merger is effective from the end of the month, after which we will be rebranded as one firm. We have some time for questions."

I concentrated hard on not looking in Anna's direction. I couldn't afford to be distracted on such a big day for both our firms.

The questions were inane and easy to answer, and I took each of them on auto-pilot.

Would there be redundancies? Did anyone really expect a straight answer to that question?

What would the new name of the firm be? "That's still being discussed" was the official answer, although in reality the names Allen and Smith were being dropped.

Would there be opportunities to work in the New York office? We hoped to create opportunities of all kinds for people across the firm.

It was all ambiguity and bullshit. Two things I hated.

That was when I let my eyes be drawn to her. She was staring at her feet, not at me. What was she thinking?

We wrapped up and everyone trailed out. The

rest of the day was spent in interviews with the legal press, meetings with clients and getting to know the other partners. Part of my role was to assess which of the partners made the cut. There was no doubt that people were going to get fired. We needed to improve profitability and quality, fast. That meant getting rid of dead wood. Frank would be the first to go. But I could tell today that he knew that and that he wouldn't be a problem.

It was about 6 p.m. when things started to slow a bit. All in all, it had gone well. Apparently the legal press had been positive. I'd not seen it but my secretary passed me various articles throughout the day. I asked for a tour of the building to fill in the time before we went to dinner— the obligatory, first night in London welcome from the Allen & Smith partners. I really needed to check my messages but I wanted to see where exactly she worked and if I could spot her again. I insisted that Frank didn't take me on the tour. He looked exhausted and could probably do with a break before dinner. Instead, Paul, a more junior partner showed me round. I tried to listen to what he was saying but really I spent my time scanning offices, trying to find her. I wasn't quite sure what I'd say if I did come across her. I grinned at the thought of seeing her again. Although I'd only seen her for a few seconds, that open mouth she had was the same one I saw just before she came. Jesus, I could feel my cock stirring. Maybe seeing her again was not a good idea.

I slapped Paul on the back and suggest we wrap up the tour and head off to the restaurant.

Anna

I was waiting for Leah when she arrived, looking a bit flustered. I was a glass ahead of her. Wine not whiskey, which I was sure to regret tomorrow but right then I didn't care.

I topped up my glass and poured Leah a glass, draining the bottle. I waved at the waiter, trying to get his attention so he could bring us more alcohol.

"Jesus, Anna, it's a Monday. I can't get hammered," Leah said as she sat down and took a sip of her wine.

"So, I saw Ethan today," I said.

Leah looked confused. "What do you mean you saw Ethan?"

I took another glug of my wine and nodded. "Ethan. In London. Announcing the merger."

Leah had emailed me when the news had broken online about the merger. I hadn't responded other than to give her a time to meet up this evening.

"What do you mean 'announcing the merger'? I'm not with you."

The waiter appeared at our table.

"We're going to need more wine," Leah said helpfully. At least she got that bit. "Start at the beginning."

"I told you the staff announcement was at 10 a.m. We filed in to the big conference room and there he was. Standing next to Frank."

"He was there?" she asked, catching on to what I was saying.

I nodded. "Yup. Representing Flanders, Case & Burling, the US firm that's taking us over. Why they bother calling it a merger, I have no idea, it's a takeover - we were about to go under. He spoke, after Frank, I think. I can't really remember."

"Shit."

I nodded again.

"Did you get to speak to him?"

"No."

"Did he see you there?"

"Yes, briefly, he looked at me."

"Do you think he knew you would be there?"

I shrugged. "I guess. I'm sure he had employee lists. I don't know," I said.

I shrugged again, and drank more wine.

"So, what was it like? Seeing him?"

It had been a shock seeing him again. A wonderful shock. A confusing shock. Excitement had coursed through me as I'd stared at him as he'd fiddled with some papers in front of him. And then, as he scanned the room, I knew he'd find me. And when he did, he snatched his gaze away as if I was the last person he wanted to see. It had stung.

"Do you think he knew in New York?" I blurted. The thought had just occurred to me.

"What? Knew where you worked? No. Do you think he did?"

I drank more. The effect of the alcohol seeped through my body. Was he just playing some weird fucking game with me? Trying to get information on Allen & Smith? It was a pretty big coincidence for him to be a partner at the law firm that was taking over the place I worked, wasn't it?

"I think he's an asshole who was using me," I stated.

"Why? What would he be using you for? And anyway, he can't have known. It's just a coincidence. It's the universe's way of bringing you two back on the same continent, in the same city because it knows how good you are together." Leah looked at me hopefully.

"Shut the fuck up and drink with me," I responded.

That's how he knew my name in New York. He'd not guessed my real name was Anna—there'd been no connection between us, which meant he could see who I really was without me having to tell him. He'd simply known. He'd played some weird mind game on me to try and get me to sleep with him. Using what he'd found in fucking due diligence to get laid. What a prick. He knew the whole fucking time. Things were starting to make sense to me now. *Thank you wine.*

"Did he try and speak to you?" Leah asked.

"No." That had stung, too. He hadn't looked at me again for the rest of the meeting. Not even a glance in my direction and I was sure about that because I hadn't been able keep my eyes off him. What was he going to say to me anyway? "Sorry I lied and mislead you but it was business"?

And now I was going to be working for him. He was effectively going to be my boss or my boss's boss or something. Well, hopefully he'd be back in New York by the end of the week and I wouldn't hear his name again.

"Well, I'm sure you two will catch up soon. This is exciting!"

"It's not exciting, Leah, it's a disaster. *I'm* a walking disaster when it comes to men."

"You are not! This Ethan thing could work out well. How long is he in London for?"

"He's a liar and he used me. Maybe he was trying to get information about Allen & Smith. He's an asshole."

"That seems pretty unlikely, Anna. You're jumping to conclusions. Wine does not bring wisdom."

I hadn't told her that he'd guessed my name in New York. It was a weird thing to have happened, so I'd kept it to myself. Now I was pleased I hadn't told her. I felt like such a fool for believing that it had been real.

The next day at work my anger at Ethan and my hangover mixed into a mood that turned me into something that was straight from Greek myth and legend. I swear to god, I think if anyone had so much as looked at me wrong, I would have turned them to stone. I wasn't taking any shit from anyone. I pounded through my work, refusing to think about anything but the contracts in front of me. The asshole that was Ethan Scott was not going to distract me or affect my career. Once again I'd proven to myself that I only attracted the lowest type of man. I was going to spend the rest of my life celibate. Decision made. It was easier all around, please move along, nothing to see here.

I was close to not having anything to do. It was never like that but because I'd been working like a machine since I'd returned from New York—contracts were flying off my desk. I needed to stay distracted so I fired off an email to my boss telling him that I had capacity to do more. I was going to get employee of the year.

CHAPTER
Three

Ethan

I sat at my desk trying to concentrate on my emails. I had twenty minutes until my next meeting and despite the fact I'd not had any sleep, I hadn't used my insomnia to keep on top of work and emails from clients were piling up. I forwarded a lot of them to my assistant in New York but he wouldn't be in the office for hours. If the volume of meetings continued like this, I was going to start to lose clients. I needed some people, a team, here in London, if this was going to work. And I needed to sleep. Despite being awake all night, I'd not been doing what I should have been and working through my in-box, instead I'd been going over the booklet of associate details I'd been handed when I arrived. Of course, there was only one associate I was interested in. It didn't tell me much. Just her department, her office number and her personal contact details.

I left the dinner earlier than was polite. I needed some time to think. I wanted to speak to her. It had been so good to see her. She had looked fucking amazing. I wanted to kiss her, touch her, bury myself in her.

Walking through the corridors at the office, I kept scanning the people scuttling around me, trying to find her . . . but nothing. It was irritating because I kept catching people's eyes as I looked for her. Everyone clearly knew me so I'd been trying to keep to my office between meetings.

I flicked open the booklet. I could call her and invite her to lunch or something. I dialed her number.

"Anna Kirby," she answered, sounding . . . irritated.

"Anna, it's Ethan," I spoke softly.

Silence.

"Anna?"

"What do you want?" she snapped.

It was not the response I'd expected and my body clenched. I hadn't thought this through.

"I want to speak to you." I would have thought it was obvious.

"I'm at work."

"Anna."

"You've got all the information you could ever need about Allen & Smith, I don't know why you need to speak to me about anything more."

She hung up. What was that? Did she understand that it was me? Did she get me confused with someone else?

My secretary Theresa, interrupted my thoughts and gave me some papers for the next meeting. Anna would have to wait.

"Can you get me in with Frank after this and before my lunch? I need to talk to him about resourcing my client work," I asked.

"No problem," she replied.

I liked her. She was efficient and pleasant but not a people pleaser and she wasn't trying to blow smoke up my ass. She was the only one not being a kiss ass and I was grateful to her for it.

Back at my desk, I tried Anna's extension again. No answer. It was 6.p.m. I'd declined a dinner invitation that evening so I could catch up on things but I wanted to speak to Anna, get to the bottom of her brush off earlier and, I don't know, hang out with her, hear about what had been going on with her. What the hell was the matter with her? I worked out from her extension that she must be on the fourth floor so I went down in search of her. She couldn't ignore me if I was stood right in front of her.

I wandered left out of the elevators. All the floors were the same layout—a mixture of open plan seating and rows of offices Where to start? What was I going to say to her when I found her?

One of the corporate partners, Al, found me before I had time to decide.

"Ethan, Frank spoke to me earlier, I was just about to brief a couple of assistants I've identified to work with you. Do you want to come with me and meet them? They're a couple of real stars, ready and eager to help you with whatever you need," he said.

"Sure," I replied. Was there another appropriate response? It was the last thing I wanted to do. I wanted to find Anna.

I followed Al as he went on about the associates he'd lined up and we walked across the floor, between the desks. I saw her before she saw me but only just. I smiled and she looked back down at what she was working on. Al charged into her office and she was forced to look up. She avoided looking at me.

"Anna, have you met Ethan?"

She stood up and came out from behind her desk.

"No, we've not met. I'm Anna Kirby."

I followed her lead and pretended not to know her. I took her hand to shake as she offered it to me. Her skin was as soft as I remembered but I wasn't used to seeing her in formal work wear. She gave me a tight smile and focused on something over my shoulder, not looking at me. What the fuck? My eyes glided down her body, taking in skin above her shirt, her tight skirt, the bump on her thigh gave away that she was wearing a garter belt. I wondered who else had noticed. Who was she wearing that for?

"Anna is one of our brightest associates and is going to be helping you out while you're in London." Al said.

Al clearly hadn't given Anna the heads up. She looked like she might vomit at the thought.

"Anna, why don't you put some time in Ethan's diary?" He paused and looked at me. "Is tomorrow morning soon enough?" I nodded. "Invite Richard as well. The two of you will be assisting Ethan." Al then turned to me. "Then if you need more resources, we can find more people. Does that work?"

"That's great, Al. I'm sure I'll enjoy working with Anna." I tried to catch her eye but she was looking everywhere except at me. I wanted to ask Al to leave us, leave me to say hello properly, to trail my hands across Anna's thighs, underneath her skirt, to push into her underwear. *Fuck, focus Ethan.*

"I have to get back but it was nice to meet you, Anna." She didn't respond.

Anna

I couldn't believe he had the nerve to request I work for him. What a total dick. He'd tried to call me again but I'd not picked up when I recognized the number. What could he possibly have to say to me that I wanted to hear?

My phone rang again and it was him. Again. He needed to stop harassing me. I sent the call to voicemail and logged off. If I wasn't in the office, he couldn't find me. Maybe I'd call in sick tomorrow. I was going to have to find an excuse not to work with him.

I picked up a bottle of wine on the way home and collapsed on the sofa with a huge glass. Hangover or no hangover, I needed some kind of sedative. I considered calling Leah but I couldn't risk her babbling on about fate or the universe or something equally ridiculous, so I switched on the TV and started to open my post. My mobile started vibrating on the coffee table, I didn't recognize the number but I answered it.

"Anna, it's Ethan. If you hang up, it will take me about thirty seconds to be at your front door."

"Are you stalking me? How do you have my home address?"

"The Partner Booklet of associate details."

"Fucking hell, isn't that a breach of my human rights or something, that's outfuckingrageous—"

"Let me in Anna."

"Where are you?" I peered through the peephole and saw him standing against the wall opposite my door.

"You know where I am. You just checked your peephole." He was very calm, just like I imagined a psychopath would be.

"Why are you even here? You got what you wanted. You made a fool out of me, now just pretend I don't exist."

"Let me in."

"No."

"Let me in."

"I said no."

"Do you really want to continue to have this conversation through the door for all your neighbors to hear? I'll stay here all night if I need to. It's not like I'm sleeping anyway."

What was the matter with this crazy guy? This flat was cursed. I couldn't wait to move.

"If I let you in, do you promise to leave after ten minutes?" I asked.

"I told you that I don't make promises I can't keep."

"You are full of total bullshit."

"What the fuck Anna? What is it that has made you so angry with me? We agreed I wouldn't call you, that we wouldn't stay in touch. I thought that's what you wanted." He raised his voice—it was the first time I'd ever known him to be ruffled.

I opened the door and looked at him, unwilling for the neighbors to further witness to my dating disasters.

"I'm not angry you didn't call, I'm angry because you used me."

He stepped toward me and I stood to the side to let him in. We might as well have this out as he was right in front of me.

He stepped inside my flat and I closed the door and lent back.

"I'm not a stupid guy but I'm having a hard time following your logic. We agreed it was going to be uncomplicated fun. I'm not pretending it wasn't about sex for me but you can't pretend it wasn't about sex for you. I thought we were on the same page. If I'd known you'd expected me to call . . ."

"What are you talking about? I didn't expect you to call." My voice had dropped to almost normal. I was exhausted from being so angry at him.

"Then I don't follow you," he said.

We stood in silence for a long minute. Thoughts were racing through my head and none of them made sense. Having him so close was not helping my clarity of thought. He was near enough to touch, to . . .

"Do you want a drink?" I asked. He nodded and I headed to the kitchen and poured two glasses of whiskey. Another thing to be mad at him for—whiskey and Ethan were synonymous for me now.

"Can you stop swearing at me for just a few minutes and talk to me?" he asked.

I didn't look at him, I couldn't look at him as I handed him his drink and then moved past him into the living room and collapsed on the sofa.

"Anna."

"You should have been honest with me from the beginning," I said calmly.

"About what? That I was a lawyer?"

I glanced at him and he looked confused.

"Jesus." Was he being deliberately stupid?

"Anna, seriously? What?"

"About the fact that you knew exactly who I was, that you wanted information about Allen & Smith, that you were using what you knew about me to get laid or something."

"What? When?" he asked.

"In New York." He couldn't think I hadn't realized what he'd been doing.

"You think I knew you worked for Allen & Smith when we met?" he asked, his voice lighter. I didn't respond. "How would I have known?" he asked.

Silence.

"What, and I arranged for you to be in New York, at the same bar as me?" I hadn't quite worked out how he'd managed to bump into me.

"And at lunch the following day." I prompted.

"Well, yes, that's true. I did know you were going to be at lunch at that place the next day."

My head snapped round to look at him.

"I didn't tell you because it made me look like a stalker but I wanted to see you again and the only information I got from the concierge about you was where you were going to be."

"Oh. My. God." *I knew it. I knew it.* "And how did you know I'd be in that bar?"

He stood up from the chair opposite me and took his jacket and tie off and came to sit next to me. I didn't move a muscle.

"Is that what you think? That I arranged the meeting with you to get information about Allen & Smith?"

I stayed silent.

"You are officially crazy," he said softly.

"Don't try and make me out as crazy. You're the one stalking me," I huffed.

"Think about it Anna. What information did you pass me about Allen & Smith?" I did think about it. I hadn't even told him I was a lawyer, let alone anything about where I worked.

"I found out you worked there during the announcement—when I saw you."

I looked at him sideways.

"Then how did you know my name was Anna?"

He reached out and pulled me onto his lap. I didn't resist him. Maybe I should have. But I wanted to believe what he was saying.

"I didn't know, beautiful. I just thought it suited you."

My stomach fluttered as he called me beautiful. *Damn you stomach.*

"And you strong-armed the concierge to find out where I was lunching the day after we met? That's weird."

He nodded. "Yes, a little out of character for me."

"Why?"

"Because I wanted to see you again. Haven't I told you, you're fantastic in bed?"

He grinned and then nuzzled into my neck and I let him.

Ethan

It felt so good to have her in my arms again. Too good. She'd calmed a little, but she seemed so stressed I wasn't sure how long it would last.

"So it was coincidence? Meeting at the bar and my name?" she recapped.

"Yes," I spoke into her neck, trailing my lips across her skin.

"And your firm's take-over or merger or whatever of my firm is coincidence?"

"You think I arranged the *merger* so I could see you again? You're not that good in bed."

She laughed and I felt her relax against me.

"So that's a lot of coincidences," she mused, ignoring my erection that was pressing against her hip.

"Uhuh," I mumbled and nodded.

She lay her head on my chest and I stroked her hair.

"It's nice to see you again," she whispered.

"It is? I was getting the distinct impression you were thinking the exact opposite," I teased her.

She moved to look at me, our noses almost touching. "I'm sorry. It's just . . ."

"Don't, it's fine." I moved my hand to cup the back of her head and she leaned forward, just a fraction. Did she want this?

"Ethan," she whispered so softly I wondered if I'd heard it in my head. "Ethan," she said, louder this time.

I pulled her head toward me took her bottom lip between my teeth.

I had to taste her. I slipped my tongue between her lips and I slid my hand under her shirt and down the back of her skirt, under her underwear to the base of her spine. I loved the feel of her skin against mine.

Sharply, her hands pushed against my chest forcing our lips apart but I continued stroking my fingers on her bare back. "Ethan, no. You're my boss now. We need to have rules."

I knew she was speaking sensibly but I didn't care. "Later, beautiful. We can agree to rules later. Right now, I want to taste you."

Her breath hitched and I knew that I would be inside her soon.

"You don't have roommates due back do you?" I asked.

"Why don't you ask the concierge?" she quipped, giggling at herself. She wasn't going to let me get away with that lightly.

I lifted her up and put her down next to me and slid to my knees in front of her. Roughly, I pulled her hips to the edge of the sofa and reached under her skirt. "You are looking for trouble, Miss Anna," I said and her cheeks pinked slightly. God she looked beautiful. I hooked my fingers into either side of her underwear and pulled them down. They pooled at her feet.

CHAPTER Four

Ethan

"I noticed something earlier," I said as I trailed my hands flat along the front of her thighs, from her knees up underneath her skirt. I stopped as I found the garter belt. I swallowed. She wore this shit to work? Fuck. I was never going to be able to practice law again with her around. "I thought so." Her eyelids fluttered and I removed my hands and fumbled for her zipper. I needed her skirt off so I could see what, exactly, she had on.

I slid the tight navy crepe from her legs, exposing her naked pussy and her stockings. She was perfect. With her skirt off, I pushed her knees wide apart, and she held them there. That was what really did it to me, the way she unashamedly wanted me and wasn't afraid to ask for it. And it wasn't just that she wanted sex. She wanted what *I* did to her. And that felt fan-fucking-tastic.

She was squirming before me, impatient for what was to come next. I watched her, eyes closed, head tilted back, lips parted. It was the best view in the world. "Ethan," she moaned, urging me on. I trailed my fingers down the back of her thighs, up to her perfect ass. I could see her glistening already.

"You are fucking gorgeous." I leaned forward and lightly trailed my tongue from her opening to her clit and down again and sat back.

"Ethan. Please. More." Jesus, my entire blood supply surged to my dick. I plunged both thumbs inside her, twisting and stroking. Her eyes flew to what I was doing. I moved my thumbs up her folds and spread her open, her clit exposed as I flicked the hard bud with the tip of my tongue.

"Ethan." She bolted up onto her elbows.

I flicked again.

"Ethan, no." She ground her hips into me, her body saying the opposite of her words.

I flicked once more and captured her ass in my hands and pulled her toward me as I sucked and licked. Her fingers went to my hair and she trailed her feet down my sides. I pushed her legs apart again with my elbows and thrust my fingers into her.

I knew she was close as she tried to push me away from her. "Ethan. Oh god. Oh god. Oh god."

She pulsed beneath my tongue and I reduced the pressure as she arched her back and screamed my name. Fuck I'd missed watching her come - come apart so completely in front of me.

She pulled my head from between her thighs and brought me up to face her. Instead of kissing me, she trailed her tongue across my chin, licking herself off me.

Jesus, the woman should be in jail for the things she did to me.

"I want you inside me Ethan. I mean it. Now." She rolled over to kneel on the sofa, stripped off her blouse and gripped the cushions at the back.

She was still so demanding.

"Ethan," she said, knocking me out of the daze of watching her bend over like that, offering herself to me. Jesus.

I found a condom in my wallet, peeled off my shirt, dropped my pants in record time and positioned myself, wanting to savor this moment before I slid into her. She pushed back impatiently.

"We have all night," I whispered. And I thrust into her and quickly withdrew completely. She gasped. "And all of tomorrow night." I pushed into her again. "And the night after that." She was whimpering. Incoherent. Crazed. I pulled at her waist, pulling her away from the sofa and toward me, her back against my chest. "Feel that beautiful?" I said as I kept thrusting as deep as I could. I'd not felt her around me for so long, and I wanted to get as deep as I could.

"Yes," she whispered.

"You're going to have my cock inside you every day now." I knew that I wasn't going to be able to stay away from her. I was going to have to have her, constantly, every day.

"Oh god yes," she responded.

I pushed on her shoulders, trying to get deeper. Her breaths were short and quick. It wouldn't be long.

I needed to see her face. I pulled out and she fell forward, limp. I picked her up and walked across the room to the dining table. Sitting her at one end, I pushed back into her, she was so tight, so perfect. She lay back and I leaned over her, scanning her face for her reaction to our bodies. Her cheeks were flushed and a sheen of sweat on her forehead captured a few strands of her hair. That sleek office look that she wore during the day was gone and the Anna only I knew was back.

I circled my hips and she twisted away from me. She was close.

"Don't resist it beautiful. You don't have to save it up. I'll make you come as often as you want."

Her body juddered, her mouth parted and I saw her peak just as I poured myself into her.

She slumped back on the table, boneless and beautiful. I grinned at her.

"Stop looking at me like that," she said, catching my grin.

"Like what?"

"Like you know something."

"I do know something."

"What do you know?"

"I know you're beautiful. I know that we're going

to do that again soon. And then again and again. And I know that I'm pleased to see you. I've missed you."

She turned her head to the side, not saying anything.

"I've missed you fucking me too," she said eventually.

"That's not what I said," I replied as I pulled her up to sit and then helped her off the table. "I've missed fucking you but I've missed all of you. Where's the bathroom?"

She indicated left and I pulled my arms around her waist and walked her backward in the direction of the bathroom. "Let's shower," I said.

She stood still and silent as I turned on the shower and adjusted the temperature. "Come here." I held out my hand to her and led under the water. "We never got a chance to fuck in the shower in New York."

"Ethan," she admonished.

"Now you're going to turn coy, after you've licked your come off my face and begged me to fuck you?"

She reached her hands around my neck and kissed my chest.

"I just need to understand the rules, Ethan."

"Later," I replied.

"Later?"

"Later." I kissed the top of her head.

Anna

It felt so strange but so comfortable having him in my flat, in my shower. He washed my hair for me, combed through my conditioner, covered my whole body in body wash and then rinsed me clean, all while trailing my body with kisses. We stood under the water facing each other, our tongues pressing together, exploring, kissing until the water ran cold.

"This isn't the Mandarin Oriental, I don't have unlimited hot water I'm afraid," I said as my skin puckered under the cool spray.

He smiled at me, led me out of the shower and pulled a towel around me. "I don't mind where I fuck you, as long as I'm inside you."

I dropped my towel and wrapped my hand around his erection. His eyes burned into mine and I fell to my knees. I'd given blowjobs before but it had always been to please the person on the receiving end. Right then, I *wanted* him in my mouth. There was a rush of liquid to my sex at the thought. I looked up at him from my knees and before my mouth had touched him, he groaned. I grasped the base of him and ran my tongue on the underside of his erection, from the very base of him right to the tip, my hand following, pulling on him. His eyes were wide with wonder when I closed mine, traced his head with my tongue and then took him deep in my mouth.

He hands thrust into my hair and I could tell he was trying to stop himself from pushing into me. I didn't want him to resist that urge. With him in my mouth

I moved both hands to the cheeks of his bottom and pushed, urging him to fuck my mouth. He growled as he went deeper and held my head tighter. I wanted him to take from me what he needed. It was the ultimate turn on that I could give him that. I sat back on my knees and he slowed. I placed my hands over his on my head, reassuring him that this was what I wanted. He was in control. He could have whatever he wanted from me. His thrusts started in earnest, pushing in and out of my mouth. My nipples tightened as I kept my eyes on his,

He angled himself right at the back of my throat and I gagged. The wetness between my thighs increased. I wanted him inside me.

He knew. He pulled his cock from my mouth and dragged me to my feet to my bed.

"You are so fucking sexy," he growled as I lay back on the mattress and he stood over me.

"Ethan." I was shaking with lust for him. I wanted to know why he wasn't inside me yet and then I heard the rustle of a condom wrapper. He crawled up my body and thrust into me. My head snapped back at the feel of him. As if he'd not been inside me half an hour ago. Like it was the first time I'd ever felt him fill me up. It was as if my body never quite got used to the size of him. I needed him close to me and I grabbed at him and pulled him against my body, wrapping my arms around his neck.

"You can't get enough, can you, beautiful?"

He was right. He'd created this insatiable woman who was drunk on lust for him and would do anything to have the man above her inside her. It scared me and thrilled me in equal measure. I didn't want to be so out of control.

He pulled his head back so he could see my answer. I shook my head slightly and he moaned and buried his face in my neck and sunk his teeth into my skin. A wave of pleasure washed over me and mixed with pain. The start of my orgasm began to fizz across my body.

My hands moved to his shoulders and I tried to push him away slightly.

"No," he said sharply. "You will come for me. You won't resist me anymore, Anna." He increased his thrusts, deeper, harder and a white light blinded me as I fell and fell and fell.

I lay boneless and limp, with Ethan collapsed on top of me, his breath on my neck slowing, starting to return to normal.

My hands trailed up and down his back. It felt amazing having him in my bed. In my city. But for how long? I didn't want to think about it.

Eventually he moved off me, went to the bathroom and emerged looking so hot it hurt. His hair was ruffled and his eyes bluer than before.

"I think you might have exhausted me. I didn't sleep at all last night," Ethan said as he dived under the duvet and beckoned me into the crook of his arm.

"Jetlag?" I asked.

"A bit, and seeing you and work. You're like a cure for jetlag and stress all mixed into one sexy little package." He kissed the top of my head. "Oh, can I stay? I just . . ."

I was pleased he couldn't see the smile twitching at the corners of my mouth. "I'd like that."

"So, what have you been up to since you left New York?" he asked.

"Keeping busy working long hours at the law firm you just took over."

"Merged with," he corrected me.

"Whatever."

"Disappointed I don't work construction?" he grinned at me.

"I never thought you worked construction, freak. Are you surprised that I'm a lawyer?"

He sucked in a deep breath. "Surprised that you were at Allen & Smith? Yes. Surprised you're smart and hardworking as well as sexy? No."

"I meant what I said about the rules. My job's important to me. If tonight is just tonight—with your non-dating policy or whatever—that's fine, but we need to be professional in the office until you go back to New York. I don't want any drama."

Ethan didn't respond, just continued to stroke my back. Was I being clingy or practical? No, I was definitely being practical. I wasn't asking him for a ring, just some boundaries. Working for the same firm complicated things.

"Look . . ." he started, clearly wanting to let me down gently.

"I'm not trying to pressure you."

He pulled me tighter. "I know. You're right, working together complicates things. You know we have a strict no-frat policy under the partnership agreement at Flanders, Case & Burling?"

"A what policy?"

"A rule that says the partners aren't allowed to fuck the staff."

"I'll let you into a little secret. You broke that rule. And you broke it good." I giggled and then stopped suddenly. He was telling me nothing was going to happen between us.

I tensed beside him and tried to shift away from his body but he pulled me closer.

"So, no bullshit," he said. I didn't know if it was a question or a statement. "This is complicated for a lot of reasons. Yes, technically I'm your superior. Technically there's a strict no-frat policy. And I've got a lot of shit to do while I'm over here."

"It's okay, Ethan. You don't owe me anything." I

tried to move away from him again but his arm clamped around me.

"Let me finish. I'm trying to tell you what I'm thinking and I don't do this with women often or well so you're gonna have to be patient with me." I stopped wriggling and his arm relaxed. "As you know, I don't date. I don't know how to date." I could feel myself tense again but I tried to keep relaxed and allow him to finish what he was saying. "But I'd like to spend time with you while I'm in London."

"Have you really never dated?" I asked.

"Anna, I don't bullshit. No, I've never dated."

"How come? I'm sure you've thought about it. You must have."

"All sorts of reasons I guess. Work has always come first. I've always been ambitious and that requires a certain focus that I've seen my friends lose because they've been dealing with relationship drama."

"Do you mean Andrew and Mandy?"

"Maybe. I meant my co-workers when I was more junior, but yes, Andrew to a certain extent. Ultimately, I've never met anyone that I've wanted to spend time with and I don't bullshit. I'm always very clear about the fact I'm not interested in a relationship and no one has made me want to change my rule on that. Not until, well you know, we had our week together."

My body warmed at his words. I wanted to hear more.

"And you've never felt like you wanted to try? You must have been under pressure to bring dates to parties. Isn't it easier to be in a relationship?"

"Is that a good reason to string someone along? So I have a date on hand when I need to go to an event?" he asked.

"I guess not but I think that's how a lot of relationships start."

"You might be right, but to me that's bullshit.. If you want to be with someone, be with someone. If you don't then don't. No ambiguity."

"When do you go back? Saturday?" I asked, satisfied with his explanation for now.

He turned his head sharply toward me. "No. I'm here three months."

My stomach flipped over and I sat up and hugged my knees to my chest. Three months. I could fall in love with this man in three months. This was more complicated than I expected.

Ethan stroked his hand down my back. "Hey. Come here."

I shifted out of bed and pulled on a T-shirt. I needed to think and I couldn't do that naked.

CHAPTER Five

Ethan

I hadn't thought this through. My dick had been the one doing the thinking so far. All it could concentrate on was getting inside her. And she felt so good. It started to stir again. There was no getting enough of her.

I stuck my hands behind my head, trying to come up with a solution. I wanted her. I'd wanted her in New York and I still wanted her in London. Fucking the staff did not go down well. The clause in the agreement had been used as a way of getting rid of low performing partners before. Although the ones that fucked their secretaries and still billed like champions seemed to get away with it. And I was bound to screw this up. I'd never dated anyone. It was new territory for me.

"Anna?" I thought she knew that I was going to be at Allen & Smith for a while. And to be honest, it kinda stung that when I gave her the news her reaction was to jump out of bed rather than straight onto my cock. She was chewing her thumb, which she did when she was thinking. Wasn't three months better than a week? Maybe not if she was getting back with her ex or had someone else she was dating. "Look, it's no big deal if you just want to keep it about work."

"No bullshit?" She spun round and looked at me. "You want to hear what I'm thinking?" That's exactly what I wanted. I nodded. "I think it's complicated for all the reasons you said. And I don't want to be fucking my boss, it doesn't feel right." Jesus, that was like a knife to my stomach. "But the idea of not fucking you feels worse." Okay, that was better. "And then . . . three months. This is new information."

She climbed back onto the bed, kneeling opposite me. "This is terrible and amazing."

"Terrible and amazing?" Jesus, I couldn't keep up.

"Well, yes," she said as if I'd missed an entirely obvious point. "Ethan, even after a week I missed you when I came back to London. How will I feel in three months when you go back to New York?" My pulse felt like it was going to jump straight out of my neck. This wasn't about another guy. This was about her wanting me. I was elated by her confession.

I pulled her toward me and she didn't resist.

"Seriously, maybe you shouldn't stay," she said.

"I'll go if you want me to go," I said.

"I don't want that. But . . ."

"But?"

"I don't want to get hurt," she whispered. "And I don't want to lose my job."

"You think I'll fire you if you don't put out?" I was half teasing but I wondered if she was genuinely worried.

"No, I'm not saying that. I'm just saying—it's complicated."

"I don't want to hurt you," I said.

"I believe you."

The next thing I knew, I was waking up to the morning light, Anna still asleep in my arms. It felt good. I reached across to look at my watch. Shit. I should be in the office already, it was 7.30 a.m.

It had been good to talk to her last night. It felt good to tell her what I was thinking and I could still punch the air at the fact she clearly wasn't seeing anyone. But we hadn't resolved the complications about the situation.

Unfortunately, we didn't have time for me to be inside her. I'd come to like morning sex. Having her fuzzy with sleep and working her up to a point where she was wide awake and screaming my name was the best feeling, but not this morning. I gently moved her off my chest and slid out of bed and into the shower.

She was still sleeping by the time I was ready to leave. I had a clean shirt in my office so I wasn't going to have to make a detour via my hotel, I could go straight to work, which was good because I was late already. I didn't want to wake her but I didn't want to leave without saying goodbye.

I sat on the bed next to her, watching her as her eyelids started to flutter. I stroked her cheek and her eyes opened.

"Hey," I said.

"Hey," she replied groggily. "What's the time?"

"Seven forty-five. I have to leave."

"I'm late." She sat up. "My alarm. I must have forgot to set it."

I smiled at her. She looked amazingly rumpled and sleepy. My dick started to harden so I stood up. I couldn't be distracted. I needed to leave.

"I need to go, beautiful." She nodded. "I'll see you at work."

"Okay," she said.

Should I suggest we see each other tonight? I didn't want her to feel pressured but I wanted to see her. We hadn't come to any conclusions last night. No rules had been established.

"I'll miss you," she whimpered. I felt that familiar stab in my stomach that only she could induce.

"Do you want to meet? Tonight? Talk more?" I asked. This was such new ground for me. I was used to knowing exactly what I wanted from the women in my life. The rules were clear. I took what I wanted and gave them what they wanted. It was clean and simple. This was anything but. I wanted her to be happy. I wanted to make her happy.

She nodded in response to my question and I couldn't help but grin. I leaned over her, trying to think about anything but her incredible naked body underneath the sheets. I swept her hair from her forehead and kissed her.

"Do me a favour," I said as I turned toward the door.

She sat up, leaning against her elbows. "Don't wear sexy underwear beneath your suit."

She giggled. "You won't know if I do or not."

"I'll know. I'll see you tonight. My number is in your phone." I looked back and she was grinning at me.

Anna

I really couldn't concentrate. Ethan being in London was completely bizarre. Sitting there with him and Richard talking about work was beyond weird. Richard was being a super suck up, hanging on every word that came out of Ethan's mouth. What a creep. But he was one step ahead of me because I wasn't listening to a word Ethan was saying. Seeing him in work mode, explaining the intricacies of a corporate structure, it was like I didn't know him at all. It was hot, but weird. Weird but I wanted him. My body was still sore from his fingers, his tongue, his hips and his cock, but I wanted him again. The blood was rushing in my ears, my nipples straining at the lace of my bra, wetness between my legs.

"Does that make sense, Anna?" Ethan asked,

looking at me, jolting me out of my head. He caught my expression and closed his eyes. "Richard, perhaps you could run with that and Anna can help me out with the Icarus file. Can you get something to me before you leave tonight?" Richard nodded and scurried out, leaving me sitting opposite Ethan. As soon as the door shut, Ethan looked at me. "Anna," he whispered.

I had no answer for him, I couldn't think about forming words, I couldn't think about anything but him. He moved around to my side of the conference table, so we were both facing the door. He took a seat beside me. "Anna," he repeated. I turned my head to his voice and the breath on my neck. I braced my hands against the table, trying to retain some control over the situation. His hand grasped my thigh. I gasped. This couldn't happen. He couldn't touch me in the office. His fingers found the hem of my skirt and trailed underneath, stopping suddenly when he found the top of my stocking. "Anna. I warned you about this."

I couldn't stop myself from moaning at his admonishment.

"Jesus woman, you'll have us both fired," he said as his fingers went higher and higher. I should make him stop but I couldn't move. I didn't want to move. He found the edge of my underwear and pushed his knuckle beneath. "Fuck, you're so wet." He slid back and forth across my slit and I collapsed forward, my elbows resting on the desk, my hands in my hair while his fingers worked across my pussy. "You're going to smell of come all day. A constant reminder of what I do to you," he whispered as he thrust two of his fingers into me. I tried to concentrate on not making a sound. I wanted to scream his name but I put every ounce of energy into keeping quiet.

"You look so fucking beautiful all the time, but especially now. With my fingers inside you, feeling your wetness. You like that, don't you?"

If I spoke to answer him I'd be lost and I'd start screaming for him to make me come.

"Anna," he cajoled.

I nodded.

"Beautiful girl." He thumb rounded my clitoris, hard and relentless. I was on the verge of trying to resist him, and remembered that he'd warned me about not doing that. It was an instinct, I wasn't sure where it came from. I didn't know if I'd ever done that with my previous boyfriends, but none of them had made me come as often or as hard as Ethan. Without a thought, I squeezed my thighs together and he roughly forced my knees apart. "I warned you about that, too. I decide when you come." Those words were all it took and I started to shudder and I snapped back, grabbing the arms of the chair, thrusting my hips in the air as I my orgasm spiraled through me. I don't know if it was the silence, the location or the fact we were so close to a thousand people, any of whom could have walked in at any moment, but it was more intense than I was used to.

As the pleasure subsided, panic took over. My eyes flew open and Ethan withdrew his hand, stood and walked across to his desk.

"Ethan." Horror flooded my quiet voice. What were we thinking?

"I know." He stopped me. "We need rules. You're right. Tonight. We'll talk about it tonight."

I started to gather up my notebook. My legs were wobbly and my hands were shaking. "I should go."

He nodded.

"What about the Icarus file?" I remembered him mentioning it to Richard before he left.

"There's no such thing. I just wanted you on your own. That look you give me sometimes, Anna . . . It drives me crazy. We're going to need some serious rules if we're going to be within a hundred feet of each other at work. He slumped in his desk chair.

"Do I look . . . er . . ."

"Like you've just come all over my hand?" He grinned as he finished my sentence for me. My cheeks were burning. "No, you look beautiful, but very professional."

I needed out of there and compose myself. "Ethan," I warned him. "Let's just keep out of each other's way until we speak later."

"Agreed."

"Oh, one last thing." I looked at him from over my shoulder. "No one makes me come like you do."

"Give me a break, beautiful, my balls are already blue." He groaned.

I grinned and left him at his desk with his hard on.

"You're in a better mood today," Lucy, one of the other associates, said as she sat on my desk. I'd been grinning to myself. "Did you get lucky?"

I scowled at her and she laughed. I tell you who I'd like to get lucky with. That guy from Flanders, Case & Burling, the tall, hot one, Ethan Scott.

I raised my eyebrows at her, worried if I said anything it would give something away.

"His eyes are so blue. Did you see that? I'm sure he could make me come just by looking at me."

"Lucy!" I hated that she was talking about him like that.

"And no wedding ring. Did you see?" she asked. "I bet he's after a bit of fun while he's in London. I'd be happy to be his fun for a few months." She winked at me.

Lucy was the office vixen and renowned for being a terrible lawyer. I wasn't sure how she still had a job. Probably because she flirted up a storm with all the male partners and was indiscriminate about it. Young, old, short, tall—it didn't bother her. I'm not sure that she had any control over it. It was her nature with men. It had never bothered me, until now. I couldn't bear the thought of Ethan being subjected to her come-ons.

"Lucy, I've got tons to get done. Get lost."

"But I wanted to pick your brain. You're working with him aren't you?" *Something like that.* "How do I get myself that gig?"

"I mean it, get lost."

"I take it back about your improved mood. You *need* to get lucky, sweetie."

Lucky was exactly what I got.

I rummaged through my bag for my phone and scrolled through to find Ethan. He'd filed himself under "Sex God" again. Of course he had.

I'm looking forward to seeing you this evening. It's good to have you in London.

He replied right away. *It's good to be here. I'm glad we found each other. See you tonight, beautiful.*

My stomach lurched.

CHAPTER Six

Ethan

I knocked on Anna's apartment door just after nine. It had been a long day and I was looking forward to seeing her. She relaxed me. When the door opened, I couldn't take my eyes of her.

"Hey," she said.

I didn't reply, I didn't want to waste a second. I walked toward her and without breaking stride, I grabbed her perfect ass and guided her backward into the hallway, at the same time, bringing the hem of her shirt up and over her head. All I could think about was being buried inside her and watching her as she came.

"Hey Anna, how was your day?" She was mocking me.

I ignored her and pulled down her jogging pants. She stood in her underwear, not helping but not hindering me either. Jesus she was beautiful. I tugged at my tie as she continued her conversation with herself. "It was great, thanks, Ethan. I got a lot done despite a number of office distractions. What about you? I had a good day too, Anna, thanks, I had a number of meetings—"

"Turn around and put your hands on the wall."

I interrupted her as I dropped my pants. Without a word, she did what I said and took position. I grabbed a condom out of my wallet. I was as hard as steel and I couldn't wait another minute. The curve of her back offering me that perfect lace-covered ass was all I could concentrate on. I moved her panties to one side and thrust straight into her.

"Fuck," she screamed. I pulled out and slammed into her again. My hands wanted to be on every part of her body at once—her hips, her tits, her pussy, in her hair, across her stomach. Jesus, I couldn't get enough. I throbbed inside her—I was going to come in about ten seconds.

"Harder, Ethan."

I pushed in again, relishing the feel of her around my cock. She was made for me. She grunted as I thrust in again and her fingernails pressed into the wall. I reached for her perfect tits. Her nipples puckered under my touch and I squeezed, perhaps too hard because her head snapped back onto my shoulder. There was too much of her to enjoy.

"You were so ready for me Anna. Have you been wet for me all day?" I whispered into her ear.

She nodded.

"Tell me, Anna."

"I've wanted you all day. I've been thinking about you inside me."

I couldn't hold anything back. The sound of my flesh meeting hers and the moans from her were all too much. The sight of her, the feel of her, the smell of her, the taste of her. She was everything. How could I have let her go back to London? How could I have not had her all these weeks? What had I been thinking?

She pushed back against me and I went deeper. I gripped her shoulder, riding in and out of her. She clenched around me, and her breath shortened. I slid my fingers around her hip and down to meet her clit. She bucked underneath me. I circled the nerves and the wetness around my cock increased.

"Yes. Just. Like. That," she breathed.

Her head dropped to between her arms as if she were defeated. She had given into me, into the pleasure of it all. She turned her head so her eyes met mine and she came with a look of vulnerability mixed with pure lust. That look ended me and I poured into her.

I stood still for a few seconds, catching my breath, her head resting on the wall in front of her. I pulled out of her and she whimpered as if my cock leaving her was the last thing she wanted. *Jesus*. She could corrupt the Pope. I picked her up and walked us into her bedroom. I lay her on the bed and quickly stripped off what was left of our clothes, then climbed under the covers with her, pulling her ass toward me.

I drew my arms around her waist and nestled my chin against her neck.

"Hey, how was your day?" I asked and she giggled.

"Oh, now you ask," she said, stroking my arm.

"Sorry, I just had to be inside you."

"I know. I like it."

"Like me being inside you?"

"Yes, and that you have to be, like nothing is going to stop you, you're going to take what you want."

"You make me sound like a Neanderthal."

"I like it," she said simply. "But that's why we need rules. And number one has got to be no orgasms in the office."

I chuckled into her neck. "You didn't like that?"

"Too much."

"I think it should be as little contact in the office as possible and certainly no physical contact. What about that?"

"Sounds awful but yes, I agree."

"What next?" I asked. She'd clearly given this a lot of thought. I didn't care what her rules were. I'd play any game she offered.

"We can't tell anyone at work. That frat thingy you were talking about and me not wanting to be the girl everyone thinks is sleeping her way to the top. It means we can't tell anyone at work, and I mean anyone."

"Okay."

"Okay? You don't agree?"

I liked that she could read the slight resistance in my words. "I do, but it's not ideal is it?"

"But—"

"I've said I agree. What's next?"

"That's as far as I got."

I pulled her legs between mine, "Do you want to come apartment hunting with me at the weekend, and then dinner at my sister's?"

She pursed her lips. "So, are we dating?"

I hadn't really put a label on it in my head. All I'd thought about was her, and how I wanted to spend time with her and get to fuck her while I was in London.

I shrugged. "I guess."

"Don't sound so enthusiastic." She prodded me in the thigh and I mock winced. "Okay, I have more rules," she continued.

I groaned and rolled to my back and she flipped over. "And then can I get a blow job?"

"If you're fucking me, you're not fucking anyone else."

"Babe, I've never even mentioned a threesome." That earned me a playful, tiny fist in my stomach but I caught her hand and drew it to my lips. "Beautiful, if I get to fuck you why would I want to fuck anyone else?"

"I'm serious," she whispered.

I pulled her closer to me. "So am I. You're gonna have to be patient with me. I've told you, I don't date so I'm not going to get this right all the time. But I don't play games and I'm not going to start bullshitting you.

If I'm with you, I'm with you and that's where it begins and ends."

I could see her trying to fight her smile. "So we're exclusive?"

"Oh my god, and you're one of our brightest associates? Fuck, we're toast." She gave into her grin this time. "Yes, we're exclusive. I don't want any guy coming near you."

Being inside her was going to fast become my favorite way to spend an evening. She was asleep, and lying in the nook of my arm like she was made especially for it. A sense of excitement washed over me about being in London. It was the job and a fresh challenge, but it was also being with her. She was as beautiful as I remembered, as funny, as wicked, as demanding but just as breakable. For the first time in my life, I was excited to be getting to spend more time with a woman.

Trying not to disturb her, I reached to the bedside table to get my phone, typing out a message to my sister

Me: Dinner on Saturday sounds good. Can I bring someone?

She texted straight back despite it being after 2a.m. That was what kids did to you.

Jessica: A girl?

Me: A woman.

Jessica: Is she a hooker?

Me: Be nice. You'll like her.

Jessica: Who are you and what have you done with my brother?

Me: I'll see you Saturday. Love you.

Jessica: I don't have ransom money, so you'll just have to keep him.

I put the phone down and grinned to myself.

Anna

We were spending the day looking at apartments. Ethan was still technically checked in at the hotel, but he'd spent every night this week with me. And I liked it. I really liked it. And I really, really liked the sex, which just seemed to get better and better, but I liked him. He made me laugh. He didn't take any of my shit, he was supremely self-confident and he seemed to like me. So far he wasn't playing any of the games I was used to. There was no pretending, no bullshit and it felt good. It felt right. It felt free.

Because I knew we only had three months, I wanted to squeeze every last drop out of our time together. I guess he felt the same, because he came 'round every night after work, without excuse or explanation. He'd even brought his laptop back last night and worked a little while we ate and before bed where he went back to work on my body.

I stood by the door, waiting for him so we could head off on our apartment hunting.

"Have you forgotten anything?" he hollered from the living room.

"Nope." I grinned.

He appeared in the doorway and took in my expression. "Are you laughing at me?" He bent his head and kissed me square on the lips.

"Maybe."

"You know, I can wipe that grin off your face in two seconds flat. Your little mouth will be all parted and panty in an instant if I let my fingers do this . . ." He reached down to cup my sex. Sure enough, my grin subsided and my underwear dampened. Part of me wanted to continue what he'd started, but we needed to go apartment hunting.

"Ethan, we need to go and I don't need to be smelling of sex while we look at these rentals."

Ethan shrugged and led us out. "This is only weekend two. We have ten more to go. Ten more when I'm going to keep you naked and tied to the bed all weekend. There will be no going out."

Had he started a countdown in his head already? Ten weekends to go? "Promises, promises," I managed to quip, disguising the clock that had just started ticking in my head.

"So if someone spots us together, what are we going

to say?" I asked as Ethan hailed a cab to take us to the first appointment.

"They won't"

"Famous last words. What if they do?"

"Then we'll deal with it when it happens, but this is a city of eight million people. Keep your panties on."

"You want me to keep my panties on? That's a one hundred and eighty degree turn for you. Am I boring you already?"

"As I said, naked and tied to the bed all next weekend."

Ethan had told me he'd changed the brief to the realtor, as he called the estate agent, and made sure that all the flats we were going to see today were close to mine. I explained to him that I was due to be moving, but he didn't seem to care. Part of me wondered whether he wanted me to offer to let him stay with me. Part of me wanted to. But I didn't suggest it and he didn't ask.

We were due to see four flats. All ten times bigger than any I'd been looking at. I'm sure any of them would be fine. Two were in the same block as each other so our hunting wasn't going to take too long. Ethan seemed enthusiastic about the day, perhaps my poky little flat was getting to him. His apartment on the Hudson was amazing and in a totally different league from my place.

We were a few minutes late to the first viewing and the realtor was waiting for us.

"I'm Marie, we spoke on the phone." She held out her hand to Ethan who shook it and then turned to me.

"This is my girlfriend, Anna."

Marie gripped my hand as my stomach clenched. Girlfriend? Fear gripped me. I didn't like the ambiguity that that word created between us. Girlfriend could mean so many things but for me it meant disappointment and heartache. I forced a toothless grin at Marie and stayed quiet.

Marie and Ethan's enthusiasm for flat hunting overshadowed any potential awkwardness that I might be projecting. The four flats were amazing and Ethan seemed to like all of them. I just nodded and smiled as he pointed out the great things about each flat.

He agreed with Marie that he'd give her his decision that afternoon. I exhaled as she left. When it was Ethan and me, everything was so much easier. I didn't need to think about a label for our relationship. I didn't need to think about the future. I could just concentrate on him.

"So, do you wanna go have lunch or go home and fuck?" he asked.

I laughed at his abruptness. "You can take the man out of New York but not New York out of the man," I replied.

"Home to fuck it is," he replied. He grabbed me and pulled me against him with one hand and held out his hand for a cab with the other.

We were within walking distance of my flat. I wasn't sure if he had his bearings or he didn't want to waste any more time with our clothes on.

"So, you look a bit brighter now that you're going to get your rocks off." He nudged me in the cab.

"Was I looking dull before?" I asked.

"You looked like you were going to puke there for a while when I called you my girlfriend. A man with a lessor ego could have been crushed."

I didn't know what to say in response. "I'm sorry. I was just surprised."

"But you didn't like it," he pressed.

"I struggle with the connotations the word brings with it."

"Hmmm," was the only reply I got.

"Anyway, I think you're just trying to get a rise out of me. You've avoided having a girlfriend for like ever."

"I'm not trying to avoid anything. I think you need to ask yourself if you are," he said and looked at me with something in his eyes that I couldn't quite name. I leaned forward and pulled down the window of the cab, trying to find more air just as we arrived back at my flat. I jumped out and tried to pay the driver, but Ethan was already handing over cash inside the cab.

We moved silently into my building, the tension bristling between us. I wished that what he was thinking would play out in subtitles above his head.

When we got inside the flat I went to the kitchen and switched on the kettle. I half thought that he'd grab me and we'd be fucking this tension away as soon as we got inside, but Ethan headed straight to the living room. I shifted from leg to leg as I tried to unscramble what I was thinking at the same time as speculating on what was going through Ethan's head. We had a few hours before we had to leave for dinner at Ethan's sister's. We had time.

Ethan was hovering in the living room, looking out the window when I brought in coffees for both of us. "Thanks, but I think I'm going to head back to the hotel and call the realtor," he said. My heart tightened. I didn't want him to go. I didn't want to have caused this.

"I thought we were going to fuck?" I said, trying to lighten the mood.

"Jesus, really? You're going to pretend this all about sex?" he asked, still looking out of the window with his back to me and reaching into his pocket and retrieving his keys. I'd not seen this side of him before. Normally, nothing ruffled him. He was always calm and in control.

"Ethan," I said and walked toward him. I went to stroke his arm and he pulled away from me. Anxiety swept through me. Had I upset him? Did I have the power to upset him? I hated this feeling. "Ethan, please. I don't want you to go."

"I don't know if I can do this with you Anna, I can't

handle it when you keep things from me." he said simply, still not looking at me.

My heart squeezed tighter and I struggled to breathe. I nodded but he couldn't see. I was trying to be calm, but inside I felt anything but. What could I say to make him stay? Maybe it would be better this way. Easier at work, anyway. The thought of seeing him in the office but knowing that we would be nothing to each other made my stomach clench and I clasped my fingers of one hand in the other and twisted, hoping to displace the pain.

"I understand. It's complicated," I said, trying to keep my voice steady but I failed and I managed an unattractive half-breath, half-sob at the end of the sentence. It didn't go unmissed by Ethan and he turned to look at me.

"What is it?" he asked. "You're upset? What's wrong?"

I shrugged my shoulders and a tear escaped.

"Anna. Would you just talk to me? I'm not a mind reader. I don't know what you're thinking. You want to be exclusive but you get freaked out by me introducing you as my girlfriend. What's that? And you're distant in the cab and then all about the sex when we come up here? What's going on?"

"I'm trying," I choked out. "Just because I've had boyfriends before doesn't mean I'm good at it."

I turned away from him and covered my face with my hands. How did I feel this upset about him leaving me? What happened to the promise I'd made to myself that men were only going to be about fun from now on?

"Then be honest with me. I can't deal with the bullshit."

"I'm not bullshitting you."

"But you're not being honest."

"I'm scared," I bit out.

"Of me? Of being honest?"

I could feel him moving closer to me. I nodded but didn't look up at him. He pulled my hands from my face and his head dipped as he tried to look me in the eye.

"Anna, talk to me. What are you scared of?"

It was like he'd uncorked a bottle of something fizzy and everything just spilled out. "I'm scared this, us, is more than sex. I'm scared that I *want* this to be more than sex. I'm scared of you leaving and I'm scared of you staying. I'm scared of how I feel about this, you. It's just complicated and this wasn't supposed to be complicated. You could hurt me, Ethan. Already, you could really hurt me."

I kept my eyes away from his, worried at what I would see if I looked. He just pulled me toward him and held me tight. "I know," he whispered in my hair.

CHAPTER
Seven

Ethan

Her reaction to me calling her my girlfriend fucking hurt. I knew it shouldn't but for the first time in my life, I wanted to be able to call someone my girlfriend and she practically fucking winced when I'd said it. I tried to not let it bother me, but it did. It really fucking bothered me.

I didn't follow what happened next. Her moods seemed to zigzag, throwing me off the scent every time I thought I'd caught up. She seemed to be quiet, angry and sad all within a sixty-second window

I'd managed to get her to open up a bit but I was in new territory. Other than my sister, I'd never had to comfort any woman who was upset.

I stood with her wrapped in my arms and wondered what I should say next. Fuck.

"Beautiful, how do we make this less complicated? How do *I* make this less complicated? I hate to see you sad." Did she know what she wanted and was just too afraid to tell me?

She made sounds against my chest but I'm pretty sure none of them were actual words. Jesus, she was usually so feisty, this sad side of her was one I'd never seen. How many did she have?

"What are you thinking? No bullshit," she asked.

Shit.

"I'm thinking about you," I replied, hoping that would placate her.

"What about me? That I'm some kind of crazy emotional person?"

"Maybe."

She laughed against my chest and I felt so fucking relieved. I didn't want her back in angry mode again.

"Sorry, I just, it's just—"

I kept hold of her. "I don't want you to be upset. I don't want you to be frightened. I don't want to hurt you. Ever. I want us to hang out, have hot sex, be together, be happy."

"I want that, too," she said quietly. "But what happens when you go back?"

I hadn't thought about what would happen in three months. I didn't even spend the night with the women I fucked, so every day with Anna felt different and special—like an adventure. I didn't know what the road I was on held. "I don't have all the answers. You might hate me in three months. All I know is that I'd rather spend this time with you and risk a broken heart than walk away. But if you don't want to take that risk then—"

She pulled away and looked at me, smiling softly. "Oh my god, you're perfect. And I do want to do all those things. I just know I won't hate you in three months." She put her head back on my chest.

"I'm anything but perfect, Miss Anna."

"Please don't break my heart," she whispered.

I had a feeling that she might be the first girl capable of breaking mine but the thought didn't scare me. I wanted to be with her more than I wanted to protect myself. I needed her to feel the same. I squeezed her close. I wanted to take all the doubt and worry away from her.

We stood there for what seemed like hours, just holding each other, not wanting to be the first one to let go.

Her phone going off finally separated us.

"Hey, Leah."

I scrubbed my face with my hands. This relationship stuff was—Anna caught my eye as she talked into her phone. She was grinning at me. She was so fucking hot, despite the mood swings. This relationship stuff was so totally worth it.

"Okay, I'll ask him. I have no idea. Er, when you hang up."

I slumped on the sofa and when she hung up she came over and straddled me.

"Leah invited us over for dinner on Tuesday," she explained.

"Great," I replied

"You want to go?" she asked

"Of course." I was looking forward to getting to see

inside her life in London. Leah had seemed nice when I'd met her in New York and Armitage sounded like a decent guy.

She took my face in her hands.

"Are we good?" she asked.

I flipped her to her back onto the sofa and her hands slid to my neck. "We're very good." I kissed her neck and she lifted her chin to give me better access. I loved the feeling of her fingers in my hair. Somehow it seemed so intimate, I was Samson to her Delilah—I knew she could ruin me in the way she thought I could ruin her.

"Shall I cancel dinner at my sister's?"

"No, why?"

"Well, we could stay home and do this all night," I replied as I sucked on the flesh just below her collarbone.

"You're going to leave a mark," she said.

"I hope so." I moved to the other side of her neck. I liked the idea of people being able to see my lips on her.

"Do you really want to cancel?" she asked.

"Yes, but it's not worth the grief I'd get from her. Do you mind?"

"No. I'm interested to meet her."

"Izzy is more interesting."

"Izzy?"

"My niece. She's adorable. She doesn't get it from my sister, that's for certain."

"Be nice."

"You haven't met her. She's a terror."

"I'm sure she just tries to keep your bad behavior in check."

"Great, talking about my sister has meant my hard-on has packed up and left, so we might as well go to dinner." I dragged myself off her and pulled her up so she was sitting.

"I thought you said we were due there at seven."

I nodded.

"We have time," she said as her hand brushed against my denim covered dick and she looked up coyly at me. "Can I see if I can convince your hard-on to stick around? You've not been inside me since this morning and I can't wait until bedtime." Her eyes were glazed and her voice was breathy. Women before her had said things to me to try and please me, because they thought they should. With Anna it sounded like she couldn't *not* say it. That what was in her head just trickled out and turned me on. I could feel the blood rushing to my dick already.

Despite an excellent blowjob and burying myself in her for what seemed like hours, my hard-on seemed to be permanent around her. I wasn't sure if it was the backless top that she was wearing, her heels or just that smile.

"Are you okay?" she asked as we pulled up outside my sister's place.

I grinned in response. "Are you okay?"

"Yeah. I'm ready for inspection."

I suppose she was going to be under a bit of scrutiny from Jessica. Was that part of what had freaked her out earlier? I was just coming to see my sister and didn't want to spend the evening without her. I'd not thought that this was an event. She was meeting my family.

"Just so you know, I don't give a shit about my sister's opinion about anything."

She playfully whacked me with her handbag as she got out of the cab. "Don't say that, it's not nice."

"I just mean this isn't a test. It's dinner."

"Stop worrying about me. You'll be the next to have a meltdown. I'm looking forward to it."

"So we're living in the moment?"

She stopped just before the gate and grinned at me. I couldn't help but grin back.

"Kiss me," she said.

I bent over to peck her on the lips and she wrapped her arms around me. She delved into my mouth with her tongue, pushing it passionately against mine. I slid my hands across her naked back, pulling her against me. Her perfect tits crushed against my chest. Fuck, she wasn't wearing a bra.

Abruptly, she pulled away. "Living in the moment.

Especially moments like that. Tell your hard-on he's off duty for a couple of hours." She grinned and I grabbed her hand and set off up the path to my sister's front door.

"You're cruel." I huffed.

"You've got the sexual appetite of a nineteen-year-old boy."

"And you're the Virgin Mary?"

"I'm thinking that you give me the appetite of a nineteen-year-old boy, too."

"Let's just go home," I whined. The last thing I wanted to do now was spend the evening with my sister. Anna stepped forward and pressed the buzzer and before I could suggest we make a run for it, shadows appeared through the frosted glass.

James threw the door open. "The women in this house are not in a good place."

"Fuck off, James," Jessica shouted from upstairs and Izzy started to wail. "Now look what you've done."

"Welcome to the happiest place on earth," James said and moved sideways so we could go inside.

"This is Anna." I deliberately did not drop the word "girlfriend".

Anna and James greeted each other and I wondered if Anna was feeling awkward. My sister screaming down the stairs wasn't the friendliest of greetings. But Anna was smiling and she seemed relaxed.

"Jessica is just trying to settle Izzy, as you can hear.

She'll be down in a minute. And then once she's downed a glass of merlot, she'll almost be human."

"I heard that." Jessica trilled as she came into the kitchen where we were gathered, James pouring us drinks. "You'd better pour me two glasses."

"Izzy down?" I asked.

"Hey, Bond. Yes, for how long, who knows?"

"Bond?" Anna asked.

"Jessica, this is my—this is Anna."

Anna turned to look at me, grinned and then turned to Jessica. "I'm Ethan's girlfriend, nice to meet you."

My heart jumped in my chest and a dull ache drummed in my stomach. As I pulled my eyes from Anna to Jessica, Jessica was looking at me as if she was waiting for me to say something. I tried to pull down the corners of my mouth but it wasn't working. She was my girlfriend and I was very fucking happy about it. I grabbed her hip and pulled her toward me.

"Well, wonders will never cease. Izzy's asleep and Bond has a girlfriend. Fuck me."

"Don't swear," James said.

"Izzy's fucking upstairs. She can't fucking hear us."

"We're trying not to swear in front of her," James explained.

I nodded, not wanting to get involved. Jessica needed her Merlot.

"So what's with calling you Bond?" Anna asked. I groaned.

"Oh this is going to be interesting. I can tell you all Ethan's embarrassing stories." Jessica was practically gleeful and I rolled my eyes at her.

"Jessica's disastrous teenage dating years can trump anything she's got on me. Bring it on," I replied.

Jessica laughed. "This is going to be fun."

Anna

Ethan's sister was pretty. Beautiful even. I suppose that should be no surprise given Ethan's god-like features. You could definitely see the resemblance. What was more interesting to me was the relationship he had with her. It was playful and teasing and sweet. Being with them reminded me of being in the Hamptons, he was relaxed and happy—Ethan's life was full of good people who loved him. Happy couples living happy lives. I wondered why he'd not dated before—didn't he want that too?

"I bet you still have all the books out, like you're trying to intellectualize a boyhood obsession," Jessica taunted him. Jessica had explained all about Ethan's James Bond obsession. There were worse obsessions to have.

"They're valuable. First editions," he replied looking slightly wounded. "At least it's more intellectual than the Boys II Men obsession you had."

"Yeah, but I don't still have my Boys II Men posters

on my wall. They came down when I started dating for real. Although I should have left them up. Rock star fantasies are so much better than the reality of dating grabby teenage boys."

"Or dating any aged men. It's not just teenage boys that are grabby," I said, forgetting my filter. "Present company excepted, of course." I cringed and Jessica laughed.

"You're probably right. The last date I went on before I met James not only made me pay for dinner but spent the night texting an ex-girlfriend, which he excused by saying she was upset over a break-up."

I nodded. "I went on a date once and came out of the loo at our restaurant to find him taking the number of the waitress."

"Jesus." Ethan recoiled.

"And in college my long-time boyfriend ended up cheating on me with my best friend. Same thing happened to Leah before she met Daniel. I'm a shit magnet, what can I say."

"So what does that make me?" Ethan asked.

"Hmmm, a knight on a white horse, his colors flying?" I grinned at him and he grinned back.

"OMG, are you quoting Pretty Woman?" Jessica asked, grinning at me expectantly.

I nodded. "I hear you're a fan of the film, too?"

"I love it. Seen it a million times. I used to make Ethan watch it over and over."

"It paid off," I said. "Did he tell you what he did in New York?"

"Holy hell, Anna, you're not telling that story." Ethan groaned. "I think I preferred the ex-boyfriend talk."

"You have to tell me now," Jessica squealed.

"No, Anna. Jessica doesn't want to hear about what her brother does naked," Ethan interjected.

"That's true," Jessica said. "No sex stories. Not ever. Well, not about my brother anyway. If they're about a sexy man I'm not related to, then dish! I've completely run out of my own stories and I need to live vicariously!"

"I don't want to hear about you naked either, for Christ's sake." Ethan rolled his eyes.

"Okay, more ex stories—my most recent ex owed money to someone he shouldn't and they ended up breaking into my flat to scare me."

Ethan pushed his chair away from the table, the legs, scraping across the tiled floor. "Are you fucking serious?" I looked at him and his face was dark, his eyes boring into me. I was stunted by his reaction, and I didn't have time to answer him. "The flat you're in now?"

"Ethan." I reached across to him, taking his hand in mine. "I'm selling it, you know I am, and the police are involved."

"How could you not tell me?" He was scouring my face, as if looking for more information.

"It hasn't come up. And there's nothing to tell."

"You're not staying there," he growled.

"Ethan, I've stayed there since, it was months ago, and you've been there with me recently." I grabbed his hand, trying to reassure him.

"You're not staying there on your own again," he said, calmer but still resolute.

"Okay," I said, meaning it. I liked that he cared enough to want to protect me. It felt nice. It felt safe. He smiled at me and squeezed my hand.

"Wow," Jessica said and we both snapped our heads 'round to her voice at the same time.

"What?" Ethan asked.

She shrugged and started to clear the plates from the table. I stood up but Ethan pulled me back down, not letting go of my hand.

"Let me help," I said, trying to get up again. Ethan pulled me and my chair toward him with one hand, his other not leaving mine.

"You two sit here. James and I will get this," Jessica said.

I leaned my head on Ethan's shoulder. "Do you work with him?" he asked after a few beats.

"No, god no. He wasn't . . . just no."

"Do you still see him?"

I shook my head. "No, not at all."

"Talk to him?"

"No, Ethan. Please. We can talk when we get home,

but drop it while we're here." I smiled at him stiffly, aware Jessica and James would be back any minute.

"I don't like it," he snapped.

"Clearly."

James came back in with two bottles of wine. "I thought we might need extra supplies. I say, if in doubt, get pissed."

"It's the only thing we have in common anymore," Jessica said as she came in with a tray of chocolate mousse. "Getting wasted to block out reality."

"I hear it's the only way to deal with children," I said.

"Absolutely," James and Jessica chorused and then laughed.

I smiled and turned to look at Ethan who was staring at me as if he'd not heard any of the interaction. I squeezed his hand and he blinked and looked away.

"What is this crap you're drinking?" He grinned and threw back a glass of whatever it was, clearly not too concerned.

"So, what do you do?" Jessica asked me.

"Oh, I'm a lawyer. I work at the firm that Ethan's firm just took over."

Jessica looked at her brother and then back at me. "So, you met working together? Is that allowed?"

"We met in New York, in the summer. It was coincidence that we work together. We didn't know," Ethan said.

It was clear, Ethan hadn't said much to his sister about me.

"So you didn't come to London to spend time with your sister and niece. Typical." Jessica was obviously joking.

"No, I came to do a job. I didn't know where Anna worked until we bumped into each other at work."

"Oh, wow," she said. "That sounds kinda romantic."

"It is what it is." Ethan sat back in his chair, his hand still not releasing mine.

"So, when are you going back to work?" Ethan asked. "Jessica's a dentist. She'll make a fortune in this country."

I elbowed him in the ribs.

"Yeah, I'm going to see a few practices next week actually. I'm a bit scared about going back. I've probably forgotten everything. It's been over a year."

"Hey, you're great at your job. You won't have forgotten anything." Ethan turned to me. "Jessica is as smart as a whip. Top of her class."

It was cute to see him so proud of her. I grinned. "I'm sure it runs in the family. What do your parents do?" I asked.

"Dad is a dentist, too. Mom stays at home. They have the perfect life. Did you hear about Uncle Alec?" Jessica asked Ethan.

Ethan nodded. "I spoke to mom yesterday."

I excused myself to pop to the restroom while they caught up on family stuff. This was a new Ethan. Family Ethan. Loyal, proud. It was nice. But I didn't need a reason to like him more.

CHAPTER
Eight

Ethan

I was mad. She'd finally told me about the ex. But despite me asking a number of times in New York and her refusing to discuss him, she casually tells my sister everything at dinner. And he turns out to be a total prick and she's not safe in her own home. I'm mad at her, I'm mad at her ex and I'm mad at myself for not getting this information out of her sooner.

I'd managed to push it to one side during dinner but after leaving my sister's it crept back into my head and I couldn't stop thinking about it.

We were in a cab, going back to her apartment, but there was no way we were staying there. I wasn't fucking her in that bed, where she'd fucked other men, especially men who didn't deserve her. Jesus, the thought made me want to punch something.

"You're quiet," she said. I'd not said anything since we'd left Jessica and James's.

Her hand was in mine, as it had been for most of the night, and I squeezed. Trying to give her reassurance of something. I wasn't sure what.

"I'm sorry I didn't tell you about Ben. I know you've asked me."

"Don't say his name to me," I said, staring straight ahead.

"I didn't bullshit you," she said finally. She was right, technically she hadn't lied but I hated that there was so much of her I didn't know. She was mine and I wanted to know everything.

When we pulled up outside her apartment, I could tell she was wondering if I was going to come in. As if I would leave her. She wasn't spending another night in that apartment, certainly not alone.

She tried to let go of my hand as I paid the driver but I wouldn't let her. We made our way into the apartment. "I need you to pack a bag. We're staying at my hotel tonight," I said, still not looking at her.

"Ethan—"

"Don't argue with me. Not about this."

She didn't. I released her hand and she made her way around the apartment gathering her things. I stayed by the front door, waiting.

I felt better when we were out of her place and back in another cab. But not good enough to be able to have a conversation with her. I was concerned I'd lose it. I wasn't used to dealing with shit like this. She hadn't done anything wrong but I was still angry at her for not telling me. And for dating other people before me. It was irrational but it was how I felt. I was angry at myself, that I'd not met her before this prick Ben, before all the other guys she dated.

When we arrived at the hotel, I picked up my messages at the desk and led Anna to the elevator bank, wheeling her suitcase behind us. She'd packed a decent amount, which was a good thing because she wasn't going back there.

"When does your apartment sale go through?" I asked as the elevator doors opened.

"The week after next."

I nodded. "Which apartment that we saw today did you like?"

"They were all amazing."

"Which one do you prefer?"

"It's not for me."

"Anna."

"The second one."

I nodded. "Okay, I'll speak to the realtor. It's empty so we should be able to move in quickly. We'll stay here until then."

"Ethan—"

"Not a fucking word, Anna."

"I don't get to speak?"

"Not yet."

"Then when?"

"When I've fucked you so hard you've forgotten what you wanted to say."

She didn't respond and as we entered the hotel room, the door slammed behind us. I set her suitcase down and walked across the living area to the bed.

"Come here," I said, trying to disguise the anger I felt. It was anger mixed with lust. I couldn't look at her as I undid her shirt and peeled it from her shoulders. I concentrated on her soft, smooth skin. I wanted to mark it and I tipped her head to one side and attached my lips to her neck. I sucked hard. There would definitely be a mark and the thought increased my need for her and took the edge off my anger. She made no complaint, just held herself steady against my shoulders. I moved to the other side and did the same.

"Take the rest of your clothes off," I ordered as I started to undress myself.

Silently, she complied. I could feel her looking at me, trying to catch my eye. I wasn't ready to face what I'd see there.

Naked, I knelt before her. I could smell her perfect pussy right in front of me. I grabbed her bottom and her hands went to my hair. I pushed my tongue against her. She was soaked and I couldn't hold back a groan. Fuck, she was delicious. I always loved going down on women. With most of them it was because it unravelled them to a point they'd do anything I cared to suggest. With Anna, it was the clouded look in her eyes that did it for me. The way she seemed to go to a slightly different place. She started to throb against my tongue almost immediately. She was so ready. One hand pushed her perfect ass against me, and I used the other to trace the wetness across her folds, then pushed my fingers into her and she tightened around me. Jesus, my cock started to pulse at the thought that it would soon replace my fingers. Her breath became shorter. She wouldn't last long but I wasn't going to make it that easy for her.

"Ethan," she mewed.

I pulled away from her, refusing to give her release against my tongue. That's not how it was going to happen. She wasn't going to be rewarded so easily. I stood up and lifted her roughly onto the bed.

"Turn around," I barked and she flipped over onto her stomach.

Kneeling behind her, I pushed her knees under her, raising that perfect ass of hers, ready for me while her face and chest remained flat to the mattress. I moved off the bed to get a condom and a better view.

"Stay still," I said as she went to push her chest off the bed. Again she complied without argument. This is what I needed. I needed her to show me that I was the man she wanted. That she would do whatever I asked of her.

Anna

I'd never experienced the Ethan that I'd seen today. He seemed on the verge of losing control. Maybe it shouldn't have been, but it was hot.

I felt a breeze over my sex as I lay there, exposed, my ass in the air. I knew he was looking at me, watching me ready for him. I had to stifle a moan at the thought. He'd brought me to the brink with his tongue and then stopped. I wanted to scream at him in frustration but I also wanted to give him what he wanted, what he seemed to need. He was trying to deal with his frustration by punishing me. Maybe I shouldn't have been, but I was okay with that. I wanted to give him everything.

His large hands covered my ass and the bed dipped behind me. I stayed still. I knew I shouldn't break position. I was his to do with what he wanted.

He ran a finger from my clit to my ass and I bit down on the comforter to stop from showing my pleasure.

"I can feel you, so ready for me, Anna. But this isn't about your pleasure." He growled and then thrust into me and pulled out straight away.

My heart was pounding and all I could focus on was him. His voice felt like it was coming from inside me, as if I were a part of him and him a part of me. He thrust again and my hands gripped the bedcovers.

"You feel this?" he asked, pushing in to me again and then starting a relentless rhythm. "You feel what my dick can do to you?"

I gasped in response.

"No one can do this to you, can they Anna? No one fucks you like I do?"

"No. No one." I gulped.

"You can't help yourself can you? You come so easily

with my dick inside you. But not yet. I'm not going to let you come yet, do you hear me?"

His words sent sweet sensations to my clit and I knew that with a few more of his punishing strokes my orgasm would overtake me.

"Answer me," he growled.

"Ethan, I'm . . ." I was close and I couldn't stop, it was like a freight train hurtling toward me. And then he was gone. He was no longer inside me and his hands had left my hips. A small whimper escaped me along with my orgasm.

I collapsed flat on my front as Ethan went into the bathroom.

Shit, he was really pissed at me. A loud bang came from the behind the door and I scrabbled to my feet and across the room, poking my head around the door.

Ethan was sitting on the edge of the bath, his head in his hands, his knuckles scrapped.

I knelt in front of him, placing my hands on his thighs. "I'm sorry," I said softly.

He didn't look at me. "You're angry because I kept something important from you. And although I didn't lie, I should have told you when you asked me and I'm sorry."

"It's more than that," he replied.

My heart lurched. What was he going to say? That he couldn't get past it? A fleeting thought of him leaving filled me with dread.

"Tell me." It was all I could manage.

"I hate the thought of you with someone else. Anyone else."

It wasn't what I was expecting and my dread gave way to warmth.

"I'm not with anyone else. I'm not sure I ever have been." Ethan was different. I knew that, right at that moment.

His eyes lifted to mine, as if trying to see more of me. I wanted him to see inside me. I meant what I'd said to Ethan. Men before him were irrelevant to me. Time before him was irrelevant to me.

He traced a thumb across my cheek. "This is difficult, I feel like I'm fucking this up."

Too difficult? "I only want you, Ethan. I've only ever been looking for you and you're not going to mess this up—I won't let you. And you've got to stop me from messing this up, too."

He looked pained and his hands dropped to my shoulders. I took one of his hands in mine and kissed the knuckle.

"What did you do?" I whispered.

"It's fine," he said.

"Don't go punching walls. Talk to me. As much as you want me to communicate to you, it's got to work both ways. We're still getting to understand each other, it's going to be lumpy but you were right when you said that talking things out is the way through the bumps."

He nodded. I stood up and held out my hand for him to take it. Instead he pulled me toward him and wrapped his arms around my waist and leaned his head on my chest. I kissed him on the head and pushed my fingers through his hair.

We stayed there for long minutes, things settling between us. We had revealed new and hidden parts of ourselves today. Not deliberately, but fundamentally. We lay exposed and vulnerable. As if we had just climbed to the summit of a mountain, it felt like we needed time to recover and recuperate before we got up and enjoyed the view.

Eventually Ethan stood and led me back to bed and we lay our limbs intertwined and our bodies as close as they could be, reassuring ourselves and each other.

Ethan kissed the top of my head. "I'm sorry for overreacting," he said.

"You have nothing to be sorry for."

"I do. I underestimated you, me, us. I tried to punish you."

"Ethan, you fucking me will never be a punishment. It's all pleasure."

He pulled me closer. "Are we okay?"

"We're more than okay."

"Can I fuck you properly now?" he grinned at me and I laughed at him.

"Anytime baby."

Before the words were out of my mouth he had my body pinned to the mattress with his hips, his hard-on pressed against my thigh, his lips on my neck.

"I've left a mark," he said.

"Always," I replied, my hands trailing down his back.

He brought his head up to look at me. "I'm serious, Anna. Your neck."

"It's fine. I like it."

"You like it?" He cocked his eyebrow at me.

"I do. It says that I belong to you."

"Jesus, you're making me hard."

"And I like that as well," I said as he started to rub himself up and down my thigh, getting higher and closer.

"You do?"

I nodded. He nudged at my entrance and I brought my legs up around his hips.

"You're insatiable," he said, trailing his cock up to my clitoris. I arched against him.

"Only for you," I whispered.

I grabbed a condom from the bedside table and he quickly sheathed his erection.

He plunged into me and stilled, filling me body and mind. He pressed himself close to me, his forehead against mine, and moved slowly, pressing deeper and deeper. His weight on me made me feel safe and protected, his hands under my shoulders were pushing me toward him. The heat and sweat built between us, intermingling.

"Anna," he breathed into my mouth and I dug my heels into his bottom, urging him closer to me. I thought it couldn't get better between us but this was different, closer, more intimate. I reached for his face and trailed across my fingers his cheekbones.

"Ethan," I whispered back.

It washed over me. Love. I loved him. All of a sudden, I was clear—all the emotions of the day had coming crashing down because I was trying to squash what we had together—what I felt for him. I was in love with this man. The beautiful man that was above me, inside me. "Ethan." I didn't say what my whole body felt. Today had been complicated enough. There would be time.

I brushed my lips against his and squeezed my muscles around him and he groaned. I loved to hear what my body could do to him—it was such a turn on. My nipples hardened against his chest, dragging across his skin as he shifted above me. His pace quickened but his movements were still small and intense. His muscles clenched as if her were putting every ounce of his energy into his small movements.

He circled his hips slightly and my moan caught in my throat. He watched me as I held my breath. He thrust again and again, reaching farther and farther inside and then we were both there. Right at the same time, in that white light, together, watching each other.

His body was rigid for a few long seconds and then he

collapsed onto me, his head against my neck—panting, licking, sucking.

"Fuck, beautiful," he growled breathlessly.

My breathing slowed "Hmmm" was all I could manage and I trailed my fingertips up and down his spine. I wanted him to stay on top of me like that forever.

CHAPTER
Nine

Anna

After that, things were still complicated but easier. Our relationship was everything it should be. What was between us was more than just a summer fling or a holiday romance—our hearts were open to each other.

My flat sold but I only went back with Ethan to pack things up. I didn't stay there again. I moved some of my things to Ethan's rented apartment and the rest I put in storage.

I should have started looking for a new place but that meant thinking about the future and what I wanted to do. I'd agreed with Ethan that for the first time ever, I was going to live in the present. I wasn't going to worry about the future. In the present Ethan was in London and that's exactly where I wanted to be. I didn't want to fast forward this relationship—the thought of him meeting my parents, or us moving in together properly, the thought of him as a father, us married—all that stuff that I used to think about with previous boyfriends, I couldn't let myself think about with Ethan. All that mattered was the here and now.

I managed to extract myself from working directly for Ethan, claiming I was too busy with another client's work and my excuse wasn't questioned. There were plenty of people lining up to take my place, wanting to impress the New York office. It was easier like that. I could separate work Ethan from my Ethan. Well, most of the time I could separate them. Every now and then we would pass each other in the corridor and our eyes would slam together and my underwear dampened and I knew he would be fighting a hard-on.

Our sexual attraction to each other didn't dip, not even for a second. He was inside me every chance he got and he was right when he said I was insatiable. I couldn't get enough of him. My body ached for him in the evenings while I waited for him to emerge from the office. Ethan worked hard, too hard. He always worked later than I did. He came home, it felt like our home, exhausted and stressed and I would pour him a whiskey, which we inevitably ended up sharing and then he would have me. My body was his. I would often be shuddering with anticipation by the time we were naked, as if his body was something I got to experience rarely, rather than every day, several times a day. Each time was better than the last as we fell deeper and deeper into each other.

Friday evening Ethan and I left at a similar time, earlier than the rest of the week, wanting to extend our weekend together to as long as possible. Even when we did leave the office at similar times, we never left together. No one at work knew we were together—it was against the rules. The other associates speculated about Ethan's love life and there were various rumors about an American girlfriend or a British gay lover. I listened, unconcerned. I was pleased they didn't know Ethan. I wanted to keep him for myself.

As I let myself into the flat, Ethan stood facing away from me, staring out the window, his forehead pressed against the glass. He turned as I closed the door and smiled at me. A tired smile, but a smile nonetheless.

Ethan

"Hey, beautiful." How did she manage to look so fucking amazing all the time? My cock stirred just at the sight of her. It had never occurred to me that I could remain physically attracted to a woman for this long. And the sex between us only got better. She seemed to know my body so exactly, she knew when to squeeze, bite, moan and beg for maximum impact. All these weeks later, I still had to concentrate on not getting a hard-on when I saw her in the corridors at work. Especially when she shot me that look. The look that made me feel like I really was her god. Fuck.

"Hey, my gorgeous man,"

I needed her right now. I needed her body to soothe my mind. Work was a bitch at the moment and it wasn't getting easier. Trying to manage the London politics and hold on to my US clients meant I was working long hours. Anna hadn't said anything but I wondered if she got pissed off at the lack of time I could spend with her, especially during the week. I bet her previous boyfriends had more time for her.

"Whiskey?" she asked.

I nodded and followed her to the kitchen.

"You look fucking amazing . . . but you know that." My eyes trailed over her perfect ass, covered by the tight red fabric of her dress.

"I don't know that. I'm glad you think so."

I stood behind her, wrapped my arms around her waist and buried my head into her neck as she fixed two whiskeys.

"Do we have plans this weekend, other than for me to make you come over and over and over?" I asked.

"I like that plan." She relaxed her body into me my dick pressing against her. How long would I have to wait before I was inside her? "I guess I should really arrange some property viewings."

That was the last thing I wanted to do—schlep around London, looking at her future without me. Fuck that. I had hoped she would consider coming back to New York with me, but if she was still talking about buying a place here, she wasn't thinking along the same lines. And I couldn't raise it. We didn't talk about the future, we had agreed to live in the here and now and I had to honor that.

"I thought we had dinner with Daniel and Leah?" I wanted off the new apartment subject. My teeth pressed into the flesh of her neck and she tipped her head to give me easier access.

"Yes, tomorrow night."

My teeth sunk deeper and Anna moaned and grasped the back of my neck. She enjoyed me marking her, and I took full advantage. I slid my hands up to cup her tits and I pushed them together. I imagined my dick buried between them and pressed harder into her.

"Work's made you horny I see," Anna breathed.

"*You* make me horny. Nothing and no one else." I wanted Anna to have no doubt that there was no one else but her for me. I never got the feeling that she needed my reassurance but I wanted to give it to her all the same.

My hands dropped from her tits to her hips and I slid her skirt up. Fuck, she was wearing stockings again. I'd warned her about that.

"Anna," I said admonishingly.

"But I didn't see you at all today to distract you, so what's the problem?"

"Then why?"

"Because I know what it does to you. And I like that thought."

I'd dropped my pants—my dick wasn't going to survive for long without her around it. I reached across her stomach and pulled her toward me. "Bend over beautiful. I curled my hand around her neck and pushed her down against the kitchen counter.

"You managed to put panties on. That's a compromise I suppose." I tugged down the lace and they pooled at her heeled feet. My fingers trailed back to her delicious pussy. I wanted to be in her as quickly as I could, but I wanted her to be ready.

"Fuck, you are soaking wet, beautiful."

She whimpered an answer, I couldn't tell what she was saying, as long as it was stop or no, I didn't really give a shit and by the way she felt, she was saying anything but stop. The way she got so wet for me was a complete turn on. Sometimes I wondered if she spent her time in a permanent state of semi-arousal, ready for my dick on a moment's notice. Jesus.

I trailed my dick along her folds and she shuddered as she lay out in front of me, waiting for me to slam into her. I parted the cheeks of her perfect ass. She glistened for me, the pink, puckered flesh above winking at me. I'd never touched her there. But it seemed so ready for me. I hardened further at the thought. Just the slightest touch. My fingers replaced my dick, sweeping up and down her folds once, then twice and then, coated in her arousal, I edged higher.

"Ethan," she said. I read curiosity rather than fear in her voice. I trailed around the puckered opening with my wet fingers and gently stroked. "Ethan," she said again, the pleasure breaking through her curiosity. I reached around her with my other hand and found her clit "Ethan, Jesus, fuck." She bucked and threw herself back against me, impaling herself on my finger. She gasped and gripped at me and we both stilled. I hadn't meant to go as far.

"Are you okay?" I asked.

She nodded but didn't speak and I didn't move. My finger still buried halfway inside her ass, my other thumb on her clit. She exhaled and her hands relaxed slightly against my arms. My heart was thumping in my chest and my blood pounding in my ears but I kept as still as I could. Slowly, she started to move, I assumed at first she was trying to remove my finger from her ass but as she rolled her hips, it was clear she wasn't moving away from me, she was pulling me in deeper. I groaned at the realization that she was enjoying it.

"You like that, beautiful?" I asked as I pushed farther into her and circled in tiny movements.

She was panting as she nodded, as if she had too much to concentrate on. I was as hard as I'd ever been in my life, watching her ass fucking my finger, her pussy dripping wet. Before I could finish my next thought, she verbalized it for me.

"I want you inside me," she gasped. "Quickly, Ethan, please."

This beautiful, sexy, insatiable girl would be my undoing.

"You want me in your tight pussy while I finger fuck your perfect ass?"

"Ethan!" She screamed as I pushed my dick and my finger into her at the same time. She fell forward, her hands slamming on the counter top as I slammed into her, again and again.

Jesus, the feel of her all around me, clamping around my dick and my finger, I couldn't hold back, I wanted to get deeper, closer and I pounded again and again until her pussy contracted in the beginnings of her orgasm. She snapped her head back and her fingers gripped the counter. She was almost there.

She no longer resisted me right before she started to come. She didn't try to escape the inevitable. She gave into it. Gave into me. She knew she had no choice but to come for me. She pulsed around me and then she sucked in a deep breath, there she was, right at the edge. I pulled my finger out sharply and she gasped.

With both hands on her hips, I concentrated on fucking every last drop of orgasm out of her before pouring myself into her. Again and again I thrust into her and as I saw her body slump, my head spun and my orgasm took me over.

Fuck she was beautiful, and she was mine.

My cheek rested on her back as I came back to earth. God, I needed her naked and wrapped around me right now. Slowly I withdrew and threw the condom in the garbage. Her elbows rested on the counter top and she was still trying to catch her breath.

She turned to look at me, her hair tousled, looking as amazing as she had ever had and I kissed her on her lips. "You're amazing," I whispered in her ear.

"*You're* amazing," she whispered back to me and I led her to the bedroom, picking up an orange shopping bag I'd brought home with me.

CHAPTER Ten

Anna

I scooted into the crook of his arm as he balanced a gift bag on his stomach.

"Whatcha got there?" I asked.

He pulled me closer to him. "It's for you. A present."

"Oh, I heard that girls who are into anal get gifts." I laughed. "You had this planned all along."

"Anna," he growled, letting me know that he didn't approve of my joke. He'd never bought me a present before. Not that I'd particularly noticed. Was this going to reveal his awful taste? Doubtful since his flat was amazing and his dress sense was impeccable ... although he didn't seem particularly interested in clothes—unless he was peeling me out of them.

I turned the bag to reveal the Hermès logo. I pursed my lips, trying not to grin.

"So what's this for?" I asked.

"Well, like you said, I appreciate your ass."

I play-thumped him on the chest. "You pig."

"You love me."

"I do," I said in a small voice.

He'd meant it as playful banter but he'd brought it

up. I loved him and we had promised not to keep things from each other. "No bullshit."

He knocked the bag to the floor and pulled me down the bed and crawled over me. "You better," he said. "Because I hear it's no fun being in love with someone if they don't love you back." He paused. "I love you, Anna. No bullshit."

I held his face in my hands as he looked at me, his eyes sparkling. He was happy. We were in love. Everything was perfect.

The Hermès bag contained scarves. Scarves to hide Ethan's marking of me. I'd been wearing turtlenecks a lot recently, and the weather wasn't really cold enough to justify it. I liked the idea of wearing a scarf, especially one that Ethan had bought for me.

"What about this one?" I posed in the bathroom doorway, naked apart from a scarf tied around my neck.

"I'm thinking this is shaping up to be the best Friday night I've ever had," Ethan replied. "And I can think of several uses for the scarf. I like the thought of tying you to the bed. I think I mentioned that before."

"One kinky step at a time, mister," I replied as I unknotted the scarf, threw it at him and crawled back into bed.

"Okay, we can leave that until next weekend."

My stomach dropped at the mention of the following weekend. It was the last full weekend we had together before he was due to leave.

We'd never spoken about him going. He'd forwarded me a couple of emails that set out details of his departure dates but I hadn't replied and he never mentioned it when we were face to face. I took a deep breath and tried to bury the thoughts of him leaving. Two weeks was plenty of time. Plenty of time for him to ask me to go with him.

"Next weekend we're carving out a bit of the USA here in London and having Thanksgiving dinner at your sister's, remember? You can't tie me to a bed for Thanksgiving."

"That's where you're wrong. I'd be very thankful if you were tied to the bed."

I bit into his shoulder in response and he pulled me over his body. I wanted to ask him what happened next. I wanted to ask him if he thought we could do long distance. I wanted him to ask me to move to New York.

"What are you thinking?" he asked, brushing my hair away from my face.

I shook my head. "I was imagining being tied to the bed."

I grinned but he didn't. "Don't bullshit me."

I looked down at his chest and traced my finger across his hard muscle. "Not now. Not yet."

He lifted my head up but I kept my eyes low. "Look at me, Anna."

I wasn't ready for the conversation about what happened next. I wasn't ready for it to be over, either. I wanted to keep enjoying what we had. I wanted Ethan for longer than three months. This wasn't how this was supposed to have gone. This was supposed to be the guy that helped me move on. This wasn't supposed to be the guy I fell in love with.

I lifted my eyes to meet his and his gaze was dark, intense—as if they were trying to pull something out of me. "When?" he asked. "We have to talk about it sometime."

I pulled my face from his hands and lay my cheek on his chest. "Soon," I mumbled.

We had dinner regularly with Daniel and Leah—Daniel and Ethan seemed to hit it off.

The boys were having a game of pool before dinner in Daniel's games room leaving Leah and I to catch up in the kitchen, pretending we were cooking, when Daniel's housekeeper had done it all and we were just warming stuff up.

"So, I'm in love with him," I said abruptly to Leah as she poked about in the oven.

She spun round to look at me. "You're finally admitting it?"

"What do you mean 'finally'?"

"Well, you've been in love with him since New York."

"I'd only known him a week in New York."

"Doesn't mean you weren't in love with him."

Leah had turned into a hopeless romantic since getting together with Daniel. There was no point in arguing with her.

"I told him."

She stared at me as she took a seat at the breakfast bar, nodding at me like a lunatic. "And?" she asked.

"And what?"

"Don't be obtuse. Did he say it back? Ask you to move to New York? Did he propose?"

"Don't be ridiculous," I said, trying to come across cool.

"He didn't say it back?" she asked, scrunching her eyebrows together.

"Yes, he said it back."

"Well, that's great. You've both finally admitted what we've all known forever."

"Stop, Leah. There are no happy endings here. We live on different continents. Our lives are on *different continents*."

"Are you telling me that if he asked you, you wouldn't go to New York? And don't you dare say no. Because he's totally worth it. He makes you happy and you love him and he loves you and treats you like a queen and—"

"I didn't say I wouldn't go, for god's sake, Leah."

"So you would go?"

"Yes!" I was exasperated. She was making me talk about things I really didn't want to verbalize but I spent every spare minute thinking about.

"Have you told him?"

I shook my head. "We agreed to live in the present and not worry about the future while he's here."

"But—"

"I know. I'm just not ready to lose him if he doesn't want what I want."

"But he loves you. What makes you think you're going to lose him?"

"It's complicated."

"What's complicated?" Daniel asked as he and Ethan clattered into the kitchen.

"Making risotto balls," I said quickly.

"Yeah, like you were talking about making risotto balls," Ethan said. "You can just about fry an egg."

"Whatever." I shrugged and he wrapped his arms around my waist.

"Don't worry, you have other skills that keep me coming back for more." He buried his head in my neck to kiss me.

"Eww. TMI!" Leah exclaimed.

We all laughed and set about dishing up dinner. I was relieved to have Leah and Ethan distracted at the same time.

Ethan

The weekend had been perfect. I didn't know how Anna would react to getting gifts. She didn't come across as one of those New York girls dripping in labels and expecting to be bought things. But the scarves suited her. I loved seeing her naked in them and I loved seeing her at work, in her suit with one neatly tied around her neck, covering the signs that she belonged to me.

It was our last full weekend together. My flight was booked for the following Sunday. I had pushed it out until that last possible chance so I was taking the latest flight out despite the fact that I had a full day of meetings on the Monday. It wasn't the smartest choice but I didn't want a minute in New York that could be spent in London with her.

Despite our agreement that we'd live in the present and wouldn't worry about what happened when I returned home, I'd gently tried to bring up going back to New York with Anna a couple of times. First, I sent her a couple of emails setting out the date I was due back in New York. She hadn't responded and so I hadn't brought it up. It had been raised again this weekend. I could tell it was on her mind but for some reason she didn't want to talk about it. I didn't want to push her, I wanted her to be happy and if not talking about it was going to to do that then I'd live with it, for now.

I'd never been in this situation before. I wasn't good at complicated, I just wanted to make things simple and to me, talking about it would make it simple. I wanted her in New York, with me. That was simple. And if she wouldn't move then we could do the long distance thing until I could work out a way for us to be together. I'd tried to extend my stay in London but my biggest client was being a pain in my ass about it and New York had said no. They wanted my billable hours back in New York. I could change firms but building a client base in London would not be easy. But she was worth it. She just needed to talk to me about it, to tell me what she wanted. If she didn't want me then I would go and she'd never hear from me again, but I didn't think that was it.

It was Friday night, I was home later than normal because I had things to tie up in London. Despite the time, I'd returned to an empty apartment. I checked my phone to see if she'd texted me. Nothing. I slung my jacket on the back of one of the dining chairs and went into the kitchen to make myself a drink. Her keys jangled in the lock and I grinned, reaching for another glass. I was looking forward to seeing her. Twice this week, when I'd had client dinners, I'd come home to find her asleep with a note asking me to wake her when I got in. I hadn't woken her and had been chastised the next morning on both occasions. She looked so beautiful when she slept, there was no way I could wake her despite wanting to bury myself in her.

"Hey, beautiful. I'm in the kitchen," I called out.

Her head popped round the door. "You're back." She grinned at me. "I have a gift for you."

"The last gift you gave me was the only gift I could ever want." Jesus, I felt my cock stir at the thought of her perfect tits wrapped in that black silk bow.

"That wasn't a proper gift. That was my body. This, I bought. I have two." She placed a shopping bag on the counter and pulled down the sides of the bag to reveal a pumpkin. She grinned at me as if she'd just bought me a boat. Fuck, she was cute.

"I like the other gift better," I said.

She ignored me "You missed Thanksgiving so I thought we could make a weekend of it. We're going to Jessica and James' tomorrow afternoon and in the morning you could teach me to carve pumpkins and do whatever else you yanks do this time of year."

"Well, we carve pumpkins at Halloween, not Thanksgiving. On Thanksgiving we fuck. We spend the whole weekend naked and fucking."

She smacked my arm. "You do not."

I grabbed her around the waist and pulled her toward me "We do. It's a huge tradition."

"You're crazy."

"Crazy in love with you."

That had the desired effect as she spun around in my arms and pressed her lips against mine. "Okay, we can carve pumpkins naked. How's that for a compromise?"

"You promise you'll be naked?"

She shrugged. "Sure."

"Deal." Naked pumpkin carving. This would be a great new tradition.

"So you've been out buying pumpkins all this time?"

"I went to see a flat as well."

"Oh, you didn't mention it." A stabbing pain jolted my stomach. She was planning her life without me. She was getting ready to move on. "How was it?"

"Vile. It only just came on the market and the agent was so pushy when she called me about it, but it was horrible."

"You know I paid the rent on this place until March. I did it earlier in the week. I didn't want you to be . . .You know, so you can take your time." Even if she was prepared to come to New York, she would have to give notice and I knew she didn't want to have to live with Leah and Daniel.

Her eyes soften as she looked at me but she didn't say anything. This was the perfect time to discuss the after, the future.

"Anna?"

"That's really . . . you're amazing." She reached around my neck and into my hair. God, I loved the feel of her hands in my hair.

"Anna? We need to talk."

One hand released my hair and rubbed against my hardening cock. She wasn't subtle in her distraction technique. "Soon," she whispered rubbing up and down. I should stop her and make her talk but she knew how to get exactly what she wanted.

"When?" I groaned.

She unzipped my zipper and her hand slid inside my pants.

"Sunday. Right now, I want you inside me."

I woke to the sound of her hairdryer and watched her at the dressing table doing her hair. For some reason, I loved watching her get ready. It was fascinating to me. The lotions and the potions and the nine different types of everything. She looked incredible before the ritual began so I wasn't sure why she bothered. She looked most beautiful just after she came, which was the argument I'd used to keep her naked all morning.

Naked pumpkin carving had quickly turned into naked fucking, my new favorite Thanksgiving tradition. I'd tried to convince her that we could cancel on my sister but it hadn't worked and so I stayed in bed while she banned me from coming anywhere near her while she got ready. For some reason she didn't like the idea of smelling of sex when we went to my sister's.

"You look beautiful," I said as she switched the hairdryer off.

"You always say that," she said, still facing away from me, but meeting my eye in the mirror.

"Because it's true."

"Get in the shower, you bum."

"Will you rub me down? My dick is really dirty."

She laughed. "Are you fifteen years old? You'd think that I deprive you? We've spent most of our day focused on your penis."

CHAPTER
Eleven

Anna

Watching Ethan play on the rug in the family room with his niece Izzy, almost made my heart burst. He knew how to handle women, young and old. He spoke to her as if she understood every word he said and she watched him as if she did, occasionally reaching her hand out to enthusiastically pat his cheek.

"He would make a great father," Jessica whispered to me as I stood watching Ethan.

I shrugged, pulling myself away from watching them and headed back over to the counter.

"Don't you think?" Jessica continued.

"I've not . . . I guess."

I'd spent the last three months trying not to think about things like that. Trying not to do exactly what I did with all my other relationships—ruin them with "what ifs" before they even started.

"Don't tell me you've not thought about it. You're a woman. That's what we do."

"We don't talk about that stuff," I responded. It was true. We'd not talked about it and although thoughts about the future had entered my mind, I swept them under my trusty rug of denial along with unpaid credit card bill from last month and my lack of gym attendance since Ethan had arrived.

"What stuff? Babies?"

"Babies. The future. We're here now and we're happy and that's what we're focusing on."

"But you must think about it. He leaves tomorrow." She was relentless. Couldn't she tell I was uncomfortable?

"I try not to. Can I help you with anything? I'm a great potato masher." *Please change the subject.*

She finally got the hint and set me up making a salad. I could tell from her silence she wanted me to offer up more about Ethan and our future but I resolutely stayed silent. I felt like a rabbit caught in the headlights, I'd been putting off these discussions for what seemed like forever but we had to talk. After tomorrow we were going to be on different continents. I just didn't know for how long. He wasn't staying or he would have told me and I wasn't leaving to go with him. There was no plan to be together, no plane ticket booked. I had a life and a job and a family and commitments in London but I wanted him—I wanted to be with him.

Ethan and James joined us at the counter, Izzy wriggling on Ethan's hip.

"You're not letting her cook are you?" Ethan asked, watching me chop the cucumber. "Really, she's terrible."

"I am not and anyway, I'm not cooking. I'm chopping."

"Thank god, I don't need food poisoning on a transatlantic flight."

My stomach lurched at the mention of his journey home and it must have shown in my face because he reached across and stroked my back in small circles. I squeezed out a grin.

"So, your flight leaves tomorrow night?" Jessica asked.

"Yeah, the late flight back and I have an all-day meeting on Monday."

"Ouch," James said.

"So you two are going to do the long distance thing?" Jessica asked. Jesus she was like a dog with a bone.

Ethan sighed. "I really hope you've not been pestering Anna about us, Jess. You'll find out soon enough, so drop it. Please."

"Ethan, it's not an unreasonable question. I just love you guys together. I love seeing my brother so happy and I want that for you. I want you to be happy."

She was right. It wasn't unreasonable. We should have talked about this before now. Even if we decided that tonight would be our last night together, I wish I knew what our plan was. I wish I knew that there *was* a plan for us.

"And I love you for it, but drop it unless you want to ruin tonight." There was no arguing with Ethan when he meant business. His sister seemed to know that and she didn't mention it again, but it hovered around us all evening. We both skirted the subject as we discussed what our plans were for Christmas. I explained that I always spent it with my parents and Ethan said he was flying to Aspen with his parents.

"And do you have plans for New Year's?" Jessica asked me.

"Umm. No, I usually end up at some party where I don't want to be and leave at ten past midnight. I'm not a huge fan of New Year's Eve."

God, starting a new year without Ethan sounded like the worst evening ever. I wanted him to tell me that he was flying back to London for New Year, that we could spend the evening naked, watching the fireworks across London's rooftops.

"And how's work?" she asked, flitting her eyes between us. "After the merger, is it all going well?"

I shrugged. Ethan nodded "Yeah, good. There's plenty to do but I think it will be great to have a European network." Ethan sounded enthusiastic. More enthusiastic than me.

"I've lost my work mojo at the moment," I murmured honestly. I'd not said it out loud before but once the words had left my lips, I realized that the thoughts that had been swirling around my head recently were more than the usual weekend blues as the prospect of another week ahead.

"Really?" Ethan turned to me, his eyebrows knitted together.

"A bit." *A lot.* The thought of having no prospect of running into him at work made the thought of going in on Monday even bleaker.

"Is Adams being a dick?" Paul Adams was the partner I did most of my work with.

"Language," Jessica hissed, pointing at the buggy where Izzy was fast asleep.

Ethan rolled his eyes.

"No more than usual," I replied. "I just . . . I'm sure it will be fine and if it's not, I can give it all up and go to India and become a yoga teacher."

Everyone laughed but Ethan's was forced. I reached across and stroked his knee. He grabbed my hand.

I wanted to leave right then. I just wanted it to be us. I turned my head sideways and he met my stare. He knew. He could see what I wanted and so we would leave at the first polite opportunity and have our last night in London together.

Ethan

As much as I loved my sister, I wanted to be alone with Anna. Our last night together should be about us. We needed to talk, finally, about our future. Did she think we had one? Why was she putting off this conversation until the very last minute?

When she looked at me, I knew she wanted to leave too. I loved the way I could see what was going on behind those beautiful eyes, most of the time.

I stood up to help Jessica clear the table.

"Thanks, Bond. James thinks I'm his personal slave."

James rolled his eyes. "If you weren't obsessed with clearing the dishes as soon as the last person has swallowed their final mouthful then I might get a chance to help before you started nagging."

God, were they still in love? I couldn't remember if they'd always been like this. Snipping at each other, throwing biting comments back and forth. It was exhausting to watch. I'd much rather be fucking Anna than fighting with her.

The four of us cleared the table and I made our excuses. Jessica, for once, didn't argue with me. I believed her when she said she wanted to see it work with Anna. Maybe that's why she didn't give me a hard time about leaving straight after eating.

"Make sure you two talk it out. I want to see you happy together," Jessica called as we made our way down their path to the street.

Anna looked at me and rolled her eyes. "Your sister is relentless."

I smiled. "She is. But she's right. The time is now. We need to talk."

Anna nodded but didn't say anything as I flagged

down a taxi. We sat close in the cab and I held her hand in both of mine, rubbing my thumb across her knuckles. The tension thickened between us. We sat in silence as the London streets zipped by. I'd miss this city. New York was part of my soul but so was Anna—and for me London was all about Anna, which made it the best place on earth.

I was trying to decide how I was going to say what I wanted to say. I'd had weeks, no months, to think about it and now the moment was almost here and I couldn't quite decide how to put what I was feeling into words. I loved her. I wanted us to be together. But I needed her to want all the same things and I wasn't sure if I was about to get my heart ripped out of my chest.

As the cab pulled up, Anna took a deep breath. I tried to catch her eye but she avoided looking at me. I felt a dull thud in my chest. Fuck. I didn't know if I'd survive this.

We made our way into the apartment in silence. Anna was first to speak, thanking me as I took her jacket.

"Whiskey?" she asked.

I nodded. I followed her to the kitchen and she set about the now familiar routine of setting out the glasses, dividing the ice and then pouring the amber liquid.

We took our drinks and Anna forced a smile at me. Fuck. Fuck. Fuck.

We settled on the sofa and I pulled her legs onto my

lap. I loved being able to touch her any time I pleased. I loved that whenever we sat on this sofa, her legs were mine.

"So," she said.

"So," I replied.

"So, you want to have the talk now?"

Of course I wanted to have the talk now. Didn't she? A lump formed in my throat. I couldn't speak, so I nodded.

"Okay," she said.

I nodded again. At work I used silence as a negotiation tactic. It was amazing how much someone would give away if you didn't respond to their initial offer. They'd often negotiate against themselves. But my silence in that moment was helping me not get on my knees and beg her to come back to New York with me. I needed to know what *she* wanted. Did she see a future for us?

"So where do we start?" she asked.

"You start," I choked out and took a gulp of whiskey, hoping that it would numb any pain and allow me to get my words out when the time came.

"What do you want me to say?" she asked.

That fucking irritated me. What did she think I wanted her to say? At least the agitation seemed to neutralize my nerves slightly.

"I want to you to tell me what you want. No bullshit, no ambiguity."

"And what about you?"

"What about me?"

"Don't I get to hear the same from you?" she asked.

"You do."

"So, go ahead."

Such a fucking lawyer. I chuckled. "No way, beautiful. I'm getting the last word here. You're going to start and you're going to tell me the truth. I want every single thought that's spinning in that beautiful head of yours coming out of that beautiful, very talented, mouth of yours. Now, go ahead."

She looked at me, trying to decide what to say. Surely, she'd thought about this? Surely she knew what she wanted?

"I like you," she said, finally.

"You like me?" I raised an eyebrow at her.

"Well, you know. I really like you." She started to laugh and she rolled her eyes at me. "You know I love you, Ethan."

I leaned forward and kissed her on the corner of her mouth. I couldn't help it. I never got tired of hearing those words coming from her. "It feels like there's a *but* coming."

"Well, the *but* is we live on different continents. You have a life and a career in New York and I have a life and career in London. I'd say that's a pretty big *but*."

I nodded. To me, it wasn't that big an issue. There were ways of making this work. Did she see them?

"So, if I wanted to be a lawyer about it," she continued, "we have various options."

I nodded again, willing her on.

"We could agree to part ways here and now. No complications, no ambiguity, no bullshit. . ." She looked at me, and I wasn't sure if I should respond. She was using my words, was she thinking that was my preferred option?

"For the record, that's my least favorite of all the options." The words tumbled out before I had a chance to stop them.

A smile spread slowly across her face. "How do you know that the other options aren't worse?"

"I can't think of anything worse than my life without you."

"Ethan." My name came out in a half whisper. "It will be complicated."

"I've been trying to hold back, to allow you to tell me what you want, but I can't wait another second. I want you, Anna. Whatever it takes."

"Whatever it takes?"

I nodded. "So, you seem to have thought about this. Do you have a plan?" The words came out through her grin.

"First I want to hear what you want. How much convincing do I need to do?"

"You think you need to convince me?"

I shrugged.

She scrambled across my lap, her knees either side of my lap. "You don't need to convince me of anything. I'm good at complicated."

I felt the air leave my chest and my body relax as I grabbed her face in my hands and pushed my lips against hers. Pulling away I said, "I fly tomorrow." Why hadn't we talked about this sooner, we could have been making plans?

"Then let's make every moment count. Don't expect any sleep tonight, Mr. Scott."

CHAPTER
Twelve

Ethan

I'd never realized you could feel physically fucking sick from missing someone.

We'd been in the air for two hours, which meant I hadn't seen Anna in three, but I still missed her. During our time in London we'd spent plenty of time apart when we were at work but it hadn't felt like this. It hadn't felt like I'd been sucker punched. In my gut. In my heart.

"I'll have another whiskey. In fact, just keep them coming," I said to the flight attendant. I don't know what she said in reply. I just kept my eyes on the screen in front of me and tuned her out. I was watching Pretty Woman. Of course I was. I was a walking fucking cliché. I'd become the chick who wallowed in post-break-up misery. Except we hadn't broken up. But it made me feel closer to her, knowing she'd watched it a million times and knew every line. She'd laugh if I told her. And I liked making her laugh.

I had a mountain of prep for the meeting the next day but I couldn't face it. For the first time in my life, I didn't care if I went into the meeting tomorrow hung-over and unprepared. It didn't matter. Nothing mattered anymore. Nothing except being with Anna. That was the goal and I was going to make it happen.

I nearly hadn't made the flight, not wanting to leave. We stood at security for what seemed like hours, until the last possible moment. Our arms clamped around each other, we didn't speak—we'd said all that we needed to say. We just needed to be with each other. And she held on to me tight, as if it were the end or at least the beginning of complicated.

The Empire State Series: Part Three

NEW YEAR
in
MANHATTAN

LOUISE BAY

CHAPTER
One

Anna

I didn't know how long I stood there watching, scanning the heads of travellers on the other side of airport security, heading into duty free. Maybe he'd turn back, change his mind about leaving. Maybe he'd come and see if I was still here, watching for him. And if he did, I wanted to make sure I was.

A small child ran into me and I moved my legs apart to keep from losing my balance. As I bent down to steady her, she ran off. It broke my concentration and I looked at my watch. Five minutes past take off time. I checked the board. It wasn't delayed. He was in the air. Gone.

The dull ache in my stomach that had been threatening to break through since last night engulfed me. I stumbled to a nearby bench and sat with my head in my hands. He was really gone. We'd finally had the discussion about the future. Ethan hadn't asked me to go to New York. I'd wanted him to, but he hadn't. But he hadn't ended it either. He'd told me he loved me. He'd told me he wanted to make it work and I'd said it all back to him. We were going to do the long distance thing. Relief and elation had held off complicated for a few hours until now. Now the reality of him heading to another country was right here, and living on different continents meant complication. That reality was almost unbearable

I fumbled in my bag, and took out my keys and my phone. What was next? I couldn't remember.

I stood resolutely. Home. That was what was next. I headed to the exit and found a cab. Had I told the driver where to go? I closed my eyes and let my head fall back.

"Miss. Miss."

I lifted my head from the back of the seat. It was the cab driver. The car had stopped. I looked out of the window. Home.

"Sorry to wake you, love," he said. "You got jet lag?"

He hadn't woken me, not from sleep anyway.

I mumbled at him and pushed some money into his hand.

I was soothed by familiar surroundings as I entered the flat. It wasn't home but it was the closest thing I had. The ache inside me pulsed as I remembered I'd have to find somewhere to live. I had this place until the end of March. What would happen between now and then? Nothing had been decided between us other than that we wanted to make it work.

I kicked off my shoes, went into the bedroom and, fully clothed, I crawled under the covers. I could still smell him. Feel him.

I woke to the sound of my phone muffled by my pillow. It was still dark. I flicked my fingers across the words "Sex God".

"Hey," I croaked.

"God, you sound so sexy when you've just woken."

I couldn't help but grin through my cloud of half-sleep.

"You sound sexy all the time," I said. "Where are you?"

"In a cab. Sorry to wake you."

"Don't be sorry. I've missed you."

"Already?"

I nodded. "Yes."

"Only three weeks, beautiful."

We had to get through Christmas first and then I was flying to New York. "Three weeks," I repeated.

"And I'm still going to make you come every day."

I groaned and squeezed my thighs together. Ethan had assured me that the long distance thing could work because he gave good phone sex, but the thought of not touching him, of him not touching me, for three weeks was horrifying.

"Hearing you groan like that is making me hard, and that's just not playing fair when you know I'm in the back of a cab."

I grinned again. I could get to him despite being three thousand miles away. That eased my ache slightly.

"Sorry. I didn't mean to."

"You don't have to try. You just have to exist."

"God, I love you, Ethan."

"I love you. Now get in the shower because you have that meeting that starts at 8:30." I loved that he knew my schedule. How long would that last? He knew what I was doing this week but what about the week after that?

"What time is it?"

"Just before seven your time," he replied.

I groaned again. I could sleep for a week, or maybe until it was time to fly to New York.

"Stop, Anna."

"Sorry. Don't go."

"You have to get in the shower. I'll speak to you when I wake up later. Stop pouting."

I laughed. I *was* pouting.

"Okay, I love you. Sleep well."

"I will, I'll dream of you."

I took the tube to work, like most of London, but I didn't feel like most of London. Somehow the city didn't seem as bright as usual, it was like someone had turned the contrast down—there was something gray about everyone. I felt disconnected, as if I knew something they didn't. I walked at my new pace, people rushing past me, bumping me from left and right but it was okay because I was different. I knew. I knew what it was to really, truly, love someone. And it was incredible and entirely petrifying. I'd never felt so exposed and vulnerable.

We hadn't talked about things too far in the future, but we'd set some boundaries, created some rules. Of course we had.

Rule one was that we would speak to each other every day. Even if it was for two seconds. Rule two was that we would see each other every month and we would always know when we would next see each other. Rule three was no bullshit. If either of us felt like it wasn't working, we would talk about it and make it work better.

But rules were meant to be broken, right?

"I can't believe that I've got to be in the office without having Sexy Scott to look at." Lucy landed her ass on my desk as I returned from my meeting.

Did she think I liked her? I was pretty sure I'd never given her reason to be so deluded.

I fingered the Hermès scarf that I'd worn to keep Ethan close to me and tried to ignore her. She kept yapping away as I opened my inbox and started going through my emails. I managed to tune her out.

"Anna? Are you listening? He totally had the hots for me."

"Whatever you say, Lucy," I said, my eyes fixated to my screen.

"Jesus, you're a miserable bitch."

"Whatever you say."

She finally left me alone and I cocooned myself in a bubble that I hoped screamed "leave me the fuck alone". I wanted to get my work done and go home. Although Lucy irritated the living crap out of me, she was right. There was no joy in this place without Ethan. Not for me. Not now.

Leah called, presumably because I wasn't responding to her emails and texts.

"We can just have a girlie night in. Daniel has a dinner," Leah said.

"I need to do a ton of laundry and call my parents. Maybe later in the week?" I was fobbing her off and she knew it. I just genuinely didn't want company. I wanted to be surrounded by Ethan. And even though he was gone, I could feel close to him back at the flat.

"Don't become a hermit. You wouldn't let me do that and I won't let you."

"I appreciate you're on hermit patrol and I thank you for your service, but it's all good. I'll speak to you later."

I delved into my work where I could be alone.

Just past midday, my phone buzzed. "Hey," I whispered.

"I dreamt of you," he said.

I got up and closed the door to my office.

"Was it a good dream?" I asked.

"You were going down on me, so I'd say so."

"How romantic. You say the sweetest things." I laughed.

"I don't like waking up without you," he said, and my heart tripped.

"I know. I don't like you waking up without me either. Only three weeks until your next real-life blow job," I said, trying to lighten the mood.

I heard him groan on the other end of the phone. I laughed. "Get in the shower, you bum. I'll call you when I'm home."

Ethan

I put the phone down and headed into the bathroom. Was jerking off when she wasn't on the end of the phone cheating? I was going to have to establish rules about that. I had the hard-on to end all hard-ons and it was ruining my concentration. I picked up my phone again to see what emails had come in overnight. That should help redistribute my blood flow better.

We'd managed two snatched conversations since I'd left. Was this what it was going to be like? I had really held myself back when we'd finally talked about our future together. What I wanted to do was throw her over my shoulder and bring her back to New York with me. But I had managed to control myself. She seemed to want to understand what I wanted and it had been difficult for me to establish what was going to make her happy. When I'd suggested trying a long distance relationship she'd seemed relieved.

I wasn't sure which alternative had made her anxious—the thought of me taking her back with me, or ending it. But I hadn't pushed her. Perhaps I feared her answer. We'd promised no bullshit, but as much as I felt she was holding something back, I was too. I hadn't demanded that she come back to New York. The thought of her in London, without me, was fucking terrifying—she could change her mind about us, or meet someone else. The thought of me without her was fucking terrifying—she had become like oxygen. I couldn't really remember myself before her and what I did remember, I didn't like. I didn't want to go back to sex without complications or ambiguity. Anna was everything I'd spent my life fighting against and now the only thing I wanted.

Three weeks. How would I survive three weeks? I was struggling to get through a few hours. I needed a plan. I'd hit the gym. That would work. I'd need to be putting plenty of hours in at the office. That would be a good distraction. And I could hang out with my old college friends, Andrew and Mandy, this weekend. That was a plan. Now I just needed to set about making sure

Anna wasn't distracted by something or someone other than me. I was going to make sure I was always front and center of her mind.

"So, are you officially pussy whipped?" Andrew asked. My smile spread across my face and I shrugged. "I knew it would happen at some point," he said.

Andrew had suggested lunch and I'd had my assistant organize reservations at the place where we'd not-so-accidently "run into" Anna and Leah the morning after our first night together. I'd been crazy about her even back then.

"What can I say? She's worth being whipped for."

"So, she's coming over for Christmas?"

"New Year's," I corrected. "I'm taking my folks to Aspen for Christmas. They're disappointed not to be with Izzy, so I thought Aspen might make it up to them. And then Anna flies in on the twenty-seventh."

"And then what?"

"And then what what?"

"Well, is she going to move over permanently? Are you going to London? Are you going to marry her?"

Yes, yes and yes? No, maybe and one day? I didn't have an answer. I shrugged again.

"But you love her right?"

I couldn't stop the grin that spread across my face. "Yeah, I love her."

"So make it happen, dude."

Andrew was a great friend. He could have been giving me miles of shit for going soft but instead he wanted me to get my girl.

"Thanks, man. I'm going to find a way for us to be together on the same continent."

"Good. Girls like Anna and Mandy don't come around very often. Don't fuck it up."

"Good advice. And so very eloquently put."

"So, do you want to spend New Year's with Mandy and me, or do you have other plans?"

"I know Anna would love to see you guys, but can we do it another night? Maybe the day before? For brunch or something? I have other plans for us on New Year's."

My idea was to make the evening special. I just hadn't decided how yet.

"Is work busy?" he asked.

"Yeah, hopefully it will be better now that I'm back in the US. The clients are so fucking demanding. It was hard managing it from London, but it should settle down." I wasn't going to be late tonight. I wanted to make it home by 7pm. I had a promise to keep. I needed to make sure my beautiful girl came every day. Shit, my dick started to stir. "How's Mandy?" I asked, knowing talking about her should settle me down.

"Good. She wants us to go out to dinner so she can give you a hard time about leaving Anna in London."

"I didn't leave her there. She lives there."

"I know man, but you know what she's like. She's excited that you've found someone."

I couldn't help but grin. I was excited that I'd found Anna, too. We just had to find a way to be on the same continent.

CHAPTER Two

Ethan

On the way back to the office, I texted Anna

E: I'll be home by 7pm. Can you wait up?

A: All night, for you.

E: Good. I want you in bed and naked by the time I call.

A: Yes, sir.

E: Stop with the "sir", you're making me hard.

A: That's how I like you, sir.

Fuck, she could get me like steel with a text from three thousand miles away. I was like a fucking teenager when it came to her. Maybe we should have a no text rule during office hours?

I slipped back into my work routine. Managing things from London for three months meant that being back in New York made everything seem easier and I got through things quickly. But I did have a conference call at eight that evening that I could take from home. It meant I got an hour with Anna. The thought of her in bed and naked—her creamy-soft skin wrapped in our sheets—had my dick twitching, so I tuned it out and got on with the day.

It was just coming up to 7pm and I was stuck in traffic. Fuckety fuck. I didn't want to waste a minute with her, so I called her from the back of the cab.

"Hey, my handsome man."

"God, I love you." I couldn't stop myself, I loved her and how she loved me.

"Are you okay?" She sounded concerned. Because I'd told her I loved her? I wasn't doing it enough if it raised questions.

"Yes, I just wanted you to know. I've missed you all day."

"I've missed you, too. I don't like being here without you. It doesn't feel right." My gut ached hearing her say that. It felt like she might be missing me as much as I was missing her.

"Where are you?"

"I'm in bed."

"Did I wake you? Were you sleeping?"

"No, I was waiting for your call. You told me to be naked and in bed, so I am."

I groaned and the taxi driver shot me a look in the mirror.

"Fucking traffic," I spat.

"Where are you?"

"In the back of a cab. The traffic's a bitch. I shouldn't be too much longer. I just couldn't wait to hear your voice."

"It's fine. There's no rush." I hadn't told her about my 8p.m. conference call because I didn't want her thinking I was fitting her in amongst other things or that there was a time limit to our call. "How was your day?"

"Good, actually. I saw Andrew for lunch and I got a lot done."

"How are he and Mandy?"

"Good. They want to see you when you come over. I'm going to have dinner with them one night this week."

"I'm glad you have them."

"Me too. I left something for you, in the top drawer, where my stuff used to be. Go take a look."

Anna

"You did? What is it?" I asked.

"Go take a look," he repeated.

I scrambled out of bed, went over to Ethan's drawer and pulled it open. The sight of the almost-empty space made my stomach flip. Another reminder that he wasn't here anymore. But it wasn't completely empty. There was a small orange box stamped with the now familiar Hermès logo. I grinned, grabbed it and headed back to bed.

"Did you find it?"

"I did. You don't need to buy me gifts."

"I want to. I think you're the only girl ever born who complains about getting gifts."

"I'm not complaining. I just don't want you to think you have to."

"I want to. Do you like it?"

"I've not opened it."

"We should be doing this by video call or something. I want to see you."

"Three weeks. Where are you now?"

"We're just pulling in. Open your gift."

I did. I loved that he'd thought about leaving me something when he was gone. He was good at this boyfriend thing, even if he hadn't had much practice. It was a beautiful blue enamel bracelet. "God, Ethan, I love it. Thank you."

"Put it on. I want to imagine you in nothing but a bracelet."

I grinned at the thought of being his fantasy. And his reality. "It fits beautifully, thank you. I'll send you a picture."

The sound of the street echoed more clearly on the other end of the phone. "Where are you?"

"I got out to walk. I'm just at the end of the block."

"I want to hear more about your day."

"It was completely uninteresting compared to you in our bed, naked."

Our bed. He still thought of it as ours.

"Tell me. I want to hear everything as if you were beside me chatting."

"If I was there and you were naked, I wouldn't be talking about my day."

I wondered how many women had flirted with Ethan today, on a day I wasn't going to be there to wrap my hands around his cock and make sure it was my eyes he was looking into when he came. I had to push the thoughts to one side

"Tell me, what would you be doing?"

"Oh, beautiful, you might be the death of me. But I'd die happy, that's for sure."

My whole body heated. The thought of being the one that made him happy? That I could do that to him? It was all I could want. The sounds of the street began to fade.

"If I were there now," Ethan continued, "I'd lay you on your back on our bed and drink you in for a few minutes. I love your skin, how soft it is, how it tastes. I love the feeling of my fingers on you, in you, all over you."

There was familiar wetness between my legs at his words. It was if he was worshipping my body.

His voice and the buzz across my skin made his absence more acute. I was aware of everything I didn't feel. Everything he would be doing to my body if he were here. The almost too-hard press of his thumbs below my hips. The drag of his lips across every inch of my skin. The feel of his hard body under my fingers, my lips, my tongue.

My nipples tightened and grazed the sheets I was wrapped in. I squeezed my thighs together. "I wish you were here with me."

"Beautiful, there's nothing I want more, right this second." On the other end of the phone keys jangled and doors slammed.

"Are you hard?" I asked, almost embarrassed, but not quite. Our relationship had been, until now, so much about the physical stuff between us. It was how we communicated, it was how we were comfortable. We were in new territory here. I got confidence from his desire for me. Now I was blind. I didn't want to make a fool of myself. I needed to be there with him, to see, to feel for myself.

"Like a fucking stone. Like I said, you just have to exist to make me hard. Having the image of you naked on the other end of the phone makes me like steel. If I were there, would you be ready for me, baby? Tell me how wet you are."

"Ethan." I wasn't sure I could do this. It felt strange and unfamiliar.

"I want you to reach between your legs. Stroke that perfect pussy of yours and tell me how wet you are."

Tentatively, I moved my free hand down across my stomach, then lower. I was ready for him, but I wanted to do what he said.

"Tell me, Anna."

My slickness quickly coated my fingers. "I'm ready for you, Ethan. Really ready for you."

"You're ready for my tongue, my fingers or my cock?"

I couldn't help but groan. "Ethan."

"That's right, you'll have all of them."

I started to circle my clit with my fingers and my back arched.

"Jesus, I want to be inside you right now. I'm so hard. I want to be surrounded by your pussy. It's my favorite place to be. I love the feel of you around me while I slide into you. The way your eyes widen every time, like I'm almost too big."

"Fuck, Ethan," I whimpered.

"That's right, beautiful, tease that pretty clit. Imagine my tongue bringing out your pleasure."

I was close and then the phone slipped out of my hand. As I pulled it back to my ear Ethan seemed to slip away from me. My body went cold and my mind was distracted by his absence.

Something left me and I wasn't going to get there. It wasn't enough for me to pretend that he was touching me. In fact, it was worse. It just made me more aware that he wasn't there with me, doing what he did best.

"I'm so hard for you. Are you close? I want us to come together," he said.

"Yeah . . . I love you Ethan." I wanted him to get off even if I couldn't. I wanted to make sure he wasn't walking around with a hard-on without me being around. I wanted this to work.

"Anna?" His tone changed quickly. He sounded serious. "Anna, are you bullshitting me?"

"I . . . I . . ." How could I answer him?

"Were you faking it with me?"

"No! Never. I would n-n-never," I stuttered.

"But you're not about to come." It wasn't a question.

"I'm sorry. I was and then I just missed you and it left me." The beginnings of tears began to gather in my eyes.

"Don't be sorry. Don't ever be sorry. Jesus I wish I were there. I want my arms around you."

I laughed. "And the rest."

That broke the tension and Ethan laughed, too. "Yeah, and the rest. But seriously, this situation sucks."

"It does."

"You've never faked it with me, have you?"

I laughed again. Ethan had never been insecure about the power he had over my body—to think that he had the slightest doubt about the way I responded to him was laughable. "I've never needed to fake a single thing about our relationship, and certainly not the way you make me come. I can't say I've never faked it, but I've never faked it with you. I couldn't stop myself from coming even if I tried when you touch me."

"You say the sweetest things. If I were with you I'd be fucking you for the second time tonight."

"Now I've left you with blue balls."

"Yeah, about that . . . is getting myself off cheating if you're not on the end of the phone?"

"No. I mean, did you when you were in London? Do you think it should be?" Why was he asking me this? It felt weird talking about it. But at the same time I was pleased. Ethan seemed to have no boundaries. He hid little from me and I loved that, but I wasn't used to it. No one in my life had ever been as open as Ethan was with me. As much as it made me slightly uncomfortable at times, it was exactly what I needed.

"I never did in London. But I spent half my time inside you."

I smiled. "Why would you think that I wouldn't want you to?"

"I just didn't know how you would feel about it. So I wanted to ask you."

"You are the best boyfriend ever. Do you want to know how I feel about it, no bullshit? I think that I want you to get yourself off twenty times a day if you need to. Anything to ensure that you're not tempted to go near another woman while we're apart."

"Okay, that's not what I was expecting you to say. You're worried that I'm going to cheat on you?"

Was I? I *was* worried that I would lose him, but would he cheat? I didn't know if he could go without until the next time we saw each other. He did, after all, have the sexual appetite of a nineteen-year-old boy and he'd never had to think about being monogamous before. "I don't think I'm worried, but it's natural to notice other women, and I guess you're more likely to act on that if you've not had sex for a while." I was trying to sound rational. I was trying to *feel* rational. "You've never had to deny yourself before Ethan."

He was quiet on the other end of the phone.

CHAPTER Three

Ethan

I was left wounded by her admission. Wounded because she thought I was capable of betraying her. Wounded because she thought I didn't have more self-control, but most of all I was fucking devastated that she couldn't feel about me the way I felt about her—not if she thought that I could ever want anyone else.

If she thought that sex with another woman could compare to her, she didn't get it. The idea of some random hook-up made my skin crawl. Apart from the fact that Anna did things to my body that no one else did. I wasn't convinced those things were entirely legal, they felt so good. The fucking was in a whole different category of sex that I hadn't realized existed. But it wasn't just fucking, it was connection, it was understanding. Or so I'd thought. But maybe it wasn't like that for her. Maybe she'd had this before. Maybe this was good, but nothing special to her. She didn't get how I felt about her. She *couldn't* feel what I felt for her because if she did, she'd understand it wasn't a possibility that I would even look at another woman. There would never be room in my brain, my heart or my soul for anyone else.

"Ethan," she breathed.

"What can I do?" I asked. "To make it better, to reassure you that there will never be anyone else?"

It was her turn at silence now.

That gave me every answer I needed. There was nothing I could do. Nothing to show her how she wasn't just another woman. I knew that she, and what we had, was different. She didn't feel it and there was nothing I could do to show her. Especially from three thousand miles away.

The grip around my heart tightened.

I would lose her.

Maybe I'd never had her to begin with.

"Tell me about your day," she said.

I didn't know if I should force the issue, make her talk about it. It was my natural instinct but I'd lost confidence in our magic formula of no bullshit. It didn't seem to be enough.

I started telling her in minute detail about everything that had happened. For some reason, it was important to get the details right. To be clear. To tell her everything. Time was ticking away. Eight was approaching, but I didn't want to end our conversation. She should be sleeping now. Was she trying to stay awake?

"How did you make it home so early?" she asked.

"What do you mean?"

"On your first day back? You must have left the office at six-thirty to be home now."

"I brought some work home. I wanted to speak to you. You . . . us. It's my priority."

More silence.

"I'm sorry I ruined it," she said.

"You didn't ruin anything."

"But it wasn't what you had planned."

"You weren't what I had planned, and look how lucky I got. I love giving you pleasure, I love getting you off, but it's not the only thing between us, beautiful. Not for me."

"Me either. But I want you to . . . you know."

I laughed. "What?"

"You know, to, er, be satisfied."

I could feel the warmth in her cheeks from here. "All the things we've done and you can't tell me you want me to come?"

"Ethan."

"What? It's pretty funny."

I loved the sound of her laugh.

"I promise to jerk off in the shower."

"Promise to think of me."

"Beautiful, I can think of nothing else any time of the day or night." It was true, she totally owned me, and I wanted her to know it. "We're going to make this work, you know."

"Should it have to be an effort?" The giggle was gone. She sounded serious.

Every part of her was having doubts. She was dripping in them. And I didn't know how to stem the flow.

"I don't know about 'should'," I replied. "I've got nothing I can compare us to. All I know is that I want you and me to work more than I want anything else."

She sighed. Was I pushing too hard? "But you've got to talk to me, I'm not there to see it in your face, you're going to have to tell me what you're thinking."

I could almost hear her brain whirring at the other end of the phone. "It's all jumbled up in my head. I'm not sure I have the words," she responded.

"They don't have to be in a particular order, just talk." Jesus, I was desperate for her just to spit it out, to talk to me. I could deal with anything if I understood what was going on in her head. I wasn't sure I'd understood what anxious meant before I'd met her. I guess because she had the power to hurt me—the power to walk away. I couldn't, didn't want to control her, I wanted her to *choose* me.

"I just wish you were here is all."

"I wish I was there, too. Or that you were here. Or that we were somewhere together. Anywhere."

"Careful, you're turning into a romantic."

"Nu-uh. I just don't bullshit and that's how it is."

"I know," she said.

"You know?"

"I do. I feel it. The same. I just . . ."

"What? You've been here before and you've been hurt before?"

"God no. No. Never. I've never been here before. Not like this. I think maybe that's it. It's because this is different." Her voice was quieter as she spoke. As if she almost didn't want to utter the words. "I'd never recover."

Her admission reassured me a little. It didn't seem to be lack of feeling that was creating the doubt—if what she was saying was the truth.

"You'll never have to."

"I thought you didn't make promises you can't keep."

"That's right."

"Ethan."

"I mean it. It's not going to happen. I won't let it." But she was right. I couldn't control it. She had her part to play as I did, and perhaps we'd need some good luck in there somewhere as well.

"You're going to have to be sure enough for the both of us sometimes." Her voice dipped a little, thickened with something.

"I can do that," I assured her.

"I'm sorry."

"You have nothing to be sorry for. Nothing."

"But I wish I could have, you know."

Fuck she was adorable—she still couldn't say that she wanted to make me come.

"Oh you will. And as you know, I don't make promises I don't keep."

She laughed again and I started to relax. But only slightly. I checked my watch. Fuck, it was coming up to my conference call. I wanted to stay on the phone to her. All night. Especially now. I didn't want to have to hang up on her while the uncertainties were still so close to the surface. I wanted to soothe her for just a few minutes longer.

"It's late. I should sleep. And you have to work. Tomorrow will be better," she said.

Tomorrow would be better. I would make sure of it.

We hung up a few minutes past eight and I quickly dialed into the call while powering up my laptop. I'd planned to send her various gifts throughout our time apart. I wanted to make her smile, and make her realize how I was thinking of her all the time, even if I wasn't with her. When I'd bought her the scarves, I'd enjoyed real pleasure from thinking what she might like. I loved it when I got it right and her eyes lit up as she unwrapped the one I'd chosen to go with her hair, or that would look so beautiful against her skin or that would go with the new suit she bought. It was an extension of the sex between us. I got pleasure from giving her pleasure. It was a revelation to me. I hadn't realized I could be happy because someone else was happy. I wondered if Andrew felt like this about Mandy, or if James felt this way about Jessica.

I'd tried to stay awake so I could speak to her before she was properly awake. I loved the sound of her drowsy, half-awake voice. I couldn't get enough of it.

At some point I must have fallen asleep because I woke to horns, my laptop and papers still spread across my bed. I was at least sleeping back in the master bedroom now. Feeling her around me, seeing her in my apartment was exactly what I wanted. It was tortuous, but it was necessary. When I left for London I did everything to avoid memories of her in my apartment. Now it was exactly the opposite.

I checked my phone. She'd be at work. I could get a head start on my day, maybe even hit the gym. I started to check my messages and found several texts from Anna. More than several. Almost a dozen. Shit, I hoped something wasn't wrong. I opened them. As the realization of what I was seeing hit me, a heat crossed my body and I was aware of the blood in my veins.

Pictures. Lots of pictures. Close up.

I scrolled through them—her lips, slightly parted, just as they were when she came. The juncture of her upper thigh, her magnificent tits pushed together, with a hint of her hand. The curve of her ass. Her fingers, where I wanted mine.

Jesus, I was hard. I wanted her with me, but this was the next best thing. She was beautiful. That skin, what those fingers could do to me, what that ass could do for me.

She answered on the first ring. I grinned. She'd been expecting my call.

"You're up early."

"And you're trying to kill me."

"That wasn't the intention. Just a little reminder of what you've got back in London—and of who is visiting you in three weeks."

I groaned and reached down to my rock hard cock.

Anna

I loved that sound he made as if he were half-crazed with lust. I must have taken about a hundred pictures and sent him about ten. I wanted to try and make them so they weren't sleazy, that they just suggested something.

"Ethan," I whispered as I closed my office door.

"I want you on my cock, right now."

"Ethan," I whispered again.

"I need you."

"You have me."

I could hear him, his breaths shortening. I imagined what he was doing and I felt my underwear dampen. The thought of him, naked, in his bed. God, I was going to have to take a cold shower.

"Stay on the phone."

"I'm here." For some reason, I liked the fact he wanted me on the phone. I hoped it would make up for last night a little. I didn't want to screw this up. I didn't want to screw us up.

"The picture of your lips. That's my favorite." He was panting now. I could hear a rhythm in his voice. "It's the shape they make when you come."

"When *you* make me come," I whispered.

He groaned again.

"Yes, when I make you. That's what you look like. And I can't get enough. It's like I'm addicted." His voice was wavering now. "I can't get enough of your body, your mind, your soul."

"It's all yours."

His breathing was heavy now, the grunts more consistent. I could imagine his neck strained as he gave into his orgasm. He was there and hearing him was the sexiest, most erotically intimate thing I'd ever heard. I wished I was back at the flat, somewhere where I could try again.

But I wasn't back at the flat and a knock at the door pulled me back to my surroundings.

Paul Adams, the partner I did most of my work for, put his head round my door and saw I was on the phone and silently indicated I should call him. I was sure he could tell that I'd just got my boyfriend off at the other end of the phone. It must have shown in my face, surely. I nodded and he closed the door behind him.

"Are you okay?" Ethan asked me.

I laughed. "I am, it was Paul. I feel like we've been caught doing something we shouldn't be."

"Well, it's a good job we weren't on Skype."

"Yeah, I think that would be a slam-dunk breach of the anti-frat."

The rest of the day was better. I loved to hear him undone like that and even though we were three thousand miles apart, it felt like this morning had brought us closer somehow.

Sometime after lunch, I came back to my office after a meeting to find two pieces of post on my desk. The first was a courier package, the second a hand written envelope marked 'private and confidential'. I opened the courier package first, expecting some documents from a client but instead I found a book. But not just a book. It was a book titled "Pumpkin Carving in New England". But before the word "Pumpkin" someone had handwritten the word "naked".

Lucy chose that exact moment to make her entrance, and it was always an entrance.

"What have you got there?" She asked seeing me with a book in my hand and a grin on my face. Not that my grin lasted long.

"What do you want Lucy?" I didn't want anything spoiling my mood.

"Just coming to say hi, that's all. What's this?" She asked picking up the book.

"Nothing." I snatched it from her fingers. I hadn't had time to enjoy it yet. To think how thoughtful and silly and perfect a gift it was. I hugged it to my chest.

"Jeez, someone's touchy. You still pissed you're not working with Sexy Scott?"

"He's back in the US."

"Yeah, but I'm still working with him. He emails me all the time. Can't keep away. He's such a flirt."

If I could have kneed her in the groin without anyone finding out I would have done. I wasn't one for physical violence but it was like she was trying to wind me up. Did she know about Ethan and me? Maybe she suspected?

"Okay, well enjoy that." I snapped. "I've got a lot to do, Lucy." I stood up and moved towards the door. She couldn't keep talking to me if I wasn't in my office. She got the hint and I went to the loo.

When I got back to my desk I grinned inanely at the book Ethan had sent to me. As I flipped through the book I saw that he'd annotated it so that every time 'pumpkin carving' was written he'd added the word 'naked'. The book was full of beautiful photographs of intricately carved pumpkins set against typical New England homes and landscapes. It was sweet and thoughtful and I loved it.

I texted a quick message.

A: I love my gift. And I love your obsession with nakedness. Oh, yeah, and I love you.

Still grinning, I turned my attention to the handwritten envelope that had been on my desk with the courier package. It wasn't Ethan's writing and I couldn't think who it could be from.

Inside was a handwritten letter. It started "Dear Anna" but I still didn't recognize the writing, so I skipped to the end.

It was from Ben. Ben the Biker. Ben the Bastard. My ex-boyfriend who had been responsible for my flat being broken into, putting me in danger. What on earth was he writing to me for?

CHAPTER Four

Anna

"Have you got it with you?" Leah asked. I had called an emergency wine meeting to discuss the letter from Ben the Bastard.

I handed it over and she began to read from the beginning. I concentrated on my wine.

For the next five minutes all I got was "God", "Oh, wow" and "Well that makes sense." And then I got a question. "And you had no idea?" she looked up at me.

I shook my head. "Like it says, he got very good at hiding it."

She nodded, like she understood. Like it was understandable that I hadn't realized he was an addict. I wasn't sure it was. What did that say about my ability to read people?

Leah continued to read. "Oh and this is him making amends. I see. It's brave." She looked up and I nodded. It was brave.

When she got to then end she exhaled dramatically. "What did Ethan say?"

"I've not told him yet. I'm going to call him when I get back. Anyway, this was all pre-Ethan. Before we met."

"So it doesn't change anything?"

"What? Between me and Ethan?" I looked at her to check she wasn't high on something. "Of course it doesn't *change* anything. What could it possibly change? Ethan and I are together."

"Okay, I just wondered if . . . well, whether you may still have feelings that might come back now you have an explanation about things."

"Leah!" I couldn't believe what I was hearing from her. She knew, she must know, how I felt about Ethan. He wasn't just another boyfriend to me.

"What? I'm just asking."

"You know what it's like between Ethan and me. How can you ask me that?"

"All I know is that you're three thousand miles away from each other without a plan."

"I have a plan. I have a fucking plan, Leah." My voice started to tremble a little and from her expression that she hadn't expected me to react as strongly as I had.

"I'm sorry. Anna, please, I didn't mean to upset you. I want you to be happy."

"I know, look, I'm going to go. I want to go home and speak to Ethan."

"I'm really sorry. Please don't go, I feel terrible."

"There's nothing to be sorry about. Really. I just need to go." I was standing already. I had to be at home. But I didn't want to make Leah feel worse than she clearly already did, so I sat down and topped up our glasses.

"I'm pleased you've found Ethan."

I stayed silent. I didn't want to carry on this discussion.

"And I'm glad you have a plan," she continued. I didn't really have a plan, other than I was determined that Ethan and I would be together.

"Maybe we'll end up having a double wedding!" Leah said, clearly trying to make me laugh.

"Fuck off Leah." She knew how I felt about the whole wedding thing.

"What? I think it would be a *brilliant* idea."

"We're not getting married."

"Ever?"

"You know how I feel about getting married. It's silly and outdated and married people end up hating each other but staying together anyway. And I can't bear the thought of wearing some meringue of a dress and having members of my family trying to hide their disdain for each other while eating over-priced chicken."

"Okay, so no double wedding. But when you're bridesmaid at mine, I'm making you wear a meringue. And you're going to be eating chicken. The rest of us will have venison."

I laughed despite myself.

Ethan

The whole world was literally talking out if its asshole. No one had made any sense since I'd gotten into the office. It was like someone had infected everyone with a virus. Clearly I was immune, but the rest of them had it bad.

"No, I don't think that's a good idea. It doesn't take into account the fact that the value in this business has not been nailed down."

Fuck, this was obvious fucking stuff. Why was I having to make these points?

I checked my phone and smiled at the text Anna had sent earlier. She'd liked the book. It was the least provocative of all the gifts I had planned for her. I was still holding my cell when another text arrived.

A: When are you free? Can we talk?

E: Are you okay? I'm in a meeting now, but I can excuse myself.

A: No, when you are home. I just had a fight with Leah and I want to hear your voice.

Jesus, the woman made me feel like a god.

E: I'll be home by 7pm again, beautiful.

For the second time in two days I left the office at six thirty. It wasn't sustainable. Just because I worked from home after I spoke to Anna wasn't enough. I needed to be in the office. Three weeks until she got here, and then we needed to talk.

I called her as soon as I reached my apartment. She sounded sleepy and the blood rushed to my dick. The feeling of being ready for her when she wasn't here wasn't getting any easier.

THE EMPIRE STATE SERIES

"How was your day?" she asked.

"A fucking nightmare. I hate dealing with stupid clients."

She laughed and the tension in my voice suddenly sounded ridiculous. I could do nothing but grin in response.

"Anyway, none of that matters. Tell me about Leah. It's not like you two to argue."

"We're okay, it's fine. It's just, I got a letter from Ben."

"From who?" The pulse in the veins on my neck throbbed.

"Hear me out."

"Hear you talk about your fucking dick of an ex?"

She sighed and I felt like a dick, but really?

"No, whatever. I thought you would want to know."

"Anna, what the fuck did the fucking letter say?" I didn't need to ask. Of course, it would be begging her forgiveness, begging her to take him back. Fucking dick couldn't keep her in the first place and now wanted a second chance.

"I need you to calm down."

"And I need you to tell me what that fucking letter says before I get on the next plane to London to read it for myself." The throb in my neck was getting wilder.

"Calm the hell down, I am going to tell you if you give me a minute and stop acting like an asshole."

318

I had nothing to say to that. She was right. Some of that asshole virus must have got to me after all.

"Okay, sorry, go on."

"I'm not one of your associates that you can boss around, Mr. Bossy Pants. Well not outside the bedroom, anyway." That made me smile. "So, I got a letter at work from Ben today."

Was it me, or was she stringing this out. She needed to get the fuck on with it. And then I could arrange to have him killed or something.

"And it was to make amends."

"I bet it was, the limp-dicked prick."

"No, it was like part of his treatment. He's in AA or something for his addiction to drugs and alcohol. And it was a really lovely letter. Telling me how sorry he was for putting me in danger, for deceiving and manipulating me. How none of it was my fault . . ."

"Of course it wasn't your fault."

"Ethan, listen. It was nice. I was shocked to hear he was an addict. I didn't know. And it kind of makes sense. But he hid it well and I'm pleased for him that he's getting the help he needs."

"And does he want you back?"

"No, that's not what this was about."

My pulse calmed.

"Okay, so why did you and Leah fight, or is it not connected?"

"Yeah, well it's kind of connected." She was reticent.

"So, talk to me."

"It's nothing, and I overreacted. It's embarrassing, really."

"Tell me."

"Okay, but you have to promise to hear me out. Don't go bat-shit crazy again."

"Go on, Anna."

"Leah just asked if I would try and reconcile with Ben now that I'd read the letter. And I got really mad that she could *ever* think that, knowing how I feel about you. She knows how different it is between us compared to other boyfriends I've had. I mean, if she feels for Daniel even a tenth of what I feel for you, she would never say that. I just lost it. Totally lost it and I feel bad. I apologized and it will be fine, but I was so irritated."

I think my heart stopped. Literally, stopped dead. I didn't think it was possible to love someone more than I knew I loved Anna but apparently it was.

"Ethan?"

"Yeah, I'm here, beautiful. I'm sorry you had that fight with Leah—no, scratch that. I'm not sorry at all. I needed to hear that from you today."

"You did?"

"It's all good. But we need a plan. We can't live three thousand miles away from each other for long. I think it might just ruin me."

"I was thinking the same thing."

"So, let's think of what we can do over these next few weeks, and then discuss the possibilities face to face when you're in New York."

"I was hoping there was going to be a little less conversation and little more action when we see each other face to face."

"You're quoting Elvis at me?"

"I am." She laughed.

"Girls aren't allowed to quote Elvis. It's the law."

"Yes, sir."

"Really? And now you're deliberately trying to make me hard?"

"Maybe." The smile pushed through her voice.

"There's going to be plenty of action, you don't need to worry about that."

"I can't wait. Can I make a request?"

"A sexual request? Of course. Anything."

"Hardy har-har, Mr. Scott. You know I love Andrew and Mandy . . ."

"I take it back, no requests involving swinging or foursomes."

"Once again, you're killing me with the funny. Can't stop laughing." She was probably the most sarcastic person I'd ever met, and I loved it. "I'd like to see them, but I want it to be you and me as much as possible."

And my heart stopped again.

Anna

The next few weeks became a gigantic countdown. Ethan and I settled into a routine of sorts. We spoke to each other when he got up and then sometimes just before I went to sleep. He'd worked every weekend since being back in New York. It was selfish of me, but I liked that his life seemed to be about work. When he went out it was always business related. He'd only seen Andrew and Mandy once since he got back.

Work was less and less interesting to me. It was difficult to know whether that was because Ethan was the ultimate distraction, or whether it was the job, the clients and the politics. Maybe it was all of the above. I just didn't see my future at the firm any more. Once I realized that, it made it difficult to get up in the morning. I needed to be working toward an alternative, but I wanted Ethan as part of that. I didn't want to be the girl whose future depended on a guy, but that ship had sailed. My future without him was unthinkable. I would never choose a job over him, it was as simple as that. Especially a job I felt, at best, ambivalent about. The more I thought about it, the more I wanted to resign.

The weekend before Christmas, Leah invited me to have her dinner with her and Daniel at their place. I was pleased to have the distraction. It was dark, wet and cold as I arrived at their place.

"It smells delicious, Leah," I said as I followed her into the kitchen. "Did you cook?"

"I did. I hope it's all right."

"I'm not sure I'd ever bother cooking if I had a housekeeper."

"I know, but I feel really guilty about her doing everything for us all the time. And anyway, I quite like cooking. Daniel's been in the study all day working, and I've been cooking. It's been like something from the fifties. Wine?"

"Of course wine. So where's Daniel now?"

"Behind you," Daniel said as he came into the kitchen. "My spidey sense told me you were about to open some shitty wine, so I've come to save you and find the good stuff."

Leah grinned. "So how's Ethan?"

"Good. He's still not asked me to go to New York. But we're going to talk about it when I go over for New Year, so it's all good."

"Have you offered to go?" Daniel asked.

"I want him to ask me. I don't want to feel I've backed him into a corner."

"He loves you. He's not going to feel backed into a corner," Leah said.

"Then why doesn't he ask me?"

"Have you asked him to move to London?" Leah asked.

I shook my head. "It's difficult for him."

Daniel started laughing. "You know how ridiculous you sound, right?" Was it ridiculous to want Ethan to show me he was sure about us? "He's in an impossible situation. He can't ask you to move to New York without running the risk of looking like a dick because he's asked a girl to give up a life and career for him."

I'd not thought about it like that. "I suppose."

"And moving to London has got to be tough for a New York lawyer. I mean, I'm not trying to say your career isn't important, but he's a partner, he's built a practice. It would be hard for him to start again."

"I know. I'm happy to go to New York. I don't love my job that much. I'm bored and I could do with a fresh challenge."

"I'm going to miss you so much," Leah said as the kitchen timer started buzzing. "Will you two go and sit down. You're distracting me."

"Are you sure you don't want us to help?" I offered.

Leah ignored me, and Daniel guided me toward to the table at the far end of the kitchen.

"So, you think you'll end up in New York?" Daniel asked.

I shrugged. "I guess we'll talk about it over New Year."

"Look, I don't know if you'd be interested, but I need a lawyer for my hotels in New York. I've put a new management team in there recently. There was a whole lot of crap that happened earlier in the year. And I want someone I can trust working with them."

My stomach churned. Was he serious? "Daniel."

"What do you think? I mean, I was planning to kick off a search process, but if you're interested . . ."

"Did Leah put you up to this?"

"What are you guys talking about? I heard my name," Leah shouted from behind the counter.

"Nothing. Tell you in a minute. Do you want a hand?"

Leah didn't respond.

"Why would Leah put me up to this?"

"Because she's my best friend and she loves me and is trying to look after me."

"Well, okay, yes, that's all true, but no, she didn't put me up to this."

"Fuck." It was all I could say. A million thoughts were whirring around my head. This could be a perfect solution—but I'd always worked in a law firm. Being corporate counsel was not something I'd ever considered. Could this work?

"You might have to tone down the f-bombs in the office." Daniel chuckled.

"Are you serious?"

"Of course. Are you interested?"

"Interested in what?" Leah interrupted as she came to the table with a huge pot of something.

"I just offered Anna a job."

"You didn't. You'd have to interview me and everything," I said, not thinking straight. This couldn't be happening.

"If you want the job, it's yours, Anna."

"What job?" Leah asked, collecting plates from the counter and setting them on the table.

"The General Counsel job at Palmerston."

"Oh my god, that's perfect!" Leah said, starting to dish out the contents of the delicious smelling food from the pot she'd brought to the table.

"You didn't know he was going to do this?" I asked.

Leah shook her head.

"And it's not a made up job? You were going to recruit someone?" I asked Daniel.

"Yes, I told you. Think about it. I'll send you the job spec. You wouldn't be working for me, it would be the guys in the US. Do some research on the business. Let's talk in a few days."

Jesus. Maybe Leah was right about the universe trying to bring Ethan and me together. Next, I'd be reading my horoscope and going to see psychics.

CHAPTER
Five

Anna

I'd always loved Christmas. Loved the chaos and the needless presents, the rush to get everything done and the time spent with my parents and my brother. This year it felt like it was just a warm up for the main event of seeing Ethan.

The actual day was fun, but not as fun as it could have been if Ethan and I had been together. Mum had sensed my distraction, telling me with a meaningful look in her eye to "take care" as I left them, which was the most demonstrative my mother ever got. Dad was oblivious, which suited me.

Back in London, I gave in to the excitement of seeing him. I'd been patient enough. Now, I wanted to be in New York already. I'd packed and repacked about seven times. I would only be there a little under a week, and I planned to spend most of it naked, but just in case we ventured out, I wanted to make sure I had every base covered.

My phone buzzed and "Sex God" flashed up on my screen. I grinned. He did, after all, live up to the self-titled nickname.

"Hey," I answered.

"Are you packed?"

"And hello to you, handsome."

"Sorry, I just want you here already."

I didn't know when the ache for him started. Maybe I'd had it since New York, since our first night together. Maybe since he'd left London. I did know it was getting bigger, more needy, more pressing. Speaking to him made it worse.

"I'm packed and just about to leave."

"Just bring a carry on. You won't need any clothes anyway. And it means you won't have to wait for your bags."

I laughed. "I'm not bringing just a carry on. Girls don't do that. Well, I don't anyway. Apart from anything else, I have to bring some of the gifts you've bought me."

"Well, any of the gifts that I want you to bring with you don't take up much space."

Every couple of days a new gift had arrived from Ethan. It was mainly underwear but I also got a framed film poster of Pretty Woman signed by Richard Gere and Julia Roberts, after which I promised him head every hour we were together over New Year. I also got a vibrator, which I refused to use without him and wouldn't need when I was with him. But there was lots of underwear. Underwear he made me try on and then take photos of myself in so he could "see if it fit". I feigned exasperation but I loved that he wanted reminders of me. And I thought it was funny that he thought he'd have to convince me to send them.

The underwear didn't take up much room, and I'd packed every single piece.

The door buzzed but I wasn't ready to hang up on Ethan so I maneuvered my case out of the flat, and outside to the waiting cab while Ethan told me about his day coming back from Aspen. I wanted to ask whether he'd told his parents about us, but I held back. I didn't know what New York would bring me on this trip. Last time it had brought me Ethan, but would this visit take him back from me? Would we find a way to be together? I pushed the thought from my head and tried to concentrate on what he was saying.

"Were your parents unhappy to only have such a short time with you?"

"I don't think so. They seem to be delighted that there may be a prospect of continuing the Scott name. I'm sure they thought I was gay."

I half choked on the breath I'd inhaled. "So you told them about me coming to visit?" I managed to push the words out of my still-winded lungs.

"Of course. Shouldn't I have?"

"Of course. I just . . . "

"Did you tell your family about me?"

Jesus, was this going to be a thing?

"Umm, kinda."

"Don't bullshit me, Anna. You didn't say anything?" He sounded puzzled more than anything.

"Well, not specifically. I really don't have that type of relationship with them. They knew something was going on. I mean, I spent my whole visit either on the phone with you or texting you."

"Wow."

"It's no big deal, Ethan."

"Apparently not," he said. I wasn't quite sure what he meant by that. "Listen, it's late. I'll see you at the airport."

"Ethan."

"Have a safe flight. I love you, Anna."

And he was gone.

My ache for Ethan intermingled with the anxiety that had sprouted out of our last conversation. I just needed to see him and it would be like it always was when we were together, wouldn't it?

Time on the plane seemed to pass at a different speed than in real life. I couldn't focus on my book or any of the films. I just needed Ethan. I wanted him to tell me everything was going to be okay.

By the time the plane arrived and I'd passed through security, my excitement and nerves had brought on full body shaking. Border control must have thought I was smuggling something illegal. I was surprised I wasn't searched.

Ethan spotted me before I saw him and the smile that spread across his face made my stomach curl. Jesus, I'd forgotten how handsome he was. I was tempted to dry hump him right there. Our eyes locked and he cupped my face with his hands and slid his lips across mine, softly, gently.

"God, you smell good," he said into my mouth. "And you taste good," he said, trailing his tongue along my bottom lip. "And you look phenomenal. Are you sure you're real?"

He dipped his tongue past my lips and pushed against mine. I moaned. God, how I had missed the feel of him. I smoothed my hands up from his shoulders to find his neck, straining and tight under my fingers. He pulled me toward him, deepening his kiss, pressing my body to his, pushing his hardness against my stomach. I needed him, in every way, right there. He circled his hips and then pulled his head back.

"We should go, or I'm going to get arrested."

"I think it would be worth it."

He growled and grabbed my abandoned suitcase in one hand, my arm in the other and started charging toward the exit. I had to half skip to keep up with his large strides and determined pace.

"Like the idiot I am, I drove," he said tightly.

"Thought it would stop me from having you in the back of the car in front of Rory."

Ethan

I heard Anna laugh and I turned my head. She was looking at me, laughing at me.

"What?" I asked, without interrupting our breakneck pace to the car.

"You."

"You're laughing at me, Miss Anna?"

"I am."

"I'm so pleased I amuse you."

"It's forty minutes. I thought I wanted you bad, but it's only forty minutes."

But I really couldn't wait, or didn't want to. It had been too long and now I wanted to feel her, touch her, taste her. I didn't want to waste a single second.

"Tell me what you have planned for us today."

We reached the car and I popped the trunk and looked at her quizzically as I put her case inside.

"My plans are all about you and me naked for the rest of the day."

"I get that. Tell me what you have planned, exactly."

I studied her for a few moments, and she returned my look. She didn't explain herself. Didn't rush me. She just waited.

"Well, I made a promise to you that I wasn't able to

keep, so I have some making up to do," I said as we got into the car.

"Yes, Mr. Scott, you told me that you'd make me come every day you were away. So I calculate that you owe me twenty-two orgasms."

I smirked at her. "You've been counting?"

"Counting the days until I had you inside me again."

"Fuck, Anna." I crunched the gears and sped out of the parking lot. "And don't look at me like that. Not now. Not yet. Not when I can't do anything about it."

"Like what?" she asked, innocently fluttering her eyelashes at me.

"You know that I need to be inside you when you look at me like that."

"I'm sure I don't know what you mean." She grinned and it was all I could do not to pull over to the side of the road and have her.

Driving had been a terrible idea. I wasn't a patient man at the best of times, but with Anna sitting beside me, practically begging to get fucked, I was close to having an accident.

"I was thinking," she said. "Do you, you know, get tested regularly?"

I quickly turned to look at her. "For STDs? Why? Is something wrong?"

"No, it's just, I got my annual check-up and I came back clear and . . . I'm on the pill, so, I just thought that if you got tested, then—"

"I got tested about six months ago. A few weeks after you were in New York."

"Oh."

I could hear the unspoken question behind that one simple syllable and I reached across and stroked her leg. "There's been no one since," I said quietly.

She slid her hand over mine and I turned my palm and clasped her fingers tightly.

"Really?"

"No one since I had you the first time. Really."

"Okay." She paused. "Me too. No one since you."

The revelation sat heavily between us. There was meaning there.

Eventually we pulled into my parking garage and I leapt out of the car, clumsily pulling her case from the trunk.

"In a rush?" she sing-songed.

"Whatever gave you that idea?" I raised an eyebrow at her and clamped my hand over hers as we headed to the elevators.

"You know that midnight-blue underwear set you sent me?" she asked coyly as we stepped inside the elevator.

"Er, yes." There had been a lot of underwear. A lot of pictures. But I knew the set she was referring to.

"You liked that a lot, I remember."

"I liked all of them a lot."

"So this one doesn't stand out?" she asked, facing me as she pulled at the sides of skirt, revealing blue barely-there underwear.

"Fuck." Instinctively, I reached for her and cupped her mound. She was hot. Her head fell back but her eyes stayed on mine and I moved my whole body, pressing it to hers. "I thought you might want to freshen up before we fool around?"

"Freshen up? I'm not dirty enough yet. I want you to make me really dirty, Ethan."

A sound erupted from the back of my throat. God, I wanted this woman. I sealed my lips against hers and the elevators doors sprang open.

My erection throbbed, desperate for her—it was almost painful. She pushed her hands against my chest, separating us. She was panting and reluctantly I pulled away from her and almost dragged her into the lobby.

I fumbled for my key as she stood behind me, kissing between my shoulder blades, rounding her hands across my ass and over my crotch. I groaned, dropped my keys, turned and grasped her face in my hands, taking her bottom lip between my teeth. The taste of her was so sweet. Had it been like this before? I ran my tongue along the inside of her upper lip, tracing the shape of her mouth, wanting to feel every inch of her, inside and out.

She trailed her hands across my back and over my shoulders. It wasn't enough, I wanted us skin to skin.

Reluctantly, I retrieved my keys and made more of a determined effort to get them to work. It took more effort and concentration than usual, but the door sprang open and then closed behind us. There we were—together, in private with no plans for the rest of the day apart from to be together. The thought calmed me. She was here. We had time.

The atmosphere changed between us. In the car the only thing I could think about was how my cock was going to feel buried in her pussy. Now, it was only one of the things I wanted to do with her.

I grinned at her and she grinned back. I didn't know where we should start. There was so much I wanted to share with her. I couldn't wait for her to get to know my place properly. I wanted to hear about her journey and how things were at work. I would tell her about the office, my niece Izzy, catch her up on the news around my sister's new job. *And* I wanted to fuck her so badly I could barely stand.

We had time.

I pulled her toward me, her head against my chest, and we stood in my hallway, our arms wrapped around each other's waists.

Finally she spoke.

"In all seriousness, it would probably be a good idea for me to shower. Can you wait?"

"Do you want company?"

My phone rang before she could answer.

"Shit." I bellowed into the phone. "Scott?" With Anna's arm still around my waist, I carried her case into my bedroom. She placed small, chaste kisses on my chest as I walked her backward into my bathroom and continued the conversation with work about nothing that I found remotely interesting or important. I had bought some toiletries that I thought she would like and I opened one of the cabinets to show her. She grinned at me in that way that she had that made me feel like a god. I turned on the shower and pulled some towels off the rack.

"I'll be ten minutes max. I'm sorry," I whispered

Don't be. This is perfect, she mouthed back.

She was perfect.

I closed the door behind me to give her privacy, despite the fact I wanted to watch her naked in the shower, I kicked off my shoes and lay on the bed.

There had been a disagreement between two associates at work on how to handle an issue that had cropped up with one of my clients. The case law was conflicting and they were taking opposing views. Trying to impress me, no doubt. Interrupting my time with Anna did not impress me in the slightest.

The sound of Anna in the shower echoed through the bathroom door and the thought of her in there, the water cascading down her skin, across her perfect tits and between her legs kept my hard-on at the center of my attention. The water shut off sooner than I expected. This call was going to have to wrap up quickly.

"I'm putting the phone down in five minutes, so if you want my decision on something then ask me. All I've heard so far is a battle of egos. And in a battle of egos, I'm always going to win, so get the fuck on with it."

I hung up a second before the door to the bathroom opened to reveal Anna wearing a smile and some underwear that should be illegal.

CHAPTER
Six

Anna

I watched him as he licked his lips. I fought a grin and nerves knotted in my stomach. The action reminded me of the night we met. I was half thrilled, half terrified at the prospect of him devouring me. I moved toward the bed.

"What are you thinking about?" he asked. "I can see your mind whirring."

"You," I said.

"And?"

He always wanted more, everything. "I'm nervous."

He reached out and pulled me onto his lap, arranging my legs so I was straddling him.

"Tell me."

His body against mine made my nerves multiply. "The expectation. We've both been waiting for so long. Maybe it's not like we thought it would be."

"The sex?" he asked.

I nodded, "And . . ."

He nodded and reached for my breast, pinching my nipple through my bra. It peaked as if bringing attention to itself, wanting more.

"You don't think I'll make it good for you, beautiful?"

"Always," I whispered. There was no doubt that he would make it good for me.

"Let's calm your nerves. You'll feel better when you've come."

He pushed me onto my back and dragged his fingers down my body, skirting the top of my underwear. I'd missed the feel of his hands. His skin, his smell. My ache for him was overwhelming. I needed him to touch me everywhere.

He hooked his fingers into either side of my underwear and pulled them off, almost irritatingly slowly. I needed him hard and fast. I didn't want to wait any longer. He placed my feet over his shoulders and dropped a kiss on my shin. I shivered as he ran his hands along my legs. It was as if everywhere he touched brought me back to life. Slowly, he ran his mouth up my inner thigh—licking, sucking, nipping at my skin. I ground my hips into the bed and grasped the bedcovers holding back the urge to fling my hips to his mouth.

As he reached the top of my thigh, he drew breath.

"You smell delicious. Like honey."

I couldn't help but moan at the prospect of him tasting me at any second.

"I can see how ready you are for me to lick you clean Anna. *So* ready."

"Ethan," I cried out in frustration and he dove his

tongue along my slit in one fluid movement and then back up to circle my clitoris. The pleasure built quickly. I'd been waiting a long time to feel him on me like this. I couldn't hold back and I pushed my hands into his hair, urging him deeper as I circled my hips beneath him.

"Oh, baby, you're crazy for my mouth today," he mumbled against me.

"Don't stop," I gasped and I couldn't help myself as my hips lifted to get closer to him. His tongue pressed deeper and faster and over and over and then his fingers thrust into me. I was lost, my breath left me and my orgasm spread across every inch of my skin like a fire. His tongue slowed but didn't stop, it kept lapping at my pulsing clit and it drew out my orgasm, pulling every last drop from me.

I moved his head away from between my legs. I wanted him face to face. He crawled up my body "You've not lost your touch, Mr. Scott," I said, breathless as I leaned forward to lick his chin.

"Good to know, Miss Anna." His tongue pushed against mine.

We lay side by side, our eyes locked, Ethan's hand trailing up and down my body as my breathing returned to normal. He was right, his tongue had brushed my nerves to one side. It was just Ethan and Anna now—no ambiguity, no promises, no bullshit.

"You look so beautiful," he whispered. "I'd forgotten just how beautiful."

"You look overdressed." I laughed. He was still fully clothed. He smiled at me as I reached out to his shirt and started undoing the buttons. He gasped as my fingers trailed the opening of his shirt and down to his belt buckle.

He seemed uncharacteristically happy to lie there as I undressed him, moving his body only to assist me as I peeled off his clothes.

His erection strained through his boxers. I couldn't take my eyes off him as I dipped my hand below his waistband and slid it down his length.

He gritted his teeth and his head snapped back. "Fuck."

Heat rose within me again and wetness pooled between my thighs. Quickly, I removed his boxers and knelt between his legs. His eyes had returned to mine and he watched me as I licked him from base to tip. He grasped my hair, bunching it up behind my head, giving him an unrestricted view. I took the tip in my mouth and moaned.

Ethan sat up. "Anna, no. Seriously, you're going to make me come."

I released him from my mouth for a second. "That's the point, handsome. I'll get you hard again. It's never a one-time deal with you."

He collapsed back onto the bed as I took him to the back of my throat, as deep as I could get, savoring the taste of him, the feel of him. He groaned, twisted his hips and I released him.

"Ethan, will you fuck my mouth." I wanted, no needed, him to be in control.

He didn't need to be asked twice and before I knew it, I was flat on my back as he dragged me to the edge of the mattress so my head tilted back. Ethan stood before me, his cock rubbing against my lips as he kneaded my breasts. I was more and more desperate for him. I reached down and found my clit with my fingers.

"Oh, beautiful, you just can't get enough can you?" he growled and I shifted, trying to get him closer to me, I wanted him in my mouth. "You want my cock, baby?"

I nodded. "Yes."

"Keep touching yourself," he growled as he pushed into me. He was trying to be gentle, but that wasn't what I wanted. I needed him to take me, to claim me.

"Jesus, Anna. Your mouth feels so good. So soft, so wet. Fuck." He started pumping deep, just how I wanted it, and all too soon his hips juddered and his saltiness slipped down the back of my throat.

"You undo me, Anna."

It was what I wanted to hear.

He pulled me into his arms and we lay front to front, skin to skin, with nothing between us.

"So I guess we needed that huh?" I asked.

"That and a lot more. I want to be inside you, with

nothing between us." He pushed his growing erection against my thigh and I hooked my leg over his hip and reached between us, rubbing him against my wetness.

He groaned. "So wet, so ready," he breathed as he dipped his head and licked the base of my neck and kissed across my collarbone. We moved together, holding each other, grinding against each other—lips, tongues, skin, sweat.

"Put your teeth on me," I whispered as his mouth trailed up my neck. My marks had faded and I wanted new reminders of where he'd been. Ethan groaned again and pushed me gently to my back and crawled on top of me, still working his mouth against my neck.

"No condom?" he asked.

I was beyond sure. "Yes Ethan."

"Are you ready?" he asked. I wasn't clear if he meant for his mouth or his cock, but I wanted them both. I nodded greedily, then gasped as he pushed into me inch by inch. Oh god. It was like the first time we'd been together—it had been so long since he'd been inside me I'd forgotten how he stretched and filled every space in me. My body had to adjust. I bent my knees at his sides, hoping to make myself wider.

"Jesus, you're so tight." The veins in his neck pulsed as he pushed the words out, as if he were holding himself back. "The feel of you, Anna."

Slowly he dragged himself out of me and I allowed

myself to breathe before he pushed in again, pulling my breath from me. I grasped at his shoulders, my nails digging into his skin, trying to hold on to him, to this feeling.

He started a slow rhythm, and brought his eyes to mine in between his kisses to my neck and the corners of my lips. It was loving and intimate and raw and perfect.

A sheen of sweat coated us both.

"Beautiful, I warned you, when you look at me like that . . ."

His pace picked up and my back arched off the bed as my orgasm started to build. It came from somewhere deeper than before, right in the center of me.

"Harder, Ethan, I'm close." I screamed and he slammed into me again and again, in a relentless rhythm. His face dipped to my neck and his teeth brushed against my skin. "Oh god, oh god, oh god." He was all over me, his teeth, his cock, his skin and my orgasm split me open a second before Ethan shuddered on top of me.

His whole weight was on me, his face still buried in my neck, as I trailed my fingertips up and down his spine. We lay panting out the remnants of our orgasm.

"Still nervous that it won't be good?" he asked.

I laughed underneath him. "It is always so good. You make it *so* good."

Ethan

For the next hours and days we stayed like that, naked, together, never going without touching each other for more than a few seconds at a time. It was as if we were trying to squeeze the lost time into the present so it was more concentrated, more intense.

We lay sweaty next to each other after Anna had ridden me spectacularly to a bone crushing climax.

"I don't think I can feel my legs."

"Baby, you rode me good." I reached across her body, brushing the back of my hand over her breasts.

"We should maybe get up, go for a walk or something," she said.

"Have you had enough of me already?" I bent over her chest and took a nipple in my mouth, teasing it with my teeth.

"Oh god, no. That's the whole problem. I can never get enough of you. I've been in New York for two days and we've not left this bed."

"Well, that's not true because we've had bathroom breaks. We've also fucked in the kitchen and the living room. And I think we ordered take-out, but things are a bit blurry, maybe I imagined it." I grinned at her.

She play slapped me. "Seriously. We should go and be normal people for, like an hour or something. We need to talk. I need to tell you things."

My phone buzzed from somewhere and I ignored it

but Anna reached over me in the most delicious way and handed it to me. "It's Mandy. Answer her."

I groaned, but accepted the call. "Hey Mandy. What's going on?" Jesus, she was talking at a mile a minute, trying to convince me to go to dinner. "I'll pass you to Anna. She's in charge."

She smiled at me and started talking to Mandy. I wasn't at all surprised that they liked each other, but it still made me grin that it seemed to happen so quickly. I wanted her to have friends in New York. Maybe she'd be more inclined to move here.

"Dinner tonight would be perfect," Anna said and I shook my head and tried to wrestle the phone from her. She twisted her body away from me and I grasped her legs and pulled them to either side of me as I sat up on my knees. I stroked the smooth skin of her stomach and watched her laughing and animated, her hair fanned out behind her. She looked fucking perfect. I didn't want to share her with anyone.

"Seven? What's the time now?" she asked, staring at me.

Without looking away, I pushed my thumb against her clit and I started circling it. Her hips started to move, suggesting my hands weren't unwelcome. I pulled her further toward me, my tip nudging at her entrance, her eyes glazed.

"Five already? Can we make it eight?" She clamped

her hand over her mouth to stifle a groan as I pushed in slowly.

"Okay, we'll see you then. Gotta run."

"Ethan" she screamed as she hung up. "Ethan," she cried as he plunged into her again. I'd never get enough of her screaming my name like that, as if I were her god.

We were going to be late for dinner.

CHAPTER
Seven

Ethan

Andrew and Mandy lived on the Upper East Side. My driver Rory was visiting his family in Ireland, so we took a cab.

"A driver is all well and good, but it's being in the back of a cab that makes you feel like you're in New York," Anna announced.

"If you say so. Getting out of bed was your idea. Doing things normal people do. Are you happy?"

"I'm always happy when I'm with you." She batted her eyelashes at me.

"Are you being sarcastic? I can't tell."

"And that's how I like it, my friend." She threw her head back and laughed. "But for the record, I wasn't being sarcastic."

I pulled her toward me. "So, what did you want to tell me?"

"You can't ask me on the way to dinner. Let's talk tomorrow."

"That sounds ominous."

"It's not meant to. I just need to catch you up with stuff. I've not seen you for three weeks and things happen."

She was trying to cover up something, I could tell. Had she seen that loser ex-boyfriend of hers?

The cab came to a stop at road works two blocks from Andrew and Mandy's apartment.

"So what? You won't take us around the road works?" I asked the cab driver. He just shrugged and sat there. Looked like we were walking the last two blocks. "Jesus, it's like minus twenty five out there." I missed having a driver.

"Come on, we can keep each other warm with our body heat. Don't be a brat," Anna said as she climbed out of the cab. "It's not even that cold."

"Are you drunk? It's artic, as you would say," I replied as I joined her on the sidewalk.

"Stop whining and put your arm around me." She grinned at me and despite a brief attempt at staying mad, I ended up grinning back at her. Her smile was infectious.

"Ethan?" A male British voice called out of the cold. Anna and I turned to face a couple wrapped up against the New York winter. "Hi." The man in front of us pulled off his hat and stuck his hand out. "Oh, Anna. I wasn't expecting . . . Hi." It was Al, a junior corporate partner from the London office. Despite being in different offices, we were still subject to the anti-frat policy. Shit. He knew me. He knew Anna. In a city of eight million people, on the wrong side of the Atlantic. "This is my wife, Beverly."

We all shook hands, and exchanged hellos.

"We're here for the holidays," Al said, clearly trying to explain why he was in the wrong city. I nodded, not knowing what to say.

"Have you had a nice time?" Anna asked. It was so uncomfortable. The elephant in the room was sitting on my lap.

Beverly nodded.

"Well, I guess, I understand things a bit more now," he said looking between us. I glanced at Anna; she was wearing a forced smile. "Let's catch up when you're back in the office, Anna."

"Yes of course, anyway, it's freezing, so we'd better be going before my face turns blue," Anna said. "Have a great evening."

We walked in silence. I turned to see how far away Al and Beverly had gotten before I let myself say another word. "Shit" was all I could manage once I'd established that Al couldn't hear me. "Shit. Shit. Shit. Don't let him bring up the anti-frat policy and fire you when you see him."

"He's not going to fire me," Anna replied. "How far is it to go until we're there?"

"It's just on this next corner. You seem very confident."

"I am."

"I suppose you're right. I guess it's me that's signed up to the anti-frat policy, not you."

Anna nodded. "You're not going to get fired."

"They take it really seriously. I'm not saying some haven't got away with it, but they have fired people before." We arrived at Andrew and Mandy's and Anna put her hand on my arm, stopping me from reaching the knocker.

"I don't want you to worry about this. They're not going to fire you. I'm working my notice period. It's not worth it to them to fire you if I'm leaving." With that, she grabbed the knocker herself.

Anna

I hadn't planned how I was going to tell him. But just as we were arriving for dinner at Andrew and Mandy's definitely wasn't the ideal situation to drop this particular bomb. Or was it a bomb? Even though I wasn't sure I would take Daniel's job offer, I decided to resign. I wanted to be with Ethan and it wasn't realistic to expect him to move. I liked New York and Daniel's offer at least proved that I had options around my career.

Ethan grabbed my hand from the knocker, but it was too late, I'd already thumped out our arrival.

"What did you say?" His eyes were boring into me, but I didn't turn to meet his glare.

"You heard what I said. Let's talk about it later." I could already hear rustling behind the door.

"No, I want to talk about it now. You handed your

notice in and didn't think I might want to know?" I couldn't tell if he was mad or just shocked. But he wasn't happy, and I suppose I'd expected him to be. Frankly, I'd expected him to be bloody ecstatic.

"Of course I thought you would want to know, which is why I said I had things to tell you."

"So do you have a new job? Are you going to India to be a yoga instructor? Or joining a cult? What the—" Mandy's wide smile and bouncy hair greeted us as she flung open the door.

"I'm so pleased you're here." She pulled me into a hug. "Get in before you let all the heat out. Andrew's in the basement trying to find some wine that Ethan won't spit out in disgust."

I avoided Ethan's glare as we stripped off our coats, boots and scarves and headed into the kitchen.

"Mandy, I just need a quick word with Anna in private—"

"No you don't." It wasn't the time to talk about this.

"Okay, fine. We'll do it in front of Mandy," Ethan said.

"No we won't."

"Are you fighting?" Mandy looked worried.

"Not fighting. I just found out about thirty seconds ago that Anna quit her job."

"Ethan!" I couldn't believe he'd just said that. This was between us, it should be private.

"You quit your job?" Mandy asked.

"Who quit their job?" Andrew emerged from the basement carrying numerous bottles of wine.

"Anna," Mandy said. Oh my god, this was ridiculous.

"Great. Are you moving to New York?" Andrew asked the sixty four thousand dollar question.

I didn't respond. My mouth opened and closed like a guppy. I was still in shock that the information I'd kept to myself so I could reveal it when the time was right was now being handed around like candy at a children's birthday party.

"You said you'd lost your mojo, but I thought that was temporary. I thought you liked your job," Ethan said, trying to catch my eye.

He didn't sound excited. He didn't sound happy. He sounded concerned, scared even.

"I do, I did."

Andrew started handing out very full glasses of wine, thank goodness. "It's just, well I have lost my mojo, and I thought about it and it's never going to work out there. If we stay together there's the anti-fraternization policy and if we were to split, I couldn't be at that firm, there's no way I'd handle it, so, I just . . ." Had I done the wrong thing? I'd been excited to tell Ethan. I thought he'd be pleased by the news, but maybe I'd been wrong.

"*If* we stay together?" Ethan asked. "When did we become an 'if'?"

"Don't get lost in the semantics, Ethan," Mandy said. "Let's sit down. Do you want us to leave you for a few minutes?"

I really could have done without the audience. This was proper personal stuff and I was British. I wasn't used to sharing this shit. But Ethan shook his head and I didn't want to be any ruder than we were being already.

"I didn't mean anything by saying 'if', Ethan. I thought this could be a good thing for us. But I understand that it might be too soon and that's fine, it doesn't have to be a big deal," I said. "I'm sorry about all this," I said turning to Mandy. Tears started to form in the back of my throat. The last thing I wanted to do was start crying.

Ethan reached for me and pulled me toward him. His arms around me felt like the best thing in the world. "I'm sorry," I mumbled into his chest.

"You have nothing to apologize for. *I'm* sorry. I just want to know these things," Ethan whispered into my ear.

"I didn't want to put pressure on us. I don't want you to feel like you have to do anything," I replied.

"What do you mean pressure?" Ethan asked.

"You're being such a guy, Ethan," Mandy said. "She doesn't want you to feel like she's pressuring you into inviting her to New York. And you need to stop being such a girl, Anna," she continued. "Ethan wants you in New York. He's desperate for you to move here, but he's been running around trying to work out how he can move to London, so you don't have to give it all up for him."

The tears started to fall. I couldn't stop them and Ethan pulled me closer. "You don't think that do you? That I'd feel pressure if you quit your job?"

I shrugged. "Maybe."

"Fuck that. If you *want* to come to New York, you've made me the happiest man in Manhattan. But if you want something else—"

"I don't, I want to be here with you."

"Do we have champagne in that cellar?" I heard Mandy ask as Ethan pulled my chin up. When I was finally looking at him he pressed his lips against mine.

"I can't believe it," Ethan said as he pushed his hands through his hair. "I thought, I don't know, I thought we'd have this long discussion about everything, and that I'd end up moving to London. I'd have to rebuild my practice and get new clients and it would be a complete ball-ache. You've just waved a magic wand and made everything so much easier. I mean, are you sure? You're okay with this? You're not going to change your mind?"

I couldn't stop myself from grinning at him as he scanned my face, waiting for me to tell him it was a big joke. I was so happy that he wanted me in New York, that he wasn't angry, that he didn't feel backed into a corner.

"Yes, I'm sure. I'm really, really sure."

"Where's that fucking champagne, Andrew?" Ethan bellowed.

"So, when are you moving?" Mandy asked.

"Well, I've only just been invited, so you know as much as I do," I replied, still beaming at Ethan. "I have to work my notice though. Three months."

"Three months my ass. There's no way you'll have to work that if you don't want to."

"Well, I'll need to plan and do things in London before I leave, so I can't just stay here."

"Please, beautiful, I can't wait three months. Say you'll be here quicker than that."

I reached up and stroked his handsome face. "I'll speak to the partners when I get back and see what I can do. Maybe they'll let me go earlier."

"This is so exciting," Mandy said. "I can show you round Manhattan properly. It's such a shame you don't live up town, there's the most fabulous nail bar three blocks from here."

"We could move if you wanted?" Ethan looked at me expectantly.

"Wow, this is all a lot to take in," I said.

"You're not smothering her are you, Mandy?" Andrew asked, emerging from the basement. "She probably wants to concentrate on getting a job rather than getting her nails done."

"You know, you don't have to worry about that," Ethan said. "But of course, if you want to work, I can speak to my contacts. I'm sure I can find something for you."

"Maybe I have my own contacts . . . and of course I want to work." I play slapped him on his arm. "Actually, Daniel might have something for me. He's hiring a lawyer based here in New York."

"Jesus, what other secrets have you been keeping from me?"

CHAPTER Eight

Ethan

It felt like my chest was going to explode. I wanted to pepper her with questions about what else she'd been thinking and planning. It was all too good to be true. I was sure that she wouldn't have to work her full three months' notice. Maybe she'd have to do a month and then she'd be here, with me, in New York.

"We should move," I blurted out.

"Ethan," her hand was on my leg, "we don't have to decide everything now. Let's have a nice evening with Andrew and Mandy."

"Don't you get it?" Mandy asked. "Ethan is our oldest friend. You can't make this evening any better than you have. He's been waiting for you his whole life."

"Mandy, you're going to make me cry," Anna said.

"I mean it. He didn't even know it himself and it took the longest time, but you're the bit that's been missing from his life. Now that you're here, ready and willing to move to New York, I think you love him as much as he deserves and that makes me very, very happy."

I turned to Anna and her eyes were welling with tears. "Don't cry, beautiful." I cupped her face in my hands and brushed my lips against hers. "We're celebrating."

"Time for a toast," Andrew said, raising his glass. "To the newest member of our family."

"You're killing me," Anna croaked out.

During the course of the evening, every now and then I pulled back and looked at the four of us as if I were an unobserved stranger, peering through a window. There was so much love and laughter, we looked so happy, all of us. Mandy was right, whether or not I'd known it, I'd been waiting for Anna my whole life. Right then, I knew how I was going to make New Year's Eve special—I was going to propose. I squeezed Anna's hand under the table, wanting to get closer to her, if that was even possible. She turned that beautiful smile on me and squeezed my hand back.

We'd only just climbed into the cab to start the journey downtown when she turned to me. "Why did you suggest moving, I thought you loved your flat and your neighborhood?"

I shrugged. "I do. But I want you to be happy. You might prefer a house? Or maybe to move closer to Mandy and Andrew or just get a place that's not been mine first, that we can start in together."

She grinned at me. "What?" I asked.

She laughed. "Nothing, it's just, I think you're the sweetest, most romantic, thoughtful man, ever."

"Fuck, don't say that in public, ever. I've got a

reputation to protect." I laughed. "The nice stuff is reserved just for you. I'm an asshole to everyone else."

"I like the asshole, too," she replied as she moved closer to me in the cab. I tightened my arm around her. "Let's not move. Not yet. I'd like to get to know your neighborhood and Manhattan a bit more."

"I don't want you to feel like you're living in my apartment though, Anna. I want it to be your home."

"My home is wherever you are."

I couldn't argue with that.

"So you'll move in here for now and then we'll think about moving when you've gotten to know the place a bit better."

"So, live together straight away?"

"Of course live together straight away. I'm not letting you out of my sight if I can help it."

"Okay."

"Okay?"

She laughed. "Okay, good. I like that plan."

"I'll speak to the partners and get them to let you go early."

"No, Ethan, I don't want you to. I don't think Al will say anything now that I'm working my notice, and there's no point rubbing their nose in it." But I wanted her as soon as possible. "I'll speak to them when I get back. They asked me to think about it over Christmas, so it's not common knowledge. I guess they think I might change my mind."

"Did you agree to that?"

"What?"

"Not telling anyone. Are you thinking you might change your mind?"

"No, of course I'm not. I told you, me staying there doesn't make sense for a hundred reasons. And you seem to be happy enough about it, so . . ."

"In case there is any doubt, I'm fucking ecstatic about it." I grinned at her and couldn't resist kissing the corner of her up-turned mouth. "Okay, I'll leave it to you, but if you don't negotiate them down to a month—max—I'll be forced to intervene."

"I'm an excellent negotiator, you'll see."

I got the feeling we weren't just talking about notice periods any longer. I'd give her anything she wanted. There was no negotiation to be had as far as that was concerned.

"So, can we go back to spending all our time in bed now? I'm not sure I like this whole being clothed and in public thing," I said.

"No, you have to do all the touristy things with me before I move. I can't live here without having been to the Statue of Liberty or Washington Square Park. I've never even been on that bridge in Central Park."

"Oh, god, really? You want me to show you the sights? My penis won't do?"

"It is an either or? I want both."

I chuckled. "Okay, I can live with that."

"Tonight though, it's all about your penis," she whispered into my ear as she rubbed her palm against my dick and then trailed her tongue along my jaw.

The next morning, I woke before her, and as quietly as I could, grabbed my boxers, a t-shirt and my phone, and made my way into my study. I had plans to make, things to buy—a night to remember to organize.

I called Mandy first. "Hey, thanks for last night. It was a lovely evening."

"It was a really great to see you both. You two are so awesome together. It's so good to see."

"Thanks. I need your help with something. I'm not good with this stuff, you know, the romantic shit . . ."

"You seem to be doing just fine."

"Yeah, but this is different. I really can't risk fucking it up when I propose to her."

All I heard was squealing on the other end of the phone. "What can I do? What do you need?" Mandy finally asked when she'd calmed down.

"So you don't think it's too soon? That she'll say no?"

"She's given up her job and is moving continents for you. She's not going to say no. When are you going to ask her?"

"This is what I wanted to ask you. Is New Year's too predictable? I don't know what girls want."

"Oh, wow. So before she goes back."

"Do you think it's too much?"

"No. And I don't think it's predictable, I think it's wonderful. And you shouldn't be asking me. You know her and what she likes much better than I do. You've got all the answers to this stuff. You don't need me to tell you."

She was right. This shouldn't be something Mandy planned and I went along with. This should be about Anna and me.

"Okay, you're right. Thanks."

When I put down the phone, I started scouting rings online. I was going to have to move quickly. I only had today. Tomorrow was New Year's.

"Baby," Anna shouted from the next room.

"In here," I responded, clearing down my search history just as Anna poked her head around the door. "I was going to go for a run. Do you mind?"

"Good idea. I can do some yoga here and then have a bath if that's okay?" She sat on my knees and looped her arms around my neck.

"This is your home now, Anna. You can do whatever makes you happy. There's a mat in the closet in the small guest room. Or go to the gym downstairs."

She kissed my shoulder. "No, a mat is good." I could

tell that it wouldn't take much convincing for her to get her naked and back in bed, but unfortunately, I had to get moving.

I reached around her waist and stood up as she wrapped her legs around me. "You're like a monkey."

"A pretty monkey, though, right?" She mock scowled.

I laughed. "A very beautiful monkey."

She hopped down, "Okay, enjoy your run." She pecked me on the lips and ran off to retrieve her mat.

I quickly changed and managed to smuggle my wallet into the pocket of my Columbia University sweatshirt and headed out the door.

I hoped Harry Winston would be open.

Anna

Whenever I finished a run, I looked like I'd escaped a kidnapping attempt—red faced, sweaty, hair everywhere. Ethan on the other hand, looked like he was mid-way through a Gucci photo-shoot when he got back to the flat. He was all tan with a slight sheen to his skin that made him look all the more male. I was desperate to jump his bones. In fact, I'd been desperate before his run, but he'd seemed determined to exercise—a desire that never seemed to grip me, unfortunately.

"So, I thought we could go to the Met, or the Guggenheim," Ethan said, breaking me from my haze of lust as he got dressed after his shower.

"Sounds good."

"You don't sound enthusiastic?"

"I am, I'll get my stuff." This was good. Normal things that normal couples did. I just couldn't get enough of him, I wanted to drag him back to bed.

"Okay, I need to make a phone call, so I'll be a few minutes." He worked so hard but it was kinda hot. I liked his drive and determination.

I was rooting through my case when Ethan came into the bedroom.

"I'll clear out my crap when you're back in London, but there are some drawers free in the closet. Why don't you unpack properly?"

My stomach flipped and I bit back a grin. There were some things I brought with me that I could leave. A couple of dresses and a pair of shoes at least. "Okay, I will, later."

"Are you ready?"

I nodded as I pulled on my hat and followed Ethan out to the hallway with my boots in my hand.

"Fuck me, I didn't realize you owned flat shoes. I've never seen you in anything other than heels, or naked. Sometimes in heels *and* naked."

"You see, this is when reality sets in. Real life starts right here, with my flats. It's not all nakedness and high heels, baby. Are you ready? Ready for taking out the garbage and buying me tampons? Ready for seeing me puking up and not wanting sex? I might wax my top lip tonight—are you ready for that?"

Ethan was laughing at me as I prodded his rock-hard stomach. "You're fucking crazy and I'm more than ready. Come on shorty."

"You see, I used to be beautiful and now I'm shorty and I've not even moved in yet." I sighed dramatically as I followed him out of his building.

"You'll always be beautiful, baby," he said, snaking his arm around my neck and resting it on my shoulders.

He went to hail a cab, but I stopped him. "No, I want to take the subway."

"Seriously? I've not taken the subway in a decade. It's disgusting down there." He winced as if he was in pain.

"Don't be a baby. I've never done it and I have to do all the things you would expect a New Yorker to do."

"Really?"

"Really. We have to do the unglamorous day-to-day stuff, Ethan. It's good for us."

"Okay, you get the subway and I'll get a cab and meet you there. That feels like a day-to-day compromise."

We stood on the sidewalk laughing at each other. "Oh baby, when did I say anything about compromise? Come on, we're going on the subway." I dragged the sleeve of his coat and started walking. He reluctantly followed.

"You know we're going in the wrong direction for the subway."

"Ethan!"

He grabbed me by my waist and kissed me hard.

"What was your favorite bit of the day?" I asked Ethan as we got home from several hours at the Met and what Ethan described as a reconnaissance trip of the Guggenheim.

"What do you mean? The day's not over and I enjoyed all of it."

"I've done favorite things since I was a kid, play with me," I said. "What was your favorite bit, the favorite thing you saw or step you took or conversation you had."

"Let me think. Just one?"

"We used to do top three."

"Okay, my favorite three things of today . . . one, I like that I got to see you in flats."

I grinned at him. Was he serious? Flat shoes sucked.

"And then I liked how I got to kiss you in the street."

"Ethan! We've just seen some of the most beautiful art ever to have been created. Your top three things of the day can't all be about me."

He raised an eyebrow at me. "Do you get to choose, or do I get to choose?"

"I want a no-bullshit response."

"The other two were no-bullshit responses, Anna. I won't lie to you."

"Okay."

"The last of my top three is a painting. The Velasquez. The one of his Moor slave. It's my favorite in there. I feel like he's trying to tell me something from the canvas. How he captured that is incredible."

His eyes softened as he spoke, but his face was serious.

"You like art?" I asked.

"What is fascinating about it was that it was a practice run for Velasquez's portrait of the Pope at the time. He was just prepping and that's what he came up with. Fucking brilliant."

"Have you been to Madrid? To see, you know, the one that Picasso did as well . . ."

"Las Meninas." He finished my sentence for me and looked at me as he nodded. There was something different in his eyes. "You like art?" he asked my question back to me.

"A bit. I'm spoiled in London, there's so much. I like baroque stuff—Caravaggio, Rubens and your man Velasquez. Did you get to see the Boy Bitten by a Lizard when you were in London? God, I love that painting. It's tiny, but wild." I caught myself making shapes in the air with my hands and quickly dropped my arms self-consciously. I looked across at Ethan to see if he had that 'is she crazy?' look on his face that he sometimes wore.

"You couldn't be any more beautiful to me than you are right now, Anna," he said as our eyes met.

My cheeks heated and he closed the distance between us and slid his arms around my waist.

"Can we stay in tonight?" I asked. "Unless you had plans? I'd just like to be with you tonight."

"That sounds perfect."

He skimmed his hands down my back and began to harden against my stomach.

"Me talking about gay boys and lizards gets you hot?"

"Anna," he growled in that disapproving tone he had that always made me laugh. He cupped my ass in his hands and he lifted me. I wrapped my legs around him. "Come on, pretty monkey."

CHAPTER
Nine

Ethan

Unsurprisingly, it hadn't been the lizard talk that had gotten me hot. It didn't take much around her, I had an almost permanent hard-on when she was nearby. But hearing how she liked art, that she knew of *Las Meninas* and liked Baroque—that was fucking hot. I guess I never thought that this was how it could be with a woman. Anna's brain could turn me on as much as her body could—she created one new experience after another in me.

"What do you think?" She flashed me a smile over her shoulder as she shook her black-lace covered ass. She'd insisted on getting changed in the bathroom so I was trying to be patient, as much as I could be with a hard on and a beautiful woman who was about to move in with me three steps away.

"I think you would look incredible in a garbage bag. Get over here already."

She stayed where she was, and ran her hands up over her body, cupping those perfect tits and pushing them together. "Do you know what would make these look even better?" She looked up at me from under her eyelashes.

"My dick between them?"

She bit her lip and nodded. It took everything I had not to come right there.

She started to walk toward me and my phone buzzed loudly from the bedside table. Fuck. *Ignore it.* I was waiting for a couple of confirmations about tomorrow night. It had to be perfect. I quickly checked my watch. Shit, I wouldn't have time to call them back if I didn't get this, it was getting late. Anna's eyes were pinned to mine.

"Honey, I have to get this," I said as she climbed on to the mattress and lay on her back as I got off the bed and grabbed my phone.

"Do whatever you have to do, baby," she said as she dipped her fingers into her underwear. "Whatever you have to do."

Jesus, the blood rushing to my cock was making me dizzy. I kept my eyes flitting between her face and her hand as she started to circle her clit. Fuck, this call was bad timing.

"Scott," I barked as I answered the phone.

It was the woman making the arrangements for after dinner. *Shit, shit, shit.* Anna's back arched as she let out a small moan. I kicked the bed frame and stalked out into the study. She couldn't overhear this.

It took about ten minutes to get back to Anna.

"Do you think we should get a TV in here?" she asked, the mood clearly having shifted.

"If I'm in here, I want to be fucking you or sleeping. I don't want to be one of those couples that just end up watching TV in bed. Beds should have only two functions. Speaking of, where were we? Did you finish without me?" I stripped my shirt off and stepped out of my pants.

"I don't work without you. I'm desperate for you."

"Desperate for me?"

"Since this morning when you came in from your run, looking so handsome it should have been illegal." She was pouting and it was fucking cute.

I couldn't help but grin at the thought of her wanting me since this morning. "What have you been desperate for me to do to you?" I asked, crawling over her lingerie covered body. "This?" I asked, pinching her nipple through the lace. She nodded. "And biting? You like my teeth, don't you beautiful? The sharp rush that the pain brings?" She squirmed below me and grabbed my hand from her breast and pushed it lower. "You want me to feel you, beautiful?"

She nodded again.

"Tell me."

"I'm so wet, Ethan. Feel how wet I am."

My fingers found the edge of her underwear and

dipped inside and pushed into the beginning of her slit. She was as wet as she described, just waiting for me to lick her dry. I dragged my fingers along her folds, coating myself in her. She squirmed under my touch, pulling away and pushing toward me as if she couldn't decide whether she could handle it.

I moved down her body, pulling her underwear from her thighs.

"I need you inside me," she whispered.

I couldn't deny her and I plunged my thumb straight into her, rubbing against the muscles that surrounded me.

"No, I need your dick in me, Ethan. Please, I need it." She whimpered.

Jesus, her begging was too much, I couldn't hold back even if I wanted to.

"Oh, baby, you're going to have my dick every fucking way."

I pulled off the bed, stripped off my boxers, stood facing the bed and pulled her across to meet me at the edge of the mattress.

"You want it?" I stroked my erection up and down her folds, coating it in her wetness.

"Ethan, please," she cried.

I positioned myself at her entrance. She was twisting her hips, trying to get me inside her, but I held her waist firmly so she couldn't move.

"Once I start, I'm not going to stop. Not ever," I warned her.

"Don't ever stop, Ethan, I want you to fuck me forever."

I couldn't wait any longer, I thrust balls-deep into her and watched as the air left her body, a mixture of pleasure and lust on her face. I pulled out quickly and pushed into her again and again and again. Quick, hard, rough strokes. She could do nothing but lie there, watching me as I drove into her over and over.

"Oh god, yes," she screamed.

Hearing her tell me what she liked, what she wanted was a huge turn on. I loved her appetite, for sex, for me. It was intoxicating.

She clenched around me, the beginnings of her orgasm flickering across her body. I wasn't going to last long, but I had to get her there first.

I palmed her breast and she arched into my hand. "Ethan, I'm close, I can't wait."

My eyes darted from her face to between us, where our bodies joined. When I looked back at her she was watching as I pushed into her, so deep.

"God, Ethan, I'm so full with you deep inside me." Her voice cracked and there she was, her mouth parted and her eyes fixed on mine as her orgasm gripped her. I watched her for as long as I could before I gave in to my own climax and collapsed over her, burying my face in her neck.

Seconds, minutes, hours later her fingers trailed down my spine and my mind wandered back into consciousness.

Anna

Somehow, he always knew what to give me. I had needed him fast and hard and that's exactly what I got. The last twenty-four hours had unsettled me and sex had reminded me how well we worked together. Our dinner with Andrew and Mandy, during which it had been decided I would be moving countries, which I didn't think he could have been happier about, had been wonderful and life changing. Then today the way this alpha male who barked into his phone and lost his temper so easily found beauty in such a modest, beautiful painting. I loved him for all of it. But it was close to overwhelming.

The deeper I fell into my world with Ethan, the better the sex got. It was like he'd crawled inside my body and looked at me from the inside. It was thrilling and terrifying in equal measure. It was like I was giving myself to him, body and soul.

"You're amazing," I said as I lay my head on his chest, trailing my fingers up and down his stomach.

"Back at you." He caught my wrist in his hand. "Stop or I'm going to have you again."

I twisted my hand free and moved off his chest and

crawled down. I wanted to suck him. I liked it when I could fit him whole in my mouth, and he hardened against my tongue.

I positioned myself on my knees between his legs and he groaned and widened his thighs before I'd even touched him. I held his hips and took him in my mouth, lapping around his length.

I looked up to find Ethan propped on his elbows, his intense stare on me. He responded quickly and soon he was deep at the back of my throat. I moaned, and found his eyes with mine, knowing how he liked me to look at him.

"No, Anna." He pulled away from me, and before I knew it I was on my back and Ethan had his fingers against my clit.

"Ethan, I want you in my mouth."

"I want inside you more. I know you're ready for me." He kept his fingers moving across my clit as he pushed into me. "You always get so wet from sucking me." He rocked into me now in a perfect rhythm. "Do you know how hot that is? I don't have to do anything to get you wet, do I? I just have to lie there and get my dick sucked and you're ready for me."

"Oh, Ethan, stop. It's too much," I screamed. The sight of his muscles shifting beneath his skin, how it felt as he held himself back—he was doing everything he could not to come right that second. It was so good, so right.

"I'm never going to stop, beautiful, I'm going to fuck you for the rest of our days."

I was grabbing at him, urging him closer, deeper despite my words. I clung to his shoulders, my nails pushing into his skin, I needed to be closer to him, still. The feel of my nails on his skin increased the ecstasy of it all, the pleasure and the pain merging and multiplying. I stretched my legs wider and moved my hips to meet his so they crashed into each other—skin slapping against skin, flesh digging into flesh.

"That's it, beautiful, I can feel you so tight, so needy," he growled against my cheek before he licked across my lips, lapping at my moans. It was dirty and urgent. "Look at me, I want to see those beautiful eyes cloud over when you come."

I knew as soon as I opened my eyes, I'd be lost to him. The feel of him over me, pinning me to the bed . . . the smell of him—sweat and sex mixed together—if I looked at him, that would be it. But I couldn't deny him anything and slowly I did as he asked. My body tensed and then juddered and my nails broke into his skin. I couldn't hold back as I screamed, "Ethan, Ethan, Ethan."

He was there too, managing to hold off for just long enough to watch the beginning of my climax as he loved to do. His blood throbbed beneath his skin, transferring his heat to me—he was sweaty and panting and his jaw tensed as he poured into me.

"Oh, beautiful," he cried and his head dropped to my neck.

Eventually, our breathing synchronized and slowed but he made no attempt to move. And I didn't want him to. I loved him on top of me like that—heavy, vulnerable and all mine.

"Do you mind if I stay here forever?" he asked.

"Not even a little bit," I whispered.

He nuzzled against my neck and then licked across the still throbbing pulse. "You taste so good," he mumbled. "I want to taste you every day, forever."

"Soon," I said, turning my head to give him better access to my neck.

He took full advantage and his teeth grazed against my skin. "You're mine,"

"I am."

"Forever," he said as he bit into my skin.

At some point we fell asleep because I woke up too hot, Ethan's arms still tight around me. I tried to move him off me without disturbing him but it didn't work. "Again, beautiful?" he mumbled and pulled me closer to him.

"I need to go to the bathroom, let me go." His limbs relaxed and I was able to pull away.

It was gone 8 a.m. when I checked the clock. I wanted to make the most of the day so when I got back in bed, I reached between our bodies and stroked his semi-erect cock to life. In response, Ethan mumbled incoherently, his eyes still closed. He usually woke before me, so seeing him like this, before he was alert and ready for the world was new. I pushed him gently onto his back and sat astride him before taking him in my fist and guiding him into to me.

"Fuck, baby," he continued to mumble, his eyes still closed, as I slowly lowered myself onto him. I could feel him inside me, hardening still, and I let out a small moan as I started to raise and lower myself. He was so deep inside me with me on top. I sat back on my heels, pushing as low as I could and I circled my hips.

Ethan's eyes suddenly sprang open. "Shit!"

I smiled at him. "It's your 8 a. m. wake-up call, sir. Is there anything else I can do for you?" I asked as I pressed my palms against his stomach and lifted myself higher.

His hands went straight to my hips to pull me down. "Do you want me on your cock, sir? You want to be deep inside me?" I let him push me onto his cock as he took over my rhythm and thrust his hips up so I didn't have to move at all.

"Jesus, Anna, what are you? Shit." He was wide awake, responding to my grinding against him, his eyes huge and wandering from my face down my body to where we were joined and back up, always checking for my reaction to whatever he was doing to my body.

"That's it, Ethan, right there," I screamed as he

pounded into me faster and faster. I wanted to stay like that forever, circling the mountain, just before the pleasure peaked. I collapsed onto his chest and his hands cupped my ass, keeping me in place as he continued to pump in and out of me, dragging me further and further toward my orgasm.

His fingers parted my ass cheeks and air curled against my sex. "You want to feel me here, baby?" he whispered into my hair as he brushed his fingers against the puckered flesh.

"I do, oh god." The thought was as erotic as the reality, and my body gave me my first warning that my orgasm was close.

He pushed his erection deep into me and stilled. "Look at me Anna."

I wasn't sure I was capable of moving, but I managed to straighten my arms so I was still leaning over him. His fingers circled and stroked and then one pushed through the barrier of muscles. The sensation was calming almost, intense, and I slowly circled my hips, allowing myself to feel more of him.

"You like that?" he asked.

"I like everything you do to me," I replied. I stopped moving and another finger followed his first and started to slowly push.

"And this?"

"I want it deeper, Ethan."

He grunted and pushed his hips up into me and then stopped again before pushing his fingers farther into me. I was full of him.

I snapped my head back in response to the sensation and I moved my hands to his chest, pushing deeper and farther onto him.

"Fuck, Ethan, I'm coming."

"Look at me, Anna."

We were both still, frozen almost from the intensity of it and my eyes met his just as a world of intense pleasure washed over me, just from him being inside me.

"Jesus, I'm going to come so hard," he growled as he removed his fingers slowly, and without breaking the link between our bodies, flipped me to my back and pounded into me, taking his pleasure.

"You. Make. Me. Feel. So. Good," he said between his final thrusts as be poured into me. It was just what I needed to hear after him making me feel like no other man ever had or ever would.

CHAPTER
Three

Ethan

"So, what do you guys do on New Year's Eve, during the day? Carve pumpkins?" Anna asked as I wandered back into the bedroom. I'd been making last minute arrangements for this evening.

"No, we don't carve pumpkins on New Year's any more than we carve pumpkins on Thanksgiving."

"Oh, so what do you do?"

I thought about it. Were there traditions that I'd forgotten? "Nothing, we can do the tourist thing again. Or wander into the village."

"What, not even tonight?"

"I've booked us a restaurant for tonight. If they're not partying, people normally watch the ball drop in Times Square on TV."

"Are we going to do that?"

"It depends, do you want to stand outside in freezing temperatures from about three o'clock to reserve your space?"

"That doesn't sound like much fun."

"I can't imagine it is. We'll have a nice evening."

"I know, I always do when I'm with you."

Just before my heart exploded the intercom buzzed.

Lucky for me Anna wasn't quite ready, so I managed to intercept the courier from Harry Winston without too much suspicion. I took the padded envelope into the study and locked the door as quietly as I could. I wanted to see the ring and there was no way I could risk her walking in on me.

I was pretty sure she'd like it, but they had said we could choose something else if it wasn't right. It was plainer than the first ones the woman behind the counter first picked out—just a simple band and a single square diamond. I didn't think Anna would like too much. She wasn't a show off. Yes—it would suit her.

My stomach began to churn. I really didn't want to fuck this up. I wanted it to be perfect. I wanted her to return to London with my ring on her finger.

"You're right, it's absolutely freezing. How did that happen?" Anna asked as we sat down in the horse and buggy in Central Park.

"If it starts shitting into that bag, we're stopping this thing and going home," I said.

Anna started laughing at me. "Just focus on how bloody cold it is, that will take your mind off the bag of poo in front of you."

"Are we done with the touristy stuff after this?"

"Yes, this experience has put me off doing anything else. I thought it would be more romantic than it is. But the cold and the poo has taken the sheen off."

"We can do romance later," I replied.

"You're the most romantic man ever."

"Your sarcasm isn't always a turn on, you know."

"I wasn't being sarcastic," she said as she pulled closer to me. "I mean it. Romance for me is someone who doesn't bullshit, doesn't play games and treats me well. Someone who loves me and doesn't just say it, but shows it in everything he does. And you do all that, Ethan. I don't want or need anything else from you."

I kissed the top of her head. "Does that mean we can get out of this buggy?"

She laughed. "Yes, we can get off. As long as we can do the bridge."

"Deal."

Luckily we were only a few short minutes from Bow Bridge. We walked to the center point and then rested side by side against the railings, looking out across the water. The pond's surface was still and the air was silent as if the rest of the world had paused while we had this moment together.

She turned and stretched her arms around my waist and looked up at me. "This is perfect. I think I'm going to like it here."

"I think I'm going to like you here, too."

Maybe I shouldn't wait, maybe I should ask her right now.

"Let's come here often," she said and the moment was gone. "Maybe it could be a new tradition that we have every Sunday or something. You can push me over to the view across the lake in my wheelchair when I'm too old to walk anymore."

It was a glimpse inside her image of our future together, a picture she didn't reveal very often.

"Deal. I like the idea of having traditions of our own. Come on, the sun is going down and it's going to get really cold."

She nodded. "Let's go home."

We found a cab and headed back toward home.

"You haven't really told me what we're doing tonight. What time are our reservations?" she asked as we got back.

"We need to leave the apartment at just before eight." I had decided to ask her just before midnight. There would be several moments tonight but there was no arrangement for a plane to carry a banner asking the question, or the ring to be in the bottom of a champagne glass. I wanted it to me more intimate than that. I wanted it to be just about us.

She paused, looked at me and the quietly said, "I'd like to see New York tonight and then I'd like to come back here, take all the pillows and blankets and quilts and pile them all on the floor. Then turn off all the lights and then lie on our mountain of bedding and watch the river and listen to the city with you, naked."

"We can do that."

"Really? It doesn't interfere with your plans? Did you have us going to some big, fancy party? I don't mind."

"Of course I didn't. Tonight was always just about you and me."

Anna

I was relieved we weren't going to some fancy benefit type thing that evening. I'd brought a full-length evening dress, just in case, but as it was just dinner, I kept things a little more casual in a tight fitting, high-waist satin pencil skirt and sheer-sleeved silk blouse. I also made a special effort with my hair, first curling it and then pinning it up loosely. When I was finished, I put some make-up in my clutch and went to find Ethan. I almost ran into him as he was coming out of his office.

"Hey, I'm ready."

"You look incredible," he said, reaching his hand out to cup my ass.

"You don't look so bad yourself." What I meant was he looked heart-stoppingly handsome. He was wearing a suit but no tie. He seemed to get better looking, if that was at all possible. "I like your hair longer like that," I said, pushing my fingers through the strands as he bent to kiss my neck.

"You'll need your coat. And gloves and a scarf."

"Thanks, Dad."

"Anna," he growled.

Ethan had hired a car for the evening and we headed uptown to the restaurant.

To my surprise we pulled up at the entrance to the Time Warner building. We seemed to be going to the Mandarin Oriental.

I looked at Ethan and he smiled at me and took my hand as we walked inside. We didn't end up going to the hotel. Instead we headed to the fourth floor, to a restaurant called Per Se.

"I thought you might like to look out from here. It's lower than from the suite, but still beautiful and I know how you love that view."

"Ethan, it's beautiful and thoughtful and—thank you."

They seated us kitty corner by the window and a stunning view of Columbus Circle and Central Park.

"Have you been here before?"

He shook his head "No. But I always wanted to come. I've never had the opportunity until now. And tonight seemed to be the perfect time to share this with you."

"You're right. It *is* perfect."

I had butterflies in my stomach. The evening felt big.

Ethan had clearly put a lot of thought into picking this place.

"Shall we have a glass of champagne?" he asked

I nodded a little too enthusiastically.

"Maybe a bottle?" he asked the waiter. "Are you okay?" he asked me when we were alone again.

"Yeah, of course. A bit overwhelmed coming back here, you know?"

He nodded. "To where it all began? It was only going to be for the night and now you're moving here."

"Are we being crazy?" I asked him. "Maybe this is a little nuts," I said, thinking out loud, my heart starting to thump in my chest.

"What do you mean crazy?"

"I mean me moving to New York and us living together. I had a job and I have friends and family in London and I'm going to start again in New York. I mean it sounds like maybe it's a little crazy?"

"Are you worried? Are you thinking you might not want to?"

I took a deep breath and thought about the question. Was I worried? I shook my head. "I don't feel worried. I know in my heart like it's the right thing to do, but I think that if I was looking at my decision, not knowing how I feel about you, then I'd think I was a little nuts. Does that make sense?"

All I could think was that this was happening so

quickly. Coming back here brought it all in to focus. I needed to calm down. It wasn't like I couldn't undo things if it all went badly wrong, right? If I could handle the worst case scenario—Ethan and I breaking up once I'd moved here—surely I would feel better.

Ethan didn't respond, he just looked at me. I couldn't read him.

"And it's not like I don't have a job. And we're getting married or anything, god forbid."

"God forbid?"

"Yeah, I mean, it will be fine. I'm looking forward to it."

Ethan was silent. I reached for his hand and he squeezed it as he looked out onto the view.

"I'm sorry. I was thinking out loud. I shouldn't do that. I just got overwhelmed coming back here, thinking back to our beginning and forgot my filter."

"I don't want you to filter anything. I've told you. I need you to talk to me and I'm glad you did," he said. There was something in his voice that told me however much he wanted me to talk to him, he was disappointed with what I'd said.

"It doesn't mean I have doubts. Not about you, or about us, Ethan."

He squeezed my hand and kissed me on the corner of my lips, in the way that made me melt. "God forbid," he said.

I lost count of the number of courses when we got to five.

"I've never tasted anything like this," I said. "I think they have wizards in the kitchen."

"Wizards?" Ethan raised an eyebrow at me.

"I think so. No human can create things to eat like this. It's magic. Is it what you thought it would be?"

"In some ways. Better because I'm sharing it with you, I think."

"Wow, you have all the lines tonight."

He chuckled. "I think maybe I lost one or two along the way tonight."

"You did?"

"So, we're going to make a stop on our way home, ring in the New Year and then go back to create an Everest of feathers in the living room to get naked on. Sound good?" he asked.

"Sure. Where are we seeing in the New Year?"

"You'll see."

I grinned at him. "I can't believe I'm flying home tomorrow."

"It's gone quickly. But you'll be back soon. You promise you'll speak to them about your notice period?"

"I promise."

"Because if they don't shorten it to a month, I'm going to step in."

"Ethan, you're not going to do anything. I'll deal with it. You've got other things to do—like clearing out closet space."

"We can go shopping for the apartment when you get back if you like?"

"What for? What do you need?"

"Well, if you want to refurnish it or change things."

"I love your apartment, just like it is. Why would I want to buy new things for it?"

"I want it to be our apartment."

I grinned at him "Well, we might need some new pillows after tonight."

"So, Miss Anna. One more view for you before we head home."

I followed his eyes up toward the sky as I stepped onto the sidewalk and realized the car had stopped outside the Empire State Building. "I know you came with Leah, but it's different at night.

"Good evening, Mr. Scott," the doorman said and we stepped into the lobby. I looked at him. The doorman knew his name? The lobby was quiet, with just members of staff peppered around, their eyes on us.

We headed toward the elevator, which was being held open for us. I looked at Ethan but he kept his eyes straight ahead, his hand clasped in mine.

"You have friends in high places," I said to him as the lift doors closed.

He grinned and looked down at me but didn't say a word. We went straight to the Main Deck on the 86th floor. The elevator doors pinged and we stepped out to the internal viewing area to the sound of Tony Bennett singing *Manhattan*. I looked around and didn't see a single other person. Did we have the place to ourselves? Was it closed?

Apparently, it wasn't closed to us. By the door there was a small table, on it an ice bucket holding a bottle of champagne and two glasses.

"I can't believe you've done this Ethan." He was fighting a grin as he expertly opened the bottle of champagne.

"I want your first New Year's in New York to be a proper introduction to the city. From up here, you get to see your future."

"Our future," I said feeling overwhelmed and breathless. "You're amazing and I'm so lucky," I managed to choke out.

"You got that wrong. I'm the lucky one," he said as he handed me a glass of champagne and kissed me lightly on the lips.

He grabbed my hand and we headed outside.

CHAPTER
Eleven

Ethan

I opened the door and we were hit by a rush of cold air.

This was meant to be it. It was just coming up to midnight and the ring box in my pocket felt like it was on fire. It was going to have to stay where it was. God forbid I ask her to marry me. God forbid.

"Is it too cold?" I asked as we walked slowly around the edge of the viewing area, stopping at various places.

"I have you to keep me warm. And it's too beautiful not to be out here. It's incredible. How did you manage to get the whole place just for us?"

It hadn't been easy and it hadn't been cheap, but it was meant to have been for a once in a lifetime moment.

"I wanted tonight to be special, I told you."

I hadn't pressed her on her earlier revelation. Did she mean she didn't want to get married to anyone, or just me? Was she bullshitting me? I knew she loved me. I felt it, but I hadn't expected this. I wanted to marry her. I wanted her to wear my ring and tell the world that she was mine. Fuck.

I could feel her looking at me and without catching

her eye, I bent down and kissed her on the corner of her lips.

"Kiss me properly, Ethan," she whispered and her hands went to my hair as she pulled me toward her. "I feel like I lost you a little." She ran her tongue across the seam of my lips and I closed my eyes and breathed her in. She was right, I needed to feel her, to taste her. I parted my mouth and she pushed her tongue against mine. She felt so good. She always felt so good.

"You'll never lose me. You have me for as long as you want me," I said, drawing away from our kiss.

"Long enough for you to push me in my wheelchair over Bow Bridge?"

"Longer."

"Long enough for you to have to remember things for me because I can't?"

"I do that already."

"That's true," she said thoughtfully. "Okay, long enough that I can't take my bra off without my boobs hitting the floor?" My mouth twitched at the corners. "And don't you dare say that happens already."

"Longer."

"Long enough for us to wave our grandchildren off to college?"

"Longer." My chest constricted but I managed to get that single word out. So kids were okay, grandkids were okay, but not marriage?

Our Q&A was interrupted by the sound of horns honking and people cheering and the distant pop of fireworks.

She grabbed my wrist to look at my watch and then up at me. "Happy New Year Ethan," she said, grinning at me.

I grabbed her around the waist and pulled her toward me. "Happy New Year, Anna."

When our fingers and toes had turned blue from cold, we headed home. Anna seemed excited by our trip and although I was pleased to have made her happy, I had hoped the evening would have turned out a little differently.

"Are you okay?" Anna asked as we carried pillows and blankets from the bedroom and arranged them on the floor opposite the views of the Hudson.

"I'm always okay if I'm with you."

"Okay, if you're sure."

I wasn't sure at all. Something hard had lodged in the pit of my stomach. "Of course. I'm just going to miss you, that's all."

"I'm going to speak to the partners as soon as I get in to the office. I'll be back before you know it and then you won't be able to get rid of me."

"I can't wait," I said and kissed her on the head, trying to give her the reassurance I needed.

My phone vibrated against the table. Andrew and Mandy were calling.

Anna looked at me. "Are you going to get that?"

I shook my head. "No, let's just be us tonight." Mandy would be dying to hear about how my proposal went. What would I say?

"Can we stay up all night in our den of nakedness?"

"You'll be begging for sleep before too long if you insist on being naked in our den."

"Betcha I won't," she teased as she started to undo her blouse.

"That's a bet I'll take."

If I'd taken much longer, Mandy would probably have called 911, but the traffic was a bitch on the way back from the airport.

"Hey," she said as she answered the door and handed me a whiskey. "I thought you might need this."

"Thanks," I said and tipped my head back to take the glass full in two mouthfuls. "Can I come in?"

"God, yes. Come in, come in."

I followed Mandy into the kitchen where she took my glass from me and poured me another.

"Hey, dude," Andrew said as he saw me. I forced a smile and then slumped on the breakfast barstool and pushed my hands through my hair. "I don't know how to feel."

"Tell us what happened. Did she say no?" Mandy asked.

I'd had about three hundred missed calls from Mandy in the past twenty-four hours and I'd texted her on the way to the airport that we were headed to the airport as planned and that things hadn't gone to plan. In response Mandy had simply told me to come to their place on the way back from the airport. At first I'd started to text back that I was going to go straight home, but I found that I wanted some company. I needed some help to understand what had happened and what it all meant.

"I didn't ask her."

"Ethan!" Mandy screamed. "She's perfect for you. You can't have changed your mind."

"Mandy, honey, just listen to him," Andrew said.

"She told me before I got the chance that she didn't want to get married. What was I meant to say? 'I know you don't want to get married, but I really do and I've got the ring already and so could you just change your mind?'"

"She said she didn't want to marry you? Are you sure?" Mandy asked, her face twisted in confusion.

I shrugged and took another slug of whiskey.

"What exactly did she say?"

"I can't really remember, it's all such a blur—we were talking about her moving to New York and I could tell she was a bit anxious about it. She was talking really fast and her barely there filter had disappeared completely. And she asked whether her moving was the right thing and she was answering her own question and said that at least she had a job and it wasn't as if we were getting married—and then this bit I remember clearly—she said 'god forbid.' Yes, she said, 'It's not like we're getting married—god forbid.' And then she was talking about something else.

I looked up from my glass and Mandy was looking straight back at me with a scowl on her face. "Had you talked about getting married before? Kids, a dog? Had you ever heard anything like this from her before?"

I took a deep breath in and exhaled slowly as I thought about her question. "No. We were all about living in the here and now. She didn't want to talk about the future in London. And then we agreed to try the long-distance thing and suddenly the future's here and I have no fucking clue what's going on. I guess I just assumed that if she was prepared to move to New York for me, she would be prepared to marry me for fuck's sake."

"More whiskey." Andrew nodded at Mandy and she hurriedly poured out another glassful.

"It doesn't sound like she doesn't want to marry you," Mandy said.

"She said 'god forbid', Mandy. Unless I've lost the ability to speak English, that's not an exact translation of 'Ethan, I'm desperate to be your wife and carry your children.'"

"What I meant was, I don't think it's personal."

The whiskey was having the desired effect and it took my brain a few seconds longer than it should to process her words. "I'm not sure it matters," I said finally.

"Maybe she just doesn't believe in marriage?" Andrew said.

"That's bullshit." I tipped back my third generous glass of whiskey.

Anna

I hadn't gotten much sleep on the plane, but I had managed to make it home to shower and change before going in to the office. I'd texted Ethan to say I'd landed, not wanting to wake him. When I next spoke to him, I wanted to be able to tell him that I'd had a conversation about my leaving date, which meant I had until about eleven to follow up with the partners.

Just as I sat down at my desk, my phone buzzed. "Happy New Year," I said to Leah as I answered.

"Happy New Year to you, too. How was it? Did you go to a party?"

"No, thank goodness." I went on to explain about the most perfect evening ever.

"He hired out the top of the Empire State Building for the two of you?" Leah asked.

"Yes, it was amazing. Cold but amazing. The lights from the city were spectacular and you could hear all the horns going off and the cheers. It was kinda special."

"Wow, fantastic. It sounds like the kind of thing you see in a movie when the guy proposes."

My stomach lurched. "He didn't propose Leah, don't be silly."

"I'm serious. He didn't propose? It sounds like the perfect setting."

My mind started running through the evening of events, it had been the perfect evening and so romantic. But we'd never talked about marriage.

"There's no way and I'm not interested in getting married. Ethan knows that."

"You would have said no? Now you're being silly."

"Leah, I don't have time to talk about this. He didn't ask. I have to speak to Paul about my notice period, so I'll catch you later." Leah and I had arranged to have dinner tonight. I hung up and headed toward Paul's office.

Would I have said no? Could I deny Ethan anything I had to give him?

I'd think about it later. I needed to focus on convincing Paul that I shouldn't work my three-month notice.

"Happy New Year, Anna," Paul said as I put my head round his office door.

"Happy New Year, Paul. Have you got five minutes?"

"As long as you are going to tell me you've had a change of heart about leaving over the break."

I could tell by his expression that he wasn't really expecting me to take anything back.

"Yes, well about that. I really haven't changed my mind. And I think I might have sorted out another job in New York. And it's just going to take a lot of organization to move and adjust and sort everything here and as it's the beginning of a year, I don't have much work to do at the moment and I was wondering if you could at all think about whether you actually could see if you could perhaps—"

"Take a breath! You're usually a lot more eloquent than this, Anna," Paul said, grinning at me. "You don't want to work your full notice period?"

I nodded.

"Is it a law firm you're going to in New York?"

"No, General Counsel of Palmerston Hotels, I think. Nothing's finalized yet."

Paul nodded. "Sounds interesting, Anna. Well, it's not a competitor and it is quiet in terms of work at the moment. We're expecting a busy quarter though. Let me have a think about it and I'll talk to some of the other partners and come back to you."

"Thank you so much. Anything you could do, I would really appreciate."

I practically skipped out of the office and down the corridor. That sounded hopeful. It would be great if I had news before the next time I spoke to Ethan.

Usually, the first week in January was all about catching up with colleagues and avoiding doing any work for as long as possible, but I set about compiling lists of things I had to do before I left. If they told me I didn't have to work my notice, I wanted to be able to go as quickly as possible. My secretary was going to hate me because she was going to be ass deep in filing by lunchtime.

By midday I still hadn't heard from Ethan, so I sent him another text.

A: Spoke to Paul. He's thinking about it. I'm hopeful. I love you.

SG: Good. Hung over, speak later. Love you.

Hung over? Ethan was never hung over. Where had he been last night?

Before I had a chance to ask him, Lucy barged into my office. "A little bird told me you were leaving," she said.

"Yes, that's right." I really wanted to be able to tell her that I was moving in with Ethan Scott, the object of her lust for the previous four months. But there was no point in making things difficult for Ethan.

"Have you been made an offer you can't refuse? I hear some firms are offering twenty percent raises to move. Have you got a good deal?"

"I'm not moving for the money. I'm going to New York."

"New York?" she spat out.

I nodded.

"To work?"

Lucy wouldn't be someone from London I missed.

"And live, yes."

"You have a job in New York?"

"Yes."

"Well, I might be out there, too. I work so closely with Ethan that I'm bound to get the secondment I've applied for," she announced.

I raised my eyebrow and then grinned because I'd caught that move from Ethan. "Good luck with that," I said.

"Wouldn't that be great? In New York together, doing the single girl thing?"

"But maybe you'd be dating Ethan by then?" I added. It was mean and I shouldn't have said it but I couldn't resist.

"That's a good point. I'd probably be busy accompanying him to parties or dinners. I'm sure I could squeeze you in at some point."

"Well, you just let me know, Lucy. You'll have to excuse me, I have to make a call."

Lucy spun around and stalked out of my office.

I spent the rest of the day working hard. My heart and mind were somewhere else now and I wanted my body to catch up.

When I left at seven thirty, there were few people left. Most of my colleagues were making the most of their clients still being distracted by the holiday season and leaving the office early.

I was headed to dinner with Leah. London was cold but not as cold as New York. The thought made me realize I'd still not heard from Ethan. I pulled out my phone and dragged off my glove so I could more easily dial his number.

He didn't answer, so I hung up without leaving a message. Then I decided that maybe I wanted to leave a message and tell him that I'd spoken to Paul, so I dialed him again.

He answered on the second ring. "Anna? What is it?"

"Nothing, I was expecting your voicemail. I just called and you didn't pick up."

"I'm in the middle of a meeting. I can't just pick up." He sounded pissed off and stressed.

"I know. I didn't mean to interrupt." I paused, wanting him to say something but he didn't. "I was just going to leave you a message."

"Well, I've picked up now, so what is it?"

He'd never been so short with me. So cold. It winded

me and left me grasping for words. "Nothing, I just . . . I spoke to Paul and I think he was open about my notice period. But it's not urgent. We can talk about it this evening."

"Fine. I'll call you later if I get a chance. Today's going to be very busy. I gotta go."

"Okay, bye, I love you."

"Later."

"Ethan?"

"Yes?"

"Are you okay?"

"Yes, busy."

"Okay," I said, and then he was gone.

I found that I'd stopped walking and I was standing with commuters rushing each side of me. What had just happened? Even when Ethan was busy and stressed with work he was never like that with me. He was never rude or snappy. Maybe Al had reported him for breaching the frat policy? But why would he be mad at me?

Something felt wrong.

I typed out a text.

A: I'm worried about you. You sound stressed. Would a naked picture help?

That would cheer him up surely? I smiled to myself and buried my phone back in my pocket and continued my walk to meet Leah at the restaurant.

CHAPTER
Twelve

Ethan

I'd snapped at Anna and I hated myself for it. I was being an asshole. But I couldn't shake the black cloud that had settled over me, and part of me blamed her for it. I kept telling myself that it was my hangover, but I knew better. Was it such big deal that she didn't want to marry me? It shouldn't be. We could be happy together without being married, surely. But somehow and suddenly, it had become a big deal.

Anna

"Daniel's just popped to the loo. Is it okay that he came?" Leah asked as she poured white wine into an empty glass opposite me at the restaurant.

"Of course." I would have preferred just Leah and me for dinner. Not that I didn't adore Daniel, but it was always slightly different when it was the three of us.

"Are you okay?" Leah asked.

"Yeah, I just—Ethan's stressed and he was a bit snappy with me on the phone. I know I'm being over sensitive, he's just never been like that with me and it just makes it worse when he's so far away." My throat began to thicken and I took a sip of my wine. "Maybe it's all getting a bit too real for him and he's having doubts?"

"He's crazy for you. He's not having doubts. It will be fine. Talk to him later."

Daniel came back to the table and kissed me on the cheek. "What's going on?" he asked. "Have you got a moving date?"

"I'm still waiting to hear. I spoke to Paul earlier and he's going to come back to me, but he sounded positive about it."

"I'm going to miss you so much," Leah said.

"God, Leah don't. The mood I'm in, I'll start bawling and you'll have to carry me home."

Daniel pulled a glum looking Leah toward him. "I go to New York all the time—you can just come with me. You'll see plenty of each other."

"The mood Ethan's in, he'll probably call it all off and I'll be stuck here anyway."

"Don't be silly," Leah said. "He was going to propose, I'm sure of it." Leah then proceeded to tell Daniel about our New Year's Eve and how Ethan had hired out the top of the Empire State Building. "Don't you think it's the sort of thing you do when you propose?" Leah asked him.

"He didn't though?" Daniel asked.

I shook my head. "Just because he did something thoughtful and romantic doesn't mean he was going to ask me to marry him. And anyway, I have no interest in getting married."

"You don't?" Daniel looked surprised.

"No, not really. I've never seen the point. So many people end up unhappy or divorced. Isn't it more romantic to stay together because you want to, rather than because you signed a bit of paper?"

Daniel looked at me, almost as if he were concerned.

"And anyway, guys hate the idea of marriage," I continued.

"Well, I'm a guy and I don't hate the idea of marriage," Daniel said. "I think it's important to be able to say to the world and each other that you love someone, and you're committing the rest of your lives together. I don't know how I'd feel if Leah didn't want to marry me. It's true, I don't care at all for the wedding, but the wedding and being married are two different things."

"Yeah, but you're Daniel Armitage. You're not most guys."

"Is Ethan most guys?" Leah asked.

"I don't even know why we're talking about this. He hasn't asked me. We didn't talk about it and after our conversation today we're never likely to." I surreptitiously checked my phone. He'd not even responded to the naked photo offer. Something must be up.

"Well, the top of the Empire State building for just the two of you on New Year's Eve sounds like he wants you to be happy," Daniel said. "And that can only be a good thing."

Back at the flat, I'd still not heard from Ethan. I wanted to call him but I didn't want to disturb him again. I decided to give Mandy a call instead. It would be about six in New York, so she was likely to be home and Andrew would still be at work.

"Hey, soon-to-be New Yorker," Mandy squealed as she answered the phone.

I couldn't help but smile. "Hey, I called to wish you happy New Year. Is now a good time?"

"Of course. Happy New Year. I'm so pleased you called. How's the jetlag? Have you got a date for moving yet?"

"No date, but I'm hopeful I won't have to work the full three months. I should hear in the next few days. I've started to pack things up in the office though, and I'll start on the flat tomorrow."

"You don't sound excited."

I didn't feel it. I felt heavy. "Well, you know there's a lot to do."

"Ethan is desperate to get you over here as soon as possible."

"Hmmm, maybe."

"What do you mean 'maybe'? Of course he is. The man would do anything for you. He's head over heels."

"He didn't sound it earlier. I think we just had our first argument. Or maybe we didn't and I'm just overreacting."

"What did you argue about? New Year's?"

"No, and what about New Year's?"

"What were you arguing about then?"

"He was just snappy with me, and told me I was disturbing him and that he had a hangover. But what about New Year's?" Was she deliberately avoiding my question?

"Yeah, he had too much whiskey last night."

"He was with you?"

"And Andrew, he came by on the way back from the airport."

Why hadn't he said anything about going to Andrew and Mandy's? It was so unlike him.

"Anna?"

I didn't know what to say. Something felt really off, but there was nothing I could put my finger on. Mandy had just confirmed that he had a hangover. I knew today was going to be a busy day for him. Although his response was asshole-like, it shouldn't have created the feeling that my heart was going to crash through my chest.

"Yeah, I'm here. Mandy, tell me about New Year's.

Why would we be arguing about it? I know you're Ethan's friend but I need you to tell me which bit of the puzzle I'm obviously missing."

"I love you guys together. I want you two to make it work."

"Mandy," I warned.

"Anna, he will kill me if I tell you."

"And if you don't, I will." My mind was racing. Did he have a secret love child or a gay past? What was Mandy about to tell me?

"Jesus, Anna, if you tell him I told you, I'll kill you. How's that?"

"I won't. I promise. Please put me out of my misery."

"He was planning to propose. On New Year's."

Shit. Leah had been right.

"Anna?"

"I'm still here. On New Year's Eve? Why didn't he?"

"Apparently you told him that you didn't want to marry him earlier in the evening."

"When earlier?" We'd not talked about getting married.

"I don't know exactly. He was planning to ask you at the top of the Empire State Building, so sometime before that."

"I didn't say I wouldn't marry him, I'd not really considered it. I just don't get marriage. It's not important to me, but he knows that, I think. Was he seriously going to ask me?"

"By the look of the ring I saw a picture of, I'd say he was as serious as he's ever been about anything."

"And now he's pissed off. I've hurt him." It wasn't a question—it just all made sense. If I thought about it, things had been off since that night. He'd seemed a bit distant and distracted. I'd not been paying attention.

"He's questioning himself and whether you want the same things that he does. You just need to talk about it. I know how you feel about him. And deep down, so does he. I reminded him that you're moving continents for him, but all he can focus on is you not wanting to marry him."

There was nothing I wanted more in that moment than to be able to transport myself to New York. I needed to explain myself. "Thanks for telling me. Thank god you did. Please don't tell him that we've had this conversation. I'm going to make this right."

I fished out my blackberry from my coat pocket and emailed Paul, saying that it was really important to me that I finish as soon as possible and that I needed to take next week off, even if they couldn't let me go for good at the end of this week.

I then found my phone and texted Ethan.

A: I love you. I miss you.

I couldn't have him doubting my heart for a second.

Then I logged on to my laptop and booked myself a one-way ticket to New York for Saturday. I had four days to pack up my life. If work didn't release me from my contract, I'd take unpaid leave or go sick or something.

I jumped at my phone's text alert.

SG: Good. Me too.

I smiled at the words. I hadn't expected him to reply given his earlier mood but I was glad that it didn't sound like he'd given up.

A: I spoke to Paul. He's talking to the other partners. I'm going to speak to him again tomorrow.

Before I'd put my phone down after I'd sent my text, it started to ring. The words 'Sex God' flashed up.

"Hey handsome. How's the hangover?" I answered.

"Hey. Not good. I went to Andrew and Mandy's last night and drank too much whiskey."

"I wish I were there so I could run you a bath and give you a head massage."

"Yeah?" He sounded tired. "I wish you were here, too."

"Really? You were pretty grouchy with me earlier."

"I know. I'm sorry. I just have a lot going on . . . "

"I thought we had a rule that we shared stuff." I really wanted him to tell me what he wanted for our future. I wanted the no-bullshit Ethan.

"It's just boring work stuff."

I wondered if that had been the first time Ethan had bullshitted me.

Ethan

I hated that I wasn't being honest with her. But I needed time. We had seemed to want the same things out of life up until now. I needed to talk to her about our future but it wasn't a conversation we could have over the phone.

I decided to go for a run. I'd spent most of the evening in the study, trying to get through a mountain of emails and I didn't seem to be making any progress. A run would help me clear my head. I changed and headed off. It was quiet out. I normally ran in the mornings, so this was different for me. I should have worn a hat. It was colder than I expected. The warmth of the apartment had lulled me into a false sense of security. I picked up my pace, eager to warm up, and headed east toward Washington Square Park. I tread my familiar route of the smaller roads to my destination, not thinking about work, not thinking about Anna. I just concentrated on my breathing as I settled into a comforting rhythm.

Nobody had told the shivering bodies in the park that it was cold and time to go home. People were scattered across the benches as if it were the middle of the summer. I grinned at a couple who looked like they were having an argument, but were still holding hands.

The laces of my running shoes loosened and when I glanced down, my left shoe had come untied. I stopped at one of the empty benches to fasten it, more aware of my heavy breathing once I'd stopped running.

"Ethan?" A female voice I half-recognized asked.

I looked up to find Clarissa, one of the Hamptons set, walking toward me. I stood and kissed her on the cheek. "Hi Clarissa. Not seen you in a while."

"No, not since the summer. How are things? How's work?"

"Yeah, good," I replied pushing my hands through my hair.

"How're Mandy and Andrew?"

"Yeah, they're fine. I saw them last night. And you? What are you doing downtown? Don't you live uptown?"

"You remembered," she said, smiling at me as if it were a secret. We'd fucked a few years ago. It had been a one-time deal but we ran in the same circles and we bumped into each other here and there. "I was just having drinks with friends and I wanted to walk through the park before I got a cab home. I love it at this time of night."

I nodded. "It's one of my favorite places."

"You could see me home if you wanted? I have an excellent single malt back at my apartment," she said.

My stomach flipped at the thought. "I'm with Anna. You met her right?"

"Oh yeah," she said. "The girl from the Hamptons. I remember her I think. But she's not here now and," she glanced down at my left hand and then back up at me, "I don't see a ring."

I stepped back from her. "There doesn't need to be a ring, Clarissa." I looked at her because I wanted to see her understand what I was saying. "There doesn't need to be a ring." I repeated. "Have a good night." I headed out of the park.

And there it was. The answer I didn't know that I'd been looking for. I didn't need to marry her. I wanted her forever and a ring wasn't what was going to guarantee that. I would just have to work hard every day to convince her to stay. I could do that.

I checked my watch. It was gone ten. Too late or too early to call her, but a darkness had been lifted from me. Just because she didn't want to get married didn't mean that I couldn't convince her to spend the rest of her life with me. And I wanted that life to start as soon as possible.

CHAPTER Thirteen

Anna

I needed to find a quiet corner of the airport to call Ethan, he'd just texted me, asking me if I was around. He still didn't know I was flying over. I wanted it to be a surprise. In the end I went into the Gucci shop and pretended to be thinking about buying a handbag. Hopefully, Ethan wouldn't guess where I was.

"Hey beautiful," he answered. His mood had shifted this week. Things were definitely better but I wanted to be there to make sure. I was eager to start our forever together.

"Hey handsome. What are you doing? Why aren't you sleeping?" It was first thing Saturday morning in London, so he was up late.

"I will in a bit. I just need to finish off sending some emails."

"Sounds like a wild Friday night you've got going on there, Mr. Scott."

He chuckled on the other end of the phone.

"What are you doing? Are you out with Leah tonight?"

"I'm shopping and then I'm hoping for an early night."

"I'm going to take you to bed early every night when you get here."

"Is that a promise?"

"It's a guarantee."

"I'll hold you to it. What are you up to tomorrow? Do you have plans?" I'd not even told Mandy I was coming, so Ethan could be out for the day when I arrived at around noon his time Saturday.

"Work. I'll go for a run. Then I thought I might call the realtor."

"Realtor?"

"Estate agent, whatever you call it. To see what the market's like. In case you decide you want to move."

"I love your place Ethan."

"Our place. I want us to live in our place. You're not a houseguest. I ordered you a credit card as well."

"You did not."

"I did. What's mine is yours."

"I'll take your penis—that's all I need."

"You're sick."

"You love me."

"I do. Can I call you tomorrow? I need to finish this and then sleep."

"Of course. I love you."

"I love you."

I hung up, grinning like a fool.

My smile didn't fade once on my journey across the

Atlantic. I would be back soon enough, to pack up and say my goodbyes but for now, I was headed toward my future.

Even the glum taxi driver who smelled of fried chicken and looked like he hadn't washed his hair since 1987 couldn't dampen my mood. He hauled my case onto the pavement, or sidewalk as I would have to get used to calling it—and didn't offer me any change. Whatever. I was here and I was grateful.

Ethan

It was coming up to lunchtime and I was still going through emails. I'd managed a run and a shower, but apart from that it had been all about work for me. When Anna got here, I wanted to make sure I had enough time for her, especially in her first few weeks. I hoped work calmed down a bit.

My phone started to buzz and my girl's picture flashed up.

"Hey, beautiful," I answered.

"Hey, yourself. How was your morning?"

"Crap. All about work. How was shopping. Did you buy anything? Hang-on someone's banging on my door. Jesus, is the doorman asleep? Who the fuck is bothering me?"

I swung the door open and my jaw hit the fucking floor when Anna looked back at me. "Hey, if I'm carrying bagels and coffee am I still technically bothering you?"

"What the fuck?" I grabbed her and put my arms around her.

"Can I put this coffee down so I can hug you properly?" she mumbled into my chest.

I released her and she handed me the coffee as she started to maneuver two huge suitcases from the hallway.

"What are you doing here?" I asked.

"I heard you needed a houseguest?"

"Anna," I warned her.

"Well, I thought we agreed I'd move in, so I'm moving in."

"You're moving in?"

"Yup."

"Now?"

"Unless you'd prefer me to get a hotel?"

I realized I was standing in the doorway. "Let me get those," I said, passing her the coffee back so I could get her bags.

"Are you here for good? Have you finished work?" I asked as I pulled the two concrete laden suitcases into the apartment.

"Yes, I finished yesterday. Paul told me on Tuesday. It's been killing me not telling you, but I wanted it to be a surprise."

"I can't think of a better one. But I wish I'd known. I could have planned something."

"Like what? A 'Welcome to New York' banner?"

I raised my eyebrow at her and hoisted her over my shoulder and carried her into the bedroom as she squealed. I threw her back onto the bed and pinned her arms to the bed.

"I've missed you," I said looking at her.

"I've not been gone a week."

"I've still missed you. I'm sorry I was grouchy when you left.." It was all fine now. I hadn't quite got up the nerve to take the ring back. Maybe I'd send Rory. But I understood now that her marrying me wouldn't change her commitment to me and our life together.

"I'm glad," she said. "Can we take a shower? I feel yucky after the flight."

I bent down and placed soft kisses along the seam of her lips, from one end to the other. Before I'd quite finished, she opened her mouth and our tongues crashed together.

I pulled away from her and off the bed. "Get in that shower. I have one more email to send and I'll see you in there in two minutes.

I charged into the study and re-read the email that I'd been drafting before I got the call from Anna. I made two small changes and then sent it off, racing back to the shower, hoping to find Anna naked and wet in all senses of the word.

"Get in here," she called from the cubicle. "My boobs are super dirty."

I grinned and pulled off my t-shirt and pants.

"God, you're so fucking perfect," I said as I stepped into the shower and ran my eyes up her body.

Her hands slipped around my neck, "I want a little less conversation and a little more action," she said as she grinned at me.

"I warned you about the quoting Elvis thing, Miss Anna," I said as I backed her against the wall of the shower and dipped my fingers between her legs.

"Ethan," she cried as I started to circle her clit with my fingers with the exact amount of pressure that I knew drove her wild. Her hand found my cock and her eyes slid down between our bodies. "I want you inside me, Ethan."

She didn't have to ask twice. I cupped her ass and lifted her against the wall and shoved myself right into her.

"Fuck," she screamed and her fingernails dug deep into my flesh. "I forgot. Even though it's been less than a week, I forgot how big you are."

Jesus, she knew just the right thing to say and I twitched inside her. She squeezed in response.

"Are you ready to be fucked so hard, beautiful?" I pulled out and her mouth formed a perfect "O" and then I slammed into her, pushing her farther up the tile. Her heels digging into my ass, urging me farther, deeper into her.

"Faster, Ethan. I need you."

I was lost from that moment. The sounds of the water sloshing between us, our skin slapping together, her breathless cries were all muted by the blood rushing through my ears as I fucked her relentlessly.

She pushed her hands through my hair as my mouth attached to her breast and I bit down hard. As my teeth sank into her flesh, she began to come apart underneath me, silently, breathlessly. I felt so powerful, being able to do that to her body, and do it so quickly. The thought pushed me over the edge and I emptied myself into her.

"You make it so good baby," she said, sounding sated and fatigued as she pulled her legs from around my waist.

"You sit while I wash your hair," I offered.

She sat on the shower bench and grinned at me as I shampooed and conditioned her hair and then took a sponge and rubbed her whole body from her neck to her toes in small circles.

"Can you do that every morning before work, Mr. Scott?"

"You'll have to earn it," I teased.

"I'll do anything you ever ask of me. Anything," she said. She sounded serious, more serious than the conversation warranted.

In response I kissed her lightly on the lips. She sat on the bench as she watched me quickly wash myself and turn off the shower. I wrapped her in a towel and gave her another for her hair. She looked at me seriously as I pulled a towel around my waist.

"You okay?" I asked.

She nodded.

"Shall I find you a comb?" I asked, looking around and then bending to open the doors of the vanity. As I stood, something caught my eye, a smear on the mirror. Except that it wasn't a smear. I looked again. It was the words "marry me" created by the steam on the mirror.

My heart started to race and I was pinned to the spot. Had I written that? No. I didn't understand. I used my hands to steady myself against the sink. I couldn't turn around as the realization of what was happening crept over me. Her front pressed against my back and her arms snaked around my waist.

"Hey," she mumbled into my back. "Turn around."

I took a deep breath and turned in her arms. She tilted her head to look at me. "Is this what you want?" I asked.

She nodded. "I want you forever. I want to make you happy."

"Who told you? Mandy?" I asked. This wasn't a coincidence.

"I didn't do this for any reason other than because I want to be married to you."

I groaned. It was what I wanted to hear but I knew

it wasn't the whole story. "Anna, I know you don't want to get married."

"I would have said yes. If you had asked me at New Year's. I would have said yes."

"Don't bullshit me."

I walked her backward into the bedroom, our arms wrapped around each other.

"No bullshit, I would have said yes. I could never say no to you, Ethan."

"But you don't want to get married. You told me that night that you didn't want to. If my memory serves me correctly, your exact words were 'It's not like we're getting married or anything, god forbid.'"

"Shit, is that what I said?"

I nodded. The words were etched onto my brain.

She pulled at me so we were both lying face up on the bed. "It's how I've always felt." I froze, not wanting to hear any more about how she didn't want to marry me. "It's how I felt right up until I heard you had been planning to propose." I didn't move, couldn't move. "I've never wanted the big, white wedding. I've never been one of those girls. The thought is horrifying to me. And I've never associated marriage with anything particularly happy. My parents seem to be together because they have to be, rather than because they want to be. I've seen so many people divorce or waste time in unhappy relationships. I don't want that. But when

I heard you were planning to ask me, I realized that's not us. We're not unhappy and I don't believe we ever could be. As long as I don't have to wear a huge white dress and parade down an aisle, I *want* to marry you. I *want* to marry you because I *want* to be with you forever and I want the world to know but even more than that, I want to make you happy and if that's what it takes, then I want it too."

I found my voice finally. "This can't just be about what I want, Anna."

She lifted herself up onto her elbow so she was looking at me. She put her hand across my chest, across my heart. "I want to make you happy. That is good enough reason for me to say yes. I'd do anything for you Ethan. But actually, I want it for us, too. I want to tell the world you're mine and I'm yours. I never thought I would feel like that but it's different with you. I never expected to be lucky enough to have what we have."

"Okay," I said.

"Okay?"

"I'll marry you, since you asked so nicely."

She grinned at me. "Do I get the ring? I hear it's awesome."

I threw my head back and laughed. "Oh, I get it. Jewelry can be very persuasive, huh?"

She prodded me in the ribs. "I've done the hard bit. I asked the question. I think I deserve a reward."

I pushed her back against the mattress, and slid my lips across hers.

"Maybe I took it back?"

Her eyebrows knitted together. "Did you?"

"Come on." I slipped off the bed and pulled her up. "Put some clothes on."

I handed her her robe that she'd left from the last time she was here and I pulled on my boxers and took her hand.

She trailed behind me as we made our way down the hall to the study. I lifted her to sit on my desk and then I sat down on my chair.

She looked at me expectantly. I couldn't help but chuckle at her.

"Gimme, gimme," she said, her fingers grabbing at the air.

I leaned forward and opened the bottom drawer of my desk to reveal a red leather ring box.

Her eyes widened as we both peered into the drawer, alternating glances between each other and the box.

Eventually I grabbed the box and put it on the desk next to her.

She wiggled off the desk and onto my lap. "Show me."

Slowly, I opened the box, revealing the ring that I'd carefully chosen for her. My heart was thumping through my chest.

"Wow."

"Wow?"

"It's huge."

I kissed her neck. "I know, but simple right? I didn't think you'd want anything too fussy."

"It's perfect. I couldn't have, wouldn't have picked better myself. Did you rent it? I'm going to be really upset if this is another Pretty Woman tribute, because I'm not giving it back," she said.

"You like it?" I asked her, genuinely concerned.

"Are you serious?" She started wiggling her fingers in front of me. I chuckled and reached for the ring and slid it onto her left hand.

It fitted perfectly.

She looked between me and the ring. I couldn't see anything but her beautiful face.

She was so fucking perfect, and she was going to be my wife.

PLAYLISTS

A WEEK IN NEW YORK

A New York State of Mind
Alicia Keys

No More Tears (Enough is Enough)
Barbara Streisand & Donna Summer

Same Kinda Man
Candice Glover

One Night Only
Jennifer Hudson

I Wanna be Your Lover
Prince

Ain't Nobody
Chaka Khan

All the Lovers
Kylie Minogue

PLAYLISTS

AUTUMN IN LONDON

Good Morning Heartache
Ella Fitzgerald

I Wish You Would
Taylor Swift

Don't You Remember
Adele

I've Got You Under My Skin
Diana Krall

King of Wishful Thinking
Go West

Life is Good
Brittini Black

Quitter
Carrie Underwood

PLAYLISTS

NEW YEAR IN MANHATTAN

Love Song
The Cure

Out is Through
Alanis Morrisette

Loving Me For Me
Christina Aguilera

As
Stevie Wonder

Kissing You
Des'ree

Manhattan
Tony Bennett

Thinking Out Loud
Ed Sheeran

OTHER BOOKS
by Louise Bay

*H*OPEFUL

Guys like Joel Wentworth weren't supposed to fall in love with girls like me. He could have had his pick of the girls on campus, but somehow the laws of nature were defied and we fell crazy in love.

After graduation, Joel left for New York. And, despite him wanting me to go with him, I'd refused, unwilling to disappoint my parents and risk the judgment of my friends. I hadn't seen him again. Never even spoke to him.

I've spent the last eight years working hard to put my career front and center in my life, dodging any personal complications. I have a strict no-dating policy. I've managed to piece together a reality that works for me.

Until now.

Now, Joel's coming back to London.

And I need to get over him before he gets over here.

Hopeful is a stand-alone novel.

Praise for *Hopeful*

"Louise skillfully combines humour and heartbreak with copious amounts anticipation to make this book **one of the great finds of 2014**. I loved every word, every feeling and every tear. " *Agents of Romance*

"It gave me the good ache! This is a true love story and **I couldn't put it down**! I highly recommend!" *Gwen the Book Diva*

"I really **loved this story** and this couple." *Slick Reads – Guilty Pleasures Book Reviews*

"This book contains **hot sex**, angst and you are so desperate to know what happens next." *Kindle Friends Forever*

"If done right, all you need are amazing characters...check...enthralling storyline to keep you wanting more...check...and sizzling hot chemistry... double check! This book **hooked me right from beginning to end** and I sunk right into the turbulent depths of their journey." *Page Turning Book-Junkies*

"**It was amazing**." *Summer's Book Blog*

"Hopeful was **simply amazing** and soul consuming." *Just One More Page*

"This intriguing book is written and played out beautifully! **I've had tears and I've had tingles** - I've laughed too. A romance can't give us much more than that." *Cariad - Sizzling Pages*

OTHER BOOKS
by Louise Bay

*F*AITHFUL

Leah Thompson's life in London is everything she's supposed to want: a successful career, the best girlfriends a bottle of sauvignon blanc can buy, and a wealthy boyfriend who has just proposed. But something doesn't feel right. Is it simply a case of 'be careful what you wish for'?

Uncertain about her future, Leah looks to her past, where she finds her high school crush, Daniel Armitage, online. Daniel is one of London's most eligible bachelors. He knows what and who he wants, and he wants Leah. Leah resists Daniel's advances as she concentrates on being the perfect fiancé.

She soon finds that she should have trusted her instincts when she realises she's been betrayed by the men and women in her life.

Leah's heart has been crushed. Will ever be able to trust again? And will Daniel be there when she is?

Faithful is a stand-alone novel.

Praise for *Faithful*

"I felt the emotions coming from the page over and over. I laughed at various points (Her friend is fab) and trust me we have some **serious hot naughty bits** to keep us warm." *Fun, Fab and Tantalising Reads*

"The **heat** level on this book is **off the charts**." *Kelly's Kindle Confessions*

"An emotional roller coaster ride from start to finish, this book has a realism to it that made it easy to get into and **impossible to put down**." *Slick Reads for Guilty Pleasures Book Reviews*

"I truly enjoyed this book. What I enjoyed most is the fact that this book could **truly happen**." *Books and Beyond Fifty Shades*

Wowza...this book was jam packed with a hot, steamy, unadulterated sexual feast. I was frantically fanning myself throughout the majority of this book. I was **completely hooked** from the beginning. *Page Turning Book Junkies*

"Such a **wonderful story** of finding that one true love." *Book Happiness*

LET'S Connect

If you enjoyed The Empire State Series, please leave a review. Good reviews really help indie authors!

I love hearing from readers – get in touch!

Tweet me
twitter.com/louisesbay (@louisesbay)

Friend me
www.facebook.com/louisesbay

Like me
www.facebook.com/authorlouisebay

Pin me
www.pinterest.com/LouiseBay

Friend me
www.goodreads.com/author/show/8056592.Louise_Bay

Circle me
https://plus.google.com/u/0/+LouiseBayauthor

Instagram me
Louisesbay

Find me at home
www.louisebay.com

Made in the USA
San Bernardino, CA
08 March 2015